Doyen

Specter Series

Book One

M. M. Lackie

DISCLAIMER

This book is a work of fiction. The characters
and events portrayed in this book are fictitious.
Any similarity to real persons, living or dead, is
coincidental and not intended by the author.

This book contains adult situations and
mild sexual content. It is intended for
mature audiences.

Editor: Ariel Perkins

Cover: LeisurelyMe by Richa

ISBN: 9798672678191

For my husband.
Thank you for throwing money at my little endeavor.
I think I'll keep you.

Also, to my family for putting up with the late nights.

CONTENTS

ACKNOWLEDGMENTS

Derek Eurales, Jr. for the advice and encouragement.

1. PRISON

~Commander

It had been more than a tenday since he saw a human's face. Hunger, his only companion. A hunger that felt like fire, molten rock filling his chest with the heave of every breath, his lungs throbbing. Deep meditation was a thankful distraction. The chains that bound his feet and wrists allowed movement in his cell. Yet, he still spent most days kneeling, with hands steepled at his chin, facing the wall that separated him from the empty cell next to him.

He understood why he was hated and feared. His capabilities not escaping him. Stealing the essence of man, the ability to crush their skull within his grasp. He could not help what he was. His only means of survival cost people their lives. The only alternative, death. Many of his kind chose death. Taking one's own life was not seen as cowardly. It took courage to end your existence. Death was not an option for him, however. He did not enjoy taking lives, but ending his own was

1

less appealing. So, he endured what he was. Taking lives as quickly as possible and easing their pain so they did not suffer.

His human captors had no reason to visit him. They would not, and could not, provide him what he needed to survive. They only came to taunt and tease him, bored with their mundane lives. He mostly sat in solitude, his only company the fire in his chest.

Starvation was the worst way to die. Even for him.

It had been more than seven moon cycles since his capture. The empty cell next to him had a window, and he could see the faint sunlight shine onto the floor as it moved from one side of the cell to the other. As it dawned, crest zenith, and traded places with the moon.

"Two-hundred and seventeen..." he said as the sunlight slipped beyond his vision. His voice, unused for so long, was a stranger to him. Two-hundred-seventeen; the number of dawns and dusks he had seen while locked in a cell, chained to the wall like an animal. A hunter. That is what he was. A thief who took what was not his to take. A hunter of man.

It was midday when the sound of scuffling broke his solitude. Two sets of boots were dragging a body toward the cells. He may be starving, but his senses were as keen as ever—the only thing left to a dying man.

A jingle of keys opened the cell next to his. Another prisoner? A thud and faint moan as a body hit the floor. A thick wall separated the two cells with a barred window from floor to knee. He would have to bend to see his prison mate. He chose not to move, and instead breathed in deeply, mouth agape to take in the scent of the human who was mere feet from him.

A human female. Her aroma was intoxicating and overwhelmed his senses. He closed his eyes as her scent filled the air around him. What could they want with a female? He had his suspicions as to what his captors would do with a female prisoner. He had seen with his own eyes what a group of males were willing to do to a female. He kept male and female prisoners separated for this reason. Yet, they call his kind monsters. Even his kind were above such things. Any male who would force himself on a female did not deserve to live.

DOYEN

Humans could be such beasts to each other.

He still pitied them in general and felt badly for their fate. Their short lives that typically ended in tragedy. Through their fault, or the fault of another.

He hissed as his thoughts were interrupted when the human called 'Greg,' a homely overweight male with short unruly hair and a face full of stubble, kicked his cell door. This one enjoyed taunting him. He saw Greg as a problem for the female.

"Specter, we brought you some company," Greg jeered as he glanced toward the female and adjusted himself.

"Let's get out of here. That thing gives me the creeps," another male said from out of view. Both males walked hurriedly down the corridor.

He maintained his kneeling position until the males were out of earshot. He was curious about his prison mate. He bent over, attempting to see her, peering through the barred floor level window in front of him. The chains around his wrists clanked against the floor at his knees.

She was lying just beyond the sunlight, surrounded by shadows caused by the approaching night. The sun was well past its zenith. His vision was keen in the darkness, as his kind preferred low light. He could see her in the dark, but the soft glow of the morning sun would offer sharper details.

Night came and went. He repositioned himself, sitting with his back against the wall opposite the window. His spine grated underneath his clothing, knees bent in front of him, watching the sunrise on the floor in the now occupied cell. Its new occupant did not move during the night. Her sleep was restless, and her breathing fluctuated between shallow and deep sharp breaths. Followed by a faint moan, then a whimper. A few times she appeared to stop breathing altogether. Then jolted her head with a sudden gasp, followed by shallow breathing.

He could see her face more clearly now. She was on her back, face turned toward him, with her right arm across her stomach, and her left beside her, adjacent to her face. She wore a simple white shift that cinched just above her breasts. Her

3

skin was kissed by the sun, and her hair was coiled, curly, and almost black, with subtle strands of white throughout. She was not young, but not old either. Forty-five summers, perhaps. Beautiful for a human. Still a lot of life ahead of her.

He always admired females. They had so much power. Without them, life could not exist. He seldom took the life of a human female. They carried more value. Females were leaders. He always preferred to deal with a female in charge, even among the humans. Most male Specter were the same. His society was matriarchal, and females were the center of their existence. It was forbidden to take the life of a Specter female. There were so few of them. Even in self-defense it was frowned upon.

He thought of his Regent and hoped that his confinement would not cost him. He was confident she would not have replaced him just yet, and he would still be favored among her men.

If he ever saw the firmament again.

When the sun rose the next morning, he saw she had shifted position. She was now on her side with her back to him. Her waist-length hair disheveled on the floor, and her left arm rested on the swell of her full hip.

A bright blinding light filled her cell. The Commander did not know there were electric lights. He had been shrouded in darkness since he first arrived. Whether they did it intentionally, or absentmindedly did not matter. He preferred it that way.

The female's cell door opened, and a light metallic sound scraped the floor. Then a sudden rush of water was thrown on her. Her body jolted awake. She jerked onto her back, hands fisted beside her, coughing and gasping.

"It's time to wake up," Greg snarled.

~Katlyn

Her sleep was nothing but a constant chill in between fits of restlessness. She dreamt of her family, but their faces only brought sadness.

She woke on a cold brick floor wearing nothing but a thin, three-quarter sleeved dress that fell just below her knees. It was night, and darkness surrounded her. Only moving her head, she looked up at the barred window above her. She could see the night, but the sky was empty, starless.

She was so tired. She rolled onto her right side, drifting back into a restless sleep.

***

Ice. Tiny icicles pierced her flesh. The sudden pain woke her and stole her breath. Confusion filled her mind as she struggled to breathe. It took a minute for her to realize cold water was thrown on her. Stealing her breath and robbing her of her children's faces. She was on her back, fighting the fear and confusion that swept through her. Violent tremors consumed her as the frigid water soaked her body.

"It's time to wake up," a man snarled.

He grabbed her ankle, dragging her across the floor. Her fear turned into anger as she kicked violently, freeing herself from his grasp. She managed a well-placed kick to his groin, forcing the man to his knees. She scurried away from him, retreating to the corner of her cell. The man moaned and clutched his groin. She heard a wry chuckle and a shuffle of metal from somewhere close. The other guard attempted to comfort his injured comrade, only to be pushed away.

"She's awake," he said. "Let's go."

"You bitch!" the injured man wailed, gasping for breath.

"What the hell did you expect, waking her up like that? C'mon, let's go," the other guard said. "There's food"—he pointed to the metal tray on the floor—"you need to eat. You've been asleep for days," he told her as his comrade staggered out of the cell, the door slamming behind him.

Rage consumed her. She screamed and bolted for the door. Only to be met with the butt of a gun to her face.

Nothing but darkness as she hit the floor, slipping into unconsciousness.

~Commander

"You think that was funny, Specter?" Greg barked. "You're going to starve to death if you don't watch it."

He breathed in deeply. "Perhaps, but not this day," the Commander said, followed by a low growl and short chuckle.

Greg scoffed and kicked the bars, then both guards stormed around the corner.

The woman was on her back, a bruise forming just above her left eye. Blood trickled onto her temple. He could smell the blood as it dripped into her hair. She was full of fire, heat, and passion. And that would be how he came to know her. This human female—woman, who would light something within him. Something that would make him betray even himself.

She was not unconscious for long. Her eyes shuddered opened, and she was facing him. For a moment, he thought she could see him, but that was impossible. His cell was shrouded in darkness—a thankful reprieve.

She blinked as if waking from a deep sleep. Her eyes were the color of the sea. He craned his neck to see her. He longed for someone to break the silence and fill the void in his mind— the forced isolation.

She turned her head, looking up at the ceiling. Her hands came up to touch her head, wincing when her finger brushed the fresh wound above her eye.

"Where am I?" she said under her breath. "Hello?" she called out shakily as she sat up.

He did not speak. He held his breath, waiting.

She pulled in a sharp deep breath and sniffled. She shifted onto her knees and wrapped her hands around the iron bars in front of her as she stood to her feet.

"Hey, you bastards!" She grabbed the food tray the guards left behind, and threw it, its contents hitting the bars and landing on the floor just beyond them. She screamed as she grabbed the sides of her head, filling her fists with hair, and sank to the floor sobbing.

He felt a pang of shame watching her in that vulnerable moment. He knew he should have spoken when she called out. He looked away, attempting to offer her the privacy she did not know she was robbed of. His chained arms shifted. He caught his breath, hoping she did not hear.

But she did.

She jerked up and stifled her sobs. She looked toward the barred window and froze. Seconds felt like minutes as she stared wide-eyed in his direction.

He had to speak. She knew he was there.

"Please accept my apology for not making my presence known sooner," he said. "I did not mean to intrude."

She took a sharp breath, jumped up, and bolted to the corner of her cell. Out of his view, where she would remain until the next day. Hiding from his unintended intrusion.

~Katlyn

Her head throbbed. The ache radiated from her eye, engulfing the entire left side of her head. She pushed into her temple trying to relieve the pressure, but it was useless.

The sun was setting in the window above her. She wrapped her arms around her knees, breathing into the thin slip-like gown surrounding her. Shivering from the cold, she couldn't get rest. The same thoughts haunted her sleep and wakefulness. Her family, her children.

The last thing she remembered was swinging on the tree swing in her yard, resting from the day's work. She had been mowing her yard and tending to her vegetable garden. She rested on the swing looking at the sky and dozing off, only to be awakened by a sudden rush of icy water.

How long have I been here? she asked herself. One guard said days. She could be anywhere.

The night passed quietly. The man in the cell next to her didn't speak another word. She heard not a sound from him. Did she imagine him? No, she wasn't crazy. Not yet. She knew he was there.

She rested her head in the corner behind her and drifted in and out of sleep. The light above her cell illuminated brightly.

~Commander

The light in the female's cell made it difficult for him to see the sunlight cast onto the floor. He surmised it to be morning or midday when he heard two pairs of boots shuffling toward them.

"What the hell is this?" Greg barked. "If you're going to pull this shit, we'll just let you starve!" he yelled as the door opened.

"Where am I?"

"Don't worry about that right now," he retorted as he walked toward her.

Greg lurched forward and dragged her by her hair to the middle of her cell. He pushed her to the floor and dumped water on her again. She yelped, mouth agape, fighting to breathe, with her hands fisted at her breasts.

"What do you want?" she yelled in defiance.

"Don't make a mess again," Greg snarled as he forced her chin toward his face.

"Don't touch me, you pig!" she hissed, pulling her face out of his hand.

Greg towered over her; his face distorted in fury. He drew his hand back above his shoulder, hitting her with such force she collapsed to the floor. The Commander could instantly smell that she was bleeding.

She remained motionless and quiet while the previous day's food mess was cleaned, a fresh tray replacing it, and the door locked. The stomping boots receded down the corridor, one of them turning the light off as they left.

After a few minutes, she rolled onto her back. Looking out the window above her, she moved so the sunlight covered her face. She inhaled deeply, then exhaled. Her breath faltered as she glanced toward him. Seemingly aware of his presence.

He could now see the passage of the day as the light shone on her skin. She moved across the floor, following the sun, inching closer to him. Although it dried, he could still smell the blood at her nose.

He was also on the floor, hands steepled at his waist. He did not know whether she ignored his movement or simply did not hear. He was but a shadow—a whisper when the situation warranted it.

The blackness in his ruby eyes was vast, able to see better now that the light was out. She feigned sleep. Her chest rose and fell with each breath. She moved again as the sun neared the night. If he were not chained, he could almost touch her through the bars. She need not speak. Her mere presence was enough to break his solitude. Her being human did not matter to him. Somehow, he knew he would never harm her, even if their captors wished it. He could not yet explain why.

Minutes turned to hours. Both lay in silence, exchanging nothing but the sound of their breathing. Suddenly, and without warning, she broke the silence between them.

"Why are we here?" Her voice was but a whisper in his ear, but it startled him from his meditation, and his breath caught in his lungs. He opened his eyes and turned his head to look at her. She was looking right at him as if she could see into him. Like she was searching the deepest parts of him that had not been touched by another in many cycles. He would not leave her question unanswered. Not this time.

He breathed in, counting on her to hear, exhaling just the same. Watching as her face fell into the shadow of the moon. "I do not know," he said. But that, in part, was a lie. He did know why he was there.

She closed her eyes, turned her back to him, and fell into a restless slumber.

2. WHAT I AM

He heard the scuffle of boots as Greg approached the cells, turning on the bright light, and rousing the woman from sleep. The Commander did not look into her cell as she slept, trying to afford her a bit of privacy she lacked in her current situation. She rolled over, still lying just beyond his window, and shielded her eyes from the blinding light. He rolled onto his side to better see her.

"Still not eating," Greg said as he dropped a bucket on the floor.

"You said not to make a mess," she snapped back, sitting upright. "It's still sitting there. All nice and neat where you left it."

"You know we want you to eat. We wouldn't be feeding you otherwise."

"I don't give a shit what you want..."

Fiery One, he chuckled to himself.

"...I'm not touching that slop until you tell me what's going

10

on!"

"I don't have to answer any of your questions. You are not in charge here!"

"Go fuck yourself!" she snarled.

She was far enough away the Commander could see the profile of her face, yet close enough he could feel the heat of her anger.

"Listen here, stubborn bitch. I don't care if you eat or starve. My superiors would prefer that you cooperate. If you don't, you're useless, and they'll probably feed you to the Specter."

"The what?" Her head shifted back, and her face contorted in confusion.

He only saw the side of her face, but he could see she never heard that word before. It was a word that instilled fear in those who heard it, but not her. She appeared confused.

Greg let out a boisterous laugh that made her jump. "Now you're just going to act stupid?"

She continued to look at him in bewilderment.

"Stupid women are only good for one thing..." Greg's voice trailed off as he approached her. She tried to move away from him, but he was quick. Quicker than the Commander thought possible for a corpulent human.

In the blink of an eye he pinned her to the floor. One hand grasped around her neck. The other aggressively pulling her shift up over her legs. She kicked, trying to get him off her, clawing at his face and neck, attempting to scream despite the hand around her throat.

The Commander had to do something. Even if only to stall. Give her the chance to fight back.

As she clawed at her attacker, the Commander banged his chains on the floor in front of him, hissing and snarling. Greg looked at the barred window that separated them.

"What the hell has you so agitated all the sudden?" he asked, loosening his grip around the woman's throat.

"I would like to speak with you now," the Commander said. "Do you still not have questions for me?"

"No, I don't," Greg snapped, letting go of her and kneeling onto his legs.

The Commander smirked as he watched the woman take advantage of the opportunity presented to her. She brought her right knee to her chest, kicking Greg in the face with such force that it knocked him across the cell, and into the bars, spilling the previous day's food tray.

Greg lost his senses for a moment. He shook his head in confusion as she hurled herself to her feet, snarling at him, "Keep your filthy hands off me!" Then spitting right into his eyes.

When Greg got his wits about him, his face dropped, then his cheeks flushed a light cerise, and his face distorted into an angry scowl. As he stumbled to his feet, she balled her hands into fists, readying herself to lay blows if he approached her again.

"Stay the hell away from me!"

"You're going to pay for that!"

He quickly closed the distance between them. Her right fist landed a blow just below his left eye, stopping him momentarily, but not long enough. Greg grabbed a handful of her lengthy hair, jerking her toward him as he laid a fist into her stomach, forcing her to the floor gasping for air.

At that moment, boots hurried around the corner.

"What is going on here?" asked an unfamiliar voice.

"She attacked me, sir!" Greg yelped as he whipped around into a stance that could be considered a form of respect to a superior.

"He attempted to force himself on her," the Commander interjected. "She merely defended herself."

"Keep your hands to yourself!" the unfamiliar man commanded.

"But, sir—"

"Not another word! Do I make myself clear?"

"Understood, Director!" Greg responded as he hurried out of the cell and locked the door. Then he scurried away.

Through the window, the Commander could see the woman sitting on her legs, holding her stomach. Her mouth opened when she gagged, then she rocked back and forth.

The Director approached the Commander's cell, arms

crossed in front of his chest. "I never would've thought such a thing would bother you."

The Commander stood to his feet and approached the barred door, his chains stopping him just as he came into the light. "We do not treat any female with such dishonor," he said, glancing down to the man's chest to see 'Nash' along the pocket.

Nash scoffed. "Right"—he rolled his eyes—"a Specter with honor."

The Commander squared his shoulders, keenly aware the woman not far from him could hear their conversation. "There are many things humans do not know of my kind," he said with defiance, raising his chin parallel to the floor. His ruby eyes peered down at the new jailor. The Commander was easily a head taller than the human. His hair was the color of dirt and loosely coiled around his collar and temples. His face appeared worn, as if aged, but he could not be more than thirty summers.

"I don't care to know. You are a weapon—a tool. If her people refuse to cooperate, she'll be joining you."

The Commander glared at him with stoicism. As if not caring one way or the other. He had no intention of harming her. He could control himself. No matter how hot the fire burned inside him.

"Now, I'll leave you both to contemplate your future together," Nash said as he rounded the corner and disappeared. The Commander remained still until he was sure Nash was gone.

He laid back on the floor so he could see as much of her as possible. She no longer crouched in the center of the room. He could not see her. His eyes darted from left to right in a futile attempt to find her.

He breathed in deeply. Deciding to speak, yet not expecting a response. Why should she? He was a Specter. "Are you all right?" His voice was barely above a whisper.

After a moment, he wondered if she heard him or was choosing not to answer.

"Thank you," she said, to his surprise. "I appreciate what you did."

"You are most welcome," he said gently. He expected nothing more from her.

She moved closer to the window, her back against the wall—her left-arm fully in his view.

"May I be so bold?" he asked.

"What do you mean?"

He gave a soft chuckle. "Watching you kick him in the face was most satisfying."

She gave a chortle, both hands going to her mouth to stifle her laughter. "That did feel good." She continued to laugh.

He longed for his people, speaking mind to mind with a touch. Talking to this woman was a delightful break from his solitude, a distraction from the fire burning within him. He felt something from her. Something told him that this woman, this human, was different. Like he was different. He fulfilled his duties, but he longed for another way—peace. A peace that many desired, but a peace that may never come. How could they coexist peacefully?

"They haven't fed you," she interrupted his thoughts. His brow furrowed as he looked in her direction.

"They are content to let me starve," he said carefully. "Besides, they are not able to provide what I need."

"What does that mean?"

"It does not matter." He cocked his head as if she could see his confusion. "Mistress," he said. Her head turned sharply toward him. "Please be careful. That man is dangerous."

She gave a soft chuckle. "I came into this world kicking and screaming covered in someone else's blood. I have no problem leaving this world in the same way."

After a brief pause, he responded, "Begging your pardon, but I do not understand."

"Well, it means I was born covered in my mother's blood. I'm okay dying covered in his. Or anyone else's blood who gets in my way."

"Indeed." He smiled. *Fiery One.*

"Would you like some water?" She scuffled to the water bucket. "I think the cup should fit through the bars," she said as she filled it, drank its contents, then dipped it into the bucket again. With a gentle push, the thin metal cup did fit.

"Thank you."

"You're welcome."

The Commander's shackles clanked against the floor when he repositioned himself and reached for the cup. Then he stopped. The cup was well within his reach from the safety of the floor. He faltered because she may see his hands—his claws—weapons. He knew he should not burden himself with such things, but so many moons of isolation left him desiring interaction with another.

She looked down at the untouched cup. Perhaps she assumed he might not be able to reach it. She picked it up by the rim and reached through the bars as far and high as they would allow, her hand a mere kiss away from his face. He could almost taste her energy. He held back a gentle moan as her sweet scent filled the air around his face.

He could have her right there. Grab her arm, pull her face closer to the bars, and breathe deep, taking her life from her. Even in his weakened condition, she would not possess the strength required to free herself from him. Another would. In their hunger and desperation, they would take advantage of her. Squelching her life to satiate their hunger, quieting the fire within. Even if for only a moment. But he would not.

He accepted the cup, allowing his hand to brush against hers. Careful not to scratch her with his disheveled nails. Her breath caught when he touched her. Then her arm retreated, and they sat in silence.

The water would not quench his thirst. It would do nothing for him except moisten his parched mouth and dry lips. He felt the cold liquid slide past his burning chest, into his useless stomach. He could taste her on the rim of the cup.

"I am finished. Thank you again."

"You're welcome," she said as she reached her arm through the bars to retrieve the empty cup. Again, her hand was within his reach. He took a sharp breath as he placed the empty cup in her waiting hand, touching her gently with the back of his own.

He thought for sure that the interaction between them would be fleeting. Once she realized what he was, she would be lost to him. Why was he so drawn to this woman? This human? Was it the last desperate act of a dying man? He should take her life to extend his own, but he could not.

"Would you like more?"

"Not at this time," he said. "May I ask you a question?"

"Sure. Only if I can ask one of my own."

Curiously, he said, "You told that man to 'Go fuck himself'..." He saw her pause mid-drink. "What does 'fuck' mean?"

The water in her mouth spewed out into a shower of laughter, and the cup tumbled to the floor. She gave an undignified snort followed by an uproarious laugh. He craned his neck to see her. Her head was thrown back, and she had a genuine smile on her face.

She brought her hands up to stifle her outburst when he moved. She whipped around, resting on the floor in front of him, still smiling, eyes shining.

"I'm sorry. I didn't mean to laugh," she said, attempting to hide the smile on her face with her hands, but failing miserably. "I'm not laughing *at* you. You just caught me off guard. I thought you'd ask where I'm from, or what my name is." She cleared her throat, and her face flushed. "That is a slang term, or vulgar word for, well, sex," she said. Her face flushed more, and she tried again to hide her smile.

"I see. So, you were telling him to propagate with himself. I can see how that would be insulting."

"Yes, well, 'Go propagate with yourself' doesn't sound as good as 'Go fuck yourself' does," she said, stifling more laughter.

The Commander chuckled. "That is true."

"My turn." Her expression dropped.

"Go ahead."

"Where are we? And what is Specter?"

Her voice shook as she spoke, and she stared at him although she could not see him. He attempted to play to her

16

obvious mischievous nature, lightening the sudden serious mood. If even for a moment.

"That is two questions."

A smile formed on her face. "You're right. You got me." Her smile faded. "Where are we?"

He considered how to answer her. It was obvious she came from a world unaffected by the Specter. How could this be? There were no planets, to his knowledge, that were unaffected. Perhaps her naivete is what he found so captivating. No, she was hardly naïve. A naïve woman would not be so filled with fire, passion. She enchanted him before he saw her fire ignite.

He leaned back against the wall with his knees bent in front of him. She waited patiently for an answer. Watching him as if she could see his mind searching. Answering should have been easy for him, but it was not.

He took a long deep breath. "I am not too familiar with this world." He could see her brow furrow and heart rate quicken as he spoke. "I came here to hunt for game. I was under the false impression this world was uninhabited."

She said nothing as her eyelids fluttered over her eyes.

~Katlyn

Uninhabited? she said to herself. *World? What is he talking about?* She squinted her eyes as she looked at the bright light above her. She tried to piece together the conversations she heard with unfamiliar words. Her head was spinning, and she felt ill.

"I have another question, if I may?" he asked, interrupting her thoughts.

She glanced in his direction from the corner of her eye. She struggled to breathe and process the information. She couldn't speak. She feared his next question.

"What world are you from?" he asked, with noticeable hesitation in his tone.

That's the question she didn't want him to ask. Why would he ask that? It didn't make sense. She began to sob. Her groans turned into hyperventilating, and she felt as though she were suffocating. She couldn't catch her breath. She bolted up off the floor and began pacing.

"Worlds!" she screamed at the window. "What are you talking about?" Her hands grabbed at her head, pulling her hair. Her sobs turned to groans of anger, then screams as she paced. "Who are you? Why are you doing this to me? What do you want?" she demanded.

She sobbed with anger. She wasn't angry at him, but why not? This unknown person... alien?... telling her about worlds and talking as if she wasn't on Earth. She was so pissed off now that she couldn't even form a coherent thought. She collapsed into the corner of her cell. Sobbing, and pushing her feet against the floor in front of her.

"Mistress," he whispered.

"Don't call me that!" She took a sharp breath, choking back tears. "Stop acting all courtly and polite," she insisted. "Leave me alone!"

***

For several days she didn't speak. Not even to the guards who brought her food. She ate it without question, retreating to the corner of her cell, out of the man's view. The guards still hadn't told her what they wanted from her. She didn't ask either. She ate, slept, and stared at the light on her ceiling.

Eventually, she laid down on the floor in front of the barred window, peering into the darkness, waiting for a sign that the stranger noticed her. She felt bad for snapping at him, but didn't want to disturb him if he was resting. She realized she hadn't heard a sound of movement from him in days. Was he dead? She squinted—a failed attempt to see him in the shadows. She reached out and tapped an iron bar with her nail.

"I am here," he said.

"Sorry for snapping at you like that."

"There is no need for you to apologize. You have every reason to be upset."

She inhaled deeply, trying to choke back tears. "I feel stupid for even needing to ask this. Like I'm losing my mind, but, is this Earth?" She covered her face before the words could escape her lips. She waited for him to tell her 'yes,' and she was having some horrible nightmare.

"I am sorry, but it is not. This world is called Veda."

She rolled onto her back and was calmer than expected. She looked up at the ceiling and burst into a fit of laughter. She quieted, then turned to face him. "Well, it seems that I've been abducted by aliens!" Then she laughed uncontrollably.

She finally settled down and was quite at ease with her situation as she peered into his cell. "Why should I believe you?"

"I understand your apprehension to believe what I have said. You have no reason to trust me. Other than I am a prisoner, same as you."

"How do I know that you're a prisoner? Not some spy sent in here to make me believe this ridiculous story?"

"You noticed yourself they have not fed me. No one has opened my cell in the days you have been here," he reminded her. His voice was almost regal. "Do you believe they would deprive their own of food and drink for so long? If you do believe this, to what end? Why would your captors wish for you to believe such a tale?"

She knelt at the window between them. The crown of her head rested against the bars. "I'm never going to see my family again." She covered her face with her hands.

"Do not despair," he said. "You were brought here. There is always a way back."

His voice was deep and soothing, yet powerful. It caressed her ears like a warm piece of dark chocolate cake caressed her tongue. Every time he spoke, her lungs fluttered, and her mouth watered.

As the day progressed, they exchanged pleasantries. Mostly her talking about her family. Telling him stories and things she enjoyed. Hobbies and such. Suddenly she asked him, "Have you ever attempted to escape?"

"No, I do not have the strength to break free. And our captors do not enter my cell."

"How long have you been here?"

"I have been here for more than seven moon cycles."

"Seven months! You've been here seven months without eating?" She scoffed in disbelief, scowling at the face she couldn't see. "How is that possible?"

After a moment, she sensed his hesitation. "You don't want to tell me, do you?"

"I do, but I do not wish for you to be frightened. I will not harm you," he tried to assure her.

She remembered the water and offering her hand to him. Although she was afraid, she still believed that he wouldn't hurt her. "You've already had the opportunity to hurt me, haven't you? But you didn't."

"That is correct."

"Okay. So, tell me."

"We are called many things. Demon, phantom, apparition, but we call ourselves, and are most commonly called Specter," he said. "Human food does not sustain me."

"So..." she hesitated, remembering what the guard said.

"I was born this way. I cannot help what I am. Please believe me when I say I will not harm you."

She chewed on her bottom lip, then sat up against the wall just out of his view. Seconds turned into minutes.

"In seven months, nobody has opened your cell?" she finally asked.

"That is correct."

"So, the only way for you to escape is if someone helps you by opening your cell?"

"Yes," he said, "and removing these." She heard his chains rattle.

She sighed. "I can't die here," she said, voice breaking. "I refuse to die here. They open my door every day. We're going to escape, but we need each other."

"Go on."

"Listen to me!" she demanded. "You need me to get you out. Do you understand? I know how to handle a weapon. I can help defend us. You can't eat me, okay! That's just bad manners, and you seem too polite to be rude like that."

He chuckled, "We do not *eat* humans. It is more complicated than that, but you have my word that I will not harm you."

"Save me the details. I don't want to know how it works," she lied. "All I care about is getting you out of those chains so you can get *both* of us off this planet. Can you handle that? Can you get us off this planet? I can't even believe that's a question I have to ask, but can you?"

"Yes. It will be easier if I have my weapon."

"Where is it?"

"The man called Greg carries it. He is the one who attacked you."

"Great! So, I have to get *him* alone, then kill him. That's just fantastic!" she said sarcastically. "Why do you need it?"

"I am able to modify it into a transmitter so my ship can detect my location."

"You go planet-hopping without telling your people where you're going? That doesn't seem very smart."

"I made an error in judgment that will not be repeated. If we succeed in escaping, I will be in your debt."

"Just get me out of here, and maybe a way home."

"I will free you from this world. As for getting you home, I must see what is available to me. I will do what I can to help you."

"Okay."

"Mistress," he said.

"Why do you call me that?"

"Because you are a female, a woman, whom I respect. And I do not know your proper name."

"Katlyn."

"Thank you, Katlyn, for honoring me with your name."

"Do you have a name?"

"I do, but names are personal among my kind, and we do not share them freely with humans."

"What do I call you then?"

21

"Commander is sufficient," he said. "Katlyn, thank you for your bravery."

She scoffed, "Sorry to disappoint you, but I am not brave." Her voice shuddered. "I just don't have much choice but to trust you. I can't stay here. Wherever 'here' is."

"Then, thank you for your courage."

"If you're planning on betraying me, can you at least wait until we get out of this wretched place? I don't want to die in this dungeon."

"I would not dishonor myself by betraying you. I have given my word."

She could feel his sincerity. As if he were able to reach within her and speak to her soul. But was it sincerity she felt? Or was she so desperate to escape that she would trust someone whose face she couldn't even see?

3. PLAN

~Katlyn

Time was now counted by the meals Katlyn received. The light in her cell always on. She could see the passage of time through the high window, but counting the days wasn't her objective.

She sat against the bars opposite the high window, looking up, watching the wind rustle the trees. Colorful leaves fell to the ground. She and the Commander needed to come up with a plan. Attacking the guard unprepared was out of the question, as there was no way she could overpower any of them. She had fire in her and would fight back, but she knew her limits.

She sighed, watching the trees sway outside the bars above her. She closed her eyes, placing her head against the bars behind her. She heard something scrape against iron. Her eyes opened and her brow furrowed. "Commander, was that you?"

"It was not."

Katlyn got to her feet and walked to the opposite wall.

"What is it?" he asked.

"I'm not sure," she said, looking at the bars with curiosity. She jumped up, attempting to reach the ledge, but her height betrayed her. "Damnit! I can't reach."

"What are you hoping to achieve?"

"I'm not sure. I thought I heard something on the bars. If I can reach the ledge, I could pull myself up to see what it is. I'm just curious, and have nothing better to do."

She looked around her cell, remembering the bucket of water. She ran to it and grabbed its edge. "Do you want water before I dump it?" she asked as she dumped the bucket. "Too late!" She chuckled as the remaining water covered the floor.

She dragged the bucket underneath her window. She looked in the Commander's direction with a smile, chuckling again as she flipped it upside down. She stood up and steadied herself on its now upturned bottom. With one good jump she reached the ledge enough to pull herself up. With her naked legs dangling beneath her, she hoisted herself up so she could rest her elbows on the ledge in front of the bars. She pushed her knees against the wall for leverage, then peered past the bars and gasped.

"What do you see?" the Commander asked, his chains scraping the floor.

"I have an idea!" Katlyn squealed as a broad smile formed across her face.

On the other side of the bars were a generous assortment of broken twigs and branches. Katlyn grabbed the bars with one hand, elbow resting on the ledge. Using her other hand, she reached past the bars, eyeing some branches that were as thick as her thumb. She grabbed as much as she could in the little time she had before her grip gave out. She pulled them through the bars and dropped them on the floor.

She tried to lower herself down to the bucket, but she couldn't sense where it was. As her knees came down, her dress snagged on the wall, exposing her thighs. The sudden gush of air caught her by surprise. She lost her grip on the ledge, and fell toward the floor, her dress billowing about her.

Her feet landed on the edge of the bucket, flipping it over. She crashed to the floor on her back, forcing the air from her lungs.

"Are you all right?" the Commander asked.

Katlyn was lying on the floor, struggling to breathe. Her dress bunched around her waist. She finally took a deep breath. "Maybe!" she gasped as she forced her dress back over her legs.

She stayed there for a moment trying to gather herself. When she rolled over to right herself, the Commander sputtered, "He is coming!"

She leapt to her feet and grabbed the bundle of branches beside the bucket. She rushed them to the Commander. "Hide these!" she whispered urgently. She was in such a hurry she didn't even notice the fingers reaching through the bars. She grabbed the bucket and sat down on her legs by the Commander's window, hiding the evidence he had not yet moved out of view.

The guard who appeared was the one she needed. He had the keys and the Commander's weapon. She wasn't ready, though. Not yet.

"What happened?" He scowled at the water on the floor.

"I leaned on it by accident," she lied, flashing a smile. "Can you bring more tomorrow?" she asked, lowering her voice to a flirtatious whisper.

"Maybe," Greg snorted.

He opened the cell door to replace her food tray. Katlyn remained seated, maintaining eye contact with him as he approached her to retrieve the empty bucket. She handed it to him and smiled. "Thank you," she said, biting her bottom lip.

As much as she hated Greg, she needed him. She was very cooperative with him the past few days for that reason. Although she and the Commander hadn't come up with a plan yet, appealing to Greg was part of it. So, she swallowed the bile that crept up, and despite her disgust, she smiled at him as if her life depended on it, because it did.

Katlyn continued to look at him as he stepped out of her cell and locked the door. She softened her face and smiled again when he glanced at her before disappearing around the corner.

"He is gone," the Commander said.

"That was close." Katlyn shuddered and let out the breath she didn't realize she was holding. "I don't know if I can do this."

"I do not yet know your plan, but I am confident in your ability to carry it out."

Katlyn inhaled slowly, scooting back so she could look in the Commander's direction. "I thought we might be able to make some kind of weapon with those."

"Yes, I can do that."

"Please make sure it's strong. If it breaks after one or two hits, Greg will kill me."

"It will be strong."

Katlyn leaned against the wall, waiting. She had to get Greg close. Within arm's reach, at least. The closer, the better.

"I've never killed anyone before," she said aloud, not directed to the Commander. Just admitting to herself what she was about to do.

She could hear the Commander as he whittled at the wood. The sounds from his cell stopped when he spoke. "I do not know how to make this easier for you, except to say that men like him do not deserve to live. I respect any soldier or warrior who fights for a cause they believe in, even if I do not believe in it myself. However, that man is without honor. He has been a nuisance since I first arrived, and I suspected he would be a problem for you as well."

Katlyn buried her head in her knees and sat quietly as the Commander resumed his work.

"See if this will fit in your hand," he said after several minutes.

She didn't wait for him to hand it to her. Instead, she pushed her hand between the bars, palm up. His touch was cool against her skin as he took her hand. She could hear him breathing as he placed his creation in the palm of her hand. He closed her fingers, wrapping them into a fist around the piece of wood.

She pulled her hand back, examining the lethal weapon. The ends stuck out of each side of her fist. Both ends sharp enough to penetrate deep, precisely what she needed.

"Wow! Is it finished?" she asked.

"Yes."

"That's better than I'd hoped for."

"I have another."

Katlyn reached down, meeting his hand at the bars. Just as he placed the weapon in her grasp, she looked down, seeing the ends of his fingers. She took a sharp breath and jumped back. His hand retreated into the shadows.

His skin was white. Almost bone white.

It didn't sink in until then that he was an alien. She had no idea what he looked like. Her situation was becoming very real. She was going to kill a man, a human, so she could escape with an alien. Of course, the human was alien to her, too, but he was human. The Commander was not. She was going to kill a human, and release what? What was she helping to escape? Katlyn closed her eyes, knowing he was still watching her, but she was frozen.

"Please do not be afraid," the Commander said. "You will see my face soon. Perhaps it is time I describe my appearance."

"Yeah, maybe."

"Ask me anything."

"I don't even know where to start."

"I will begin," he said, "by showing you what I am able."

Katlyn remained unmoving as the Commander's hands came out of the shadow of his cell. He moved them toward her, as far as the shackles would allow, turning them palm up. Except for their color, they appeared human. They were almost as white as the dress she wore, and claw-like nails on the thumbs. The other nails were broken and uneven.

He turned them over so she could see the tops. They were large. One hand looked like it could cover her entire face. Despite his slender fingers, they were strong and muscular. She saw a hint of a tattoo peeking out from the shackle around his right wrist. The tattoo intrigued her—a tattooed alien.

Her pulse slowed, and her tension eased. "You may touch me if you wish." She shook her head. "Very well," he said as his hands retreated into the shadows.

"Do you look human?" she asked, still unmoving.

"Mostly."

"What does that mean?"

"I am," he paused, "substantially larger than humans. As well as stronger and faster."

"So, you're big? Tall?"

"Yes."

"How tall?" she asked, cocking her head to the side.

He hesitated, then said, "I am a head taller than the Director who came here several days ago." Katlyn furrowed her brow, trying to remember how tall he was. "My facial features are human. All but my eyes and skin tone." She raised an eyebrow. "My eyes," he continued, "their shade is... the same as the vital fluid in your body. Your eyes are of the sea. Humans do not have the color we have."

"What about your hair?"

"Like my skin, but with strands of dark throughout."

Katlyn inhaled deeply and retreated to the corner of her cell. After a moment's silence, she said, "I have to admit, if they were showing any sign of releasing me, I'd have second thoughts about helping you."

"I understand."

Katlyn began to weep. "I'm helping you because I'm selfish," she said, exhaling sharply as tears flowed down her cheeks. "I don't want to die here. Trusting you is a risk, but it beats living in this cage for God knows how long. Even if I only make it down the hall, at least I'll die fighting."

"You need not free me to die fighting."

"That's true," her voice faltered, "but you shouldn't die in a cage either."

"You are not freeing me out of selfishness then."

"Why do you say that? I'm helping you escape so I can get out of here. That seems pretty selfish to me."

"No, you are helping me so that I do not die in this cage."

"I guess," she sniffled.

"Freeing you from this planet is an incentive."

She chuckled, "You have a point."

As night came, both sat in silence. Katlyn's mind reeled with what she was about to do. Will she have the strength? The ability? Will this save her, or end her life? She thought about what the Commander said—getting off the planet being her incentive. And go where? Would he be able to get her home? Or was she helping him only to become his prisoner in the end? Why was she so willing to trust him? Why was she willing to risk her life to help a man, an alien to her, whose face she couldn't see? Did she even want to see? She did. Her curiosity often got her into trouble.

The Commander spoke of honor and courage. His voice was deep, but soft, strong, courtly, and regal—a gentleman. People didn't talk like that where she was from. Of course, they're polite. Mostly. Some men would open doors for women and even pull out their chairs for them. *I've never had my chair pulled out for me*, she scoffed to herself, rolling her eyes as she laid her head in the corner behind her.

Feed you to the Specter. She remembered the guard's threat. What did that mean? Would she be his next meal? She shook that awful thought from her head. She couldn't think about that.

Hunger tore at her stomach. She fought sleep, but it consumed her.

4. CHOICES

The Commander continued kneeling in his cell with his hands steepled at his chest. For the first time since his capture he allowed his mind to wander. He did not fight it as his mind shuffled through the countless memories—millennia of images. The memories finally rested on his maturity.

On the precipice of manhood, yet still a boy. His mother stood over him, watching, teaching. He saw her slender face and long defined neck. Her hair was as black as a starless night sky. Delicate braids surrounded her face and fell past her shoulders. Her skin was white, like his. Her dark ichor pulsed through the venations of her body like the lines on a star chart. Specter had keen senses. In the dark, especially. The vital fluid coursing through the body of another could be seen with clarity. Like a roadmap leading them, showing them the heart of their essence.

His mother sauntered behind him with her hands clasped in front of her. Her blue silk gown flowed gently about her ankles.

30

"You must not allow them to suffer," she said as her son stood over the human kneeling before them. *"They honor us with their life. Never forget that. Without them, we are nothing."* Her voice was calm, gentle, yet fierce.

"Mother, is there no other way?"

"You always have a choice, son."

"What is the alternative?"

She circled to face him, arms at her sides. *"Death,"* she said, waving her hand toward him. *"Your death."*

Kel, the boy in front of her, squared his shoulders, accepting that fate despite the hunger growing within him. Having yet to take the life of a human, he was still a boy. His body was changing without his consent, and he must choose. Which life would he take? The human who knelt before him, or his own?

He looked at his mother obstinately. Head high, committed and refusing to choose.

"Sacrificing oneself for another is a noble deed, my son, even if that sacrifice is for a human. There is no shame in choosing to spare his life over your own," she said compassionately, *"but never forget, not choosing is still a choice. By not choosing to take his life now, you are choosing death for yourself, and you are choosing for him to die by the hand of another."*

Indifference showed on his face, but he knew that his mother knew who he would become. His temperament was passionate and fierce.

"If you *take their life, you can do it quickly, and ease their pain,"* she said. *"Another may not afford such a luxury."*

He looked down at the human. He made his choice, but still, he hesitated.

"Your victuals need not suffer to nourish your body," she insisted. *"Stop hesitating! You only prolong his suffering. You must choose!"*

He breathed in deep, lungs fluttering as he inhaled the scent of the human who was about to die to prolong his own life, to complete his transition. He was young, and not yet able to heal, ease pain, or give life to another. This was the first task leading to maturity. He must do this before the other gifts would come. He knew the man would suffer, even for a fleeting moment. He *was unable to provide solace to the first, but everyone who followed would not befall the same fate if he could help it.*

The boy knelt onto one knee in front of the man. Even though he had not yet reached his full height, he still had to look down to the human. He raised the man's chin and lowered his own, so their eyes met. His mother turned, walking away to leave them in private. This was not a moment to be shared with onlookers or prying eyes. Nourishing one's body was personal to only those involved.

"Please forgive me," the boy said as he grasped the man's neck, set his claw, and inhaled deeply. The fire in his lungs dissipated, and a wave of euphoria washed over him as his body filled with the essence of the man in his grasp. It happened so quickly; his victim let out barely a whimper. One deep breath and the man was limp in his arms, his cloudy eyes the only confirmation of what was taken from him.

The man was elderly and lived a full life. He did not have much to give, but it was enough to turn a boy into a man—a warrior who would one day be a great Commander.

He joined his mother on the balcony, gazing at the binary moons. Sapphire, amethyst, and emerald colors danced across the night sky of their homeworld. She looked at the man standing before her and caressed his hand as he laid it on the railing. She wished to touch his mind, the mind of her son who was passionate and fierce—Ardent.

'Compassion is not a sign of weakness.' Her thoughts washed over him like a tide. 'Some will hunt for the thrill. Others, out of necessity. It is up to you to decide which you will be. You can serve our Queen, your fleet's Regent, and your comrades honorably without killing for sport.'

He nodded in obedience.

"There is no honor in the suffering of others," she said aloud.

The weight of his mother's words carried with him, from that moment, through the next, until now. He opened his eyes and breathed in deeply. His mother's face was always a comfort to him. Why did his mind choose that moment out of all the others? Perhaps because of Katlyn – Fiery One, who was willing to kill a man to help another. A faceless man—a ghost. She owed him nothing. Even after knowing what he was, she still showed him kindness.

No, he would not betray her. Nor would he allow any harm to come to her by the hand of another. Would his actions be considered weak? Never. His kind lived by a code. Something most humans were never in the position to understand. Why would they? None he knew of had laid their lives down for a Specter. Not even the followers or those who served them were known for such things. Not of their own volition anyway. They would make the sacrifice when commanded or forced to do so, but never of their own free will.

He could hear the Fiery One's shallow breathing on the other side of the barred window, just out of reach. He suspected it was night. He closed his eyes again, sitting back on his feet, hands clasped at his waist, waiting patiently for the new dawn.

~Katlyn

"What are you so excited about?" Katlyn asked. James was always happy, but he had an unusual pep in his voice.

"How would you feel if I joined the military?"

"I would be proud of you no matter what you decided to do," she told him honestly.

"What about dad?"

"Of course! He has spent his entire adult life serving this country. Why?" she asked.

James hesitated as if worried about her response. "I joined the military."

"Which branch?"

"The Space Force."

"Really? Why that one?" she asked with a short chuckle.

"Well, you know I'm into that type of thing. I want to fly, but I also enjoy anything and everything having to do with space. Maybe I can do both in the Space Force," he said with enthusiasm.

"I hope you get everything you want, son. I'm proud of you," she said, holding back tears. *"And you know your dad will be proud of you, too."*

"The recruiter said—"

"Let me stop you right there. Never believe the recruiter. They are number crunchers. They have a quota to fill. They will tell you what you want to hear to get you to join. So, don't join hanging on their word."

"Okay, mom. I hear you. I go to boot camp in a couple of months."

"Natalie and I will have to throw you a going away party."

James laughed, *"I know you love to throw parties."*

"Any excuse. I don't even need one to throw a party." They both laugh. *"I love you, James."*

"I love you, too, mom!"

***

Gnawing hunger pulled Katlyn from sleep. She looked up at the window above her; it was daylight. She sighed, crossing her feet in front of her.

"Commander," she said toward the low window, "the sun is up."

"Are you able to see where it is in the sky?"

"Not really," she said, getting to her feet, trying for a better view.

"Perhaps you could stand in the middle of the room and attempt to catch its rays on your shift."

"My what?" she asked, scowling at him.

"The clothing you wear. It is worn between your body and outer clothing."

She growled quietly. "You know, I wasn't wearing this thing before. When I was at home," her voice broke with the word, "which means someone stripped me naked..." her voice trailed off. "Whatever! I know what you mean about the sun."

She walked to the center of the cell and looked out the window until she could feel the sun's warmth on her face. "Right here." She backed up, so the light shone on her clothing.

"It is not yet midday," the Commander said. "You have time."

Katlyn swallowed hard, continuing to stand in the warmth of the sun.

"Mistress—" he stopped abruptly. "Katlyn. My apologies."

She smiled down at the window. "It's all right. I don't mind." She crossed her arms in front of her, looking back out the window above. "Men don't talk like that where I'm from."

"That is unfortunate," he said. "You should eat. The guard will be cross with you if you do not."

"I know," she hesitated. "I don't know if I can keep it down."

"You must try."

"Maybe I can just dump it down the hole," she laughed.

"You will need your energy. I do not know how long it will be before you are able to eat again."

Katlyn trudged to the food tray sitting untouched by the door. She picked up the bowl and brought it to her lips, taking in a short sip of the thick sludge. "Oh my, fuck me! It's even more disgusting. Can you just kill me now and get this over with?" she pleaded. The Commander chuckled. "Bottom's up, I guess. Here's to getting the hell out of here," she declared as she moved the bowl, making a toast with the air in front of her.

She put the rim of the bowl to her lips and threw her head back, taking all of it in three loud gulps. She dropped the bowl and fought the urge to vomit, then belched. "Dear God in heaven, sweet baby Jesus!" she yelped, then grabbed the bread and shoved it in her mouth, trying to force the disgusting liquid to stay in her stomach.

She choked the bread down, only gagging once, followed by the water to finish. "Not what I had in mind as a last meal," she chuckled as she sat on the floor with the window to her right.

"You will have a proper meal soon."

"We both will," Katlyn said, mind lapsing. She froze, sucking air in through her teeth. "Sorry, that came out wrong."

"You have no reason to apologize."

Katlyn wanted to ask, but couldn't find the courage. How did he do it? Did he enjoy it? Did they suffer? She resisted the urge. Her curiosity would be her undoing. She was sure she'd find out soon enough anyway, whether she fell victim or someone else.

"You must not hesitate," the Commander said, interrupting her thoughts. "Once you strike, you must continue to do so until you are sure he is dead."

"I know." She felt the sludge in her stomach gurgle and lurch into her throat. She gagged, then forced it back down.

"After he is down, you must keep moving. Do not freeze. We will not have much time before another guard arrives."

"Okay," she mumbled in acknowledgment. "Commander?"

"Yes."

"Please don't watch me."

"I will not."

"I know you watch me sometimes."

She could hear his breath catch. "Please forgive my intrusion," he said.

"It's okay. I know you've been alone down here for a while. I don't know how you've done it."

"Deep meditation."

"I would just feel better if you didn't watch me do this. I don't know why."

"I understand."

5. ESCAPE

~James

"Sir, my mother is missing," James told the Commodore when he stepped into the office.

"I'm sorry to hear that, Captain. Do you have any idea what happened?" he asked.

"No, I spoke to her Saturday. She was going to mow the yard, as usual. I hadn't heard from her all week, which isn't usual. So, I went over there this morning. The house was unlocked, the mower was sitting in the backyard, and the shed was open. Her cellphone was on the tree swing. It was like she finished the yard and just walked away, which she would never do. I already notified the police."

"Are you going to request leave?"

"I'm not sure what to do, to be honest, sir. I want to stay here with my sister, but this upcoming mission is too important."

"Focus on your family for now, and we'll see what happens when it's time for you to leave. I hope your mother turns up soon."

"Thank you, sir," James said as he stood at attention, then turned around on his heel and left the office.

~Commander

The Commander stood silently by his cell door as he listened to Katlyn pace back and forth in her cell.

"What's taking so long?" she snapped. "I'm going to throw up."

"Perhaps you can try—" he started but stopped to listen.

"Try what?"

"He is coming!" A quiet squeal escaped Katlyn and she stopped pacing. "You can do this," he assured her. She let out a faint whimper, then inhaled deeply.

The Commander, having not had nourishment in many cycles, was visibly weakened. Yet he closed his eyes and took a long slow breath, attempting to transfer a feeling of calm over her. He heard her exhale slowly. In the hopes he was successful, he held his concentration, focusing his mind for the first time in many moons. He was frail, and his chest ached with the fire of an erupting volcano. He pushed past the discomfort, willing Katlyn to do what needed to be done for them both.

His other senses dulled as he focused his mind on the task at hand. He was helpless to assist her in any other way until she retrieved the keys. He held his breath as long as he could to increase his focus.

A sudden wave of heat bore down on his chest, causing him to stumble. The sounds of his shackles broke his concentration. He could no longer focus. He was too weak, and his chest ached with hunger.

He raised his chin and listened to the movements in the next cell. He heard a loud thump and water splashing, and a metallic clatter on the floor. His lips parted as the aroma of blood filled the air.

~Katlyn

Katlyn squealed and stopped dead in her tracks when the Commander told her the guard was coming. She spun around to face the bars and clutched the weapons in her fists. Her stomach lurched toward her throat, and she closed her eyes as she swallowed hard, resisting the urge to vomit.

Now or never, she said to herself.

She took a deep breath, opened her eyes, and exhaled as a wave of calm washed over her. She didn't know where it came from, but she welcomed it.

She could hear the guard's boots scuffle against the floor as he approached the cells. She stepped back to the middle of her cell and dropped to her knees. She sat on her legs, hands fisted and tucked in her lap. Her eyes were down as the guard rounded the corner.

Greg sat a fresh bucket of water on the floor so he could unlock the door. Leaving the keys in the lock, he opened the door, picked up the bucket, and stepped into the cell. Katlyn looked up at him, smiling. "Thank you for the water," she said sweetly as she rose to her feet.

Greg pushed the tray toward her as he began to set the bucket down. Katlyn froze. She couldn't take it because of the weapons concealed in her hands. Suddenly, they both heard the Commander's chains clank together. Greg's head craned toward the sound.

A wave of panic washed over Katlyn. Her target was right in front of her—vulnerable and unknowing. And well within her reach. Her world was moving in slow motion. She took a sharp breath as she plunged the spear hidden in her right hand into the jugular in his exposed neck. At the same time, her left hand came up, piercing his left eye, warm blood coating her hand. The bucket dropped, and the food tray crashed to the floor. Greg's hands shot up, grasping at the weapon in his eye. She quickly pulled the spear from his neck.

"Strike again!" The words were thick and demanding. She obeyed, hitting her target again with a sickening blow.

Warm blood spurted toward her, covering her hands and face. She remembered the Commander's words, "... until you are sure he is dead." The words echoed in her mind. She felt as if she were a marionette. A puppet being pulled on a string. The Commander seemed to control her movements and thoughts. His words pushed her beyond her known ability.

Greg stumbled, and his knees buckled as she laid blow after blow in his neck. His hands grasped at her as they both fell to the floor, Katlyn landing on top of him. Nothing came from his mouth. No sound as he clenched his neck, wide-eyed. Shock took over his dying body as blood poured out of him. Katlyn pulled away and sat back on her legs, straddling him. Before her mind had time to register what she had done, a heavy but gentle voice beckoned from the shadows. "Do not hesitate!"

She pulled herself to her feet. Body heavy, but moving as if not touching the ground. She rushed to remove the key from her cell door. Not breathing, her hand shook as she inserted the key into the lock of her prison mate and turned it.

"Give them to me," the Commander said as she opened the door. She passed her hand through the darkness, not looking up as he took the keys from her. "My weapon."

While the Commander freed himself, Katlyn stepped back into her cell, not looking at the dead man's face lying on the floor. She knelt at his legs, searching his body for anything that resembled a weapon.

As the chains in the next cell fell to the floor, Katlyn's hands found something on the dead man's right hip—a firearm. She laid it on his stomach to continue her search. Out of her peripheral vision, she saw a shadow. She resisted the urge to look at him. Her vision was tunneling, and his form was blurry.

"Check his back," the dark figure suggested as he knelt beside her on one knee, his right foot at the dead man's head. The material surrounding him moved around his feet like water rippling over river rocks.

He helped her roll the body onto its side and lifted the jacket up to reveal a concealed weapon. Its odd shape was unfamiliar to her. It didn't look like any weapon she ever saw before. It wasn't shaped like a gun, but rather a baton or like the rounded handle of a large sword. It appeared to be chrome, and the pommel was round like an orb.

The Commander retrieved the mysterious weapon, placing it on the side of his left thigh. It slid into the strapped holster as if meant to be there, like two pieces of a puzzle. He took the other weapon, handing it to her. She sat motionless with her hands resting on her thighs. She swallowed the knot in her throat, and without looking up, she accepted the weapon.

"Hold it for now," he said as he grasped the upper part of her right arm and pulled her to her feet. She did not resist as he guided her to the safety of the wall that separated the hallway from the cells. He positioned her behind him, standing between her and anyone who might come around the corner.

Katlyn's eyes shifted down and to the right, resting on the pool of blood drying on the floor of the open cell. The Commander stood at the corner just out of view of anyone who might be in the hall—listening for the foot falls that would inevitably come.

He squared his shoulders in front of her. Her breath was staggered and heavy. He looked over his right shoulder as she looked at the floor of her cell. He shifted his head back toward the corner, then turned to face her.

Katlyn could see the Commander's thick chest in her peripheral vision. His hand came up next to her hip, but he hesitated. Instead, he placed his heavy finger against the side of her chin. His touch was cool on her skin. She didn't recoil from him. In fact, she welcomed his touch, exhaling slowly as he turned her head, redirecting her eyes away from the cell floor.

"You have done your part," he whispered. "Leave the rest to me."

She inhaled deeply, squeezing her eyes shut. Her balance wavered, and she felt as if a feather could knock her over. She looked straight ahead, still hesitating to see the Commander's face. His head turned suddenly—long white hair with black wisps falling over his shoulder, inches from her face.

"Someone is coming," he said.

"What's taking so long?" a voice called out from down the hall.

The Commander turned toward the voice and straightened himself. "I must silence this man before he is able to alert the others," he whispered.

Katlyn knew the Commander was starved. She had a good idea of what he needed. He must nourish himself to continue their escape.

She could see nothing but dark blurs and shadows as she stood motionless, staring at the Commander's back, now dependent on him. Putting her trust, her very life in the hands of a man, a creature she didn't know.

He lurched forward, grabbing the approaching guard, slamming him against the wall beside them. Holding him in place with his left hand wrapped around the front of his neck, and his arm pressed against the man's chest. The Commander's right hand covered the man's mouth. His left knee came up, pinning the man's right hand against the wall to stop him from reaching for his weapon.

The wide-eyed guard had to have known his life was about to end as he stared into the eyes of a hungry Specter. In an act of desperation, he clawed at the Commander's face with his free hand, only to lose the ability to move when it was pinned above his head. Even in his weakened state, the Commander was able to overpower the guard. He was about to take the man's life but hesitated. He looked at Katlyn standing next to him. She was looking, but was unmoved by his actions.

She suddenly looked away, forcing her eyes closed. She wanted to see, but at the same time, she didn't. It seemed the Commander was still in control of her body. She heard nothing as she kept her eyes closed as firmly as she could. The guard made no sound until his body hit the floor; his head cracked as it contacted the brick. Katlyn jumped, head bolting forward as if shaken. The Commander stood in front of her facing the wall. He inhaled deeply, eyes closed, squaring his shoulders as if he just enjoyed an expensive cigar.

He looked down to her, and she finally met his gaze. She saw a man. He had the face of a man. The light by the cells was low, and with his back to her cell, his face was in shadows, but she could see that he was a man. Not a monster. His face had sharp lines and a steely appearance. His chin was sharp, and his full lips a shade darker than his white skin. If it weren't for the blacks in his eyes, she would have thought his irises were polished rubies. Despite being in shadow, they glistened, capturing what little light surrounded them. And he had to be a foot and a half taller than her.

"It is time to go. Stay behind me," the Commander said as he took the firearm from her and pulled out his weapon. Then disappeared around the corner, coat billowing behind him.

~Commander

He moved with grace. His steps effortless and with purpose. His strides long and quiet as he glided down the dimly lit corridor. His heavy boots created no sound as they contacted the floor. Katlyn must move quickly to keep up with him. Her bare feet slapped softly against the brick as she tried to stay in his shadow, behind him as he commanded.

The corridor was long and empty; no doors or archways graced either side. The Commander reached the end quickly, Katlyn following closely behind. The next room was large and smelled of grass and dirt. Several half-walls of brick and stone lined both sides. Perhaps for boarding domesticated animals centuries ago when Veda was populated and thriving.

He took cover in one of the stalls on the left, guiding Katlyn to crouch behind him. His right hand rested along her hip, urging her against the wall. He listened as a single man approached from the other side of the room, strolling along the dirt path between the stalls toward them. Seemingly unaware of his fate.

The Commander placed the firearm on the ground between him and the wall. He would stun the man with his own weapon before taking his life.

As the guard came into view, the Commander fired. The weapon was quiet like a gentle wind kissing your cheek. The shot hit the unsuspecting man in the chest. His body lurched and stiffened. Then he fell to the ground. The Commander grabbed him by the feet, dragging his body into the stall, where he promptly extinguished his life—not even noticing whether Katlyn saw him or not. He could not think about that. He knew the next room had several guards to contend with. He could hear their idle conversations, and the clacking of dice dropped on a wooden table.

He listened for footfalls, quickly peering past the half-wall and through a set of sliding barn-style doors. He and Katlyn would need to cross that room to reach the exit. When he was sure no one was coming, he picked up the weapon he laid on the ground and looked behind him. Katlyn was looking down, motionless and appearing to have detached herself.

"Remain here," he instructed her.

He crept to the doors that were slightly ajar. There was no one directly on the other side. They all sat just out of view. He crouched with his back to the door, listening. He counted at least seven men, perhaps more. Out of his peripheral vision, he saw Katlyn peering around the corner. She was not looking through the gap in the door. She was watching *him*. As if studying him. His eyes were on her as his head turned to face her. He raised his chin, motioning for her to hide behind the wall. She promptly fell back, taking cover.

He knew he could take out all the men, but he must act quickly so they could not notify their comrades. He stood upright, rising from the ground like a spirit rising from the grave. He was one with the air around him. He moved like water, liquid and fluid. In one quick motion he turned to the right. His coat rippled like waves behind him. He slid the doors open, entered the room, and fired both weapons.

***

The doors slid open to reveal a Specter bearing down on them. Their prisoner escaped! Before the men could react, there was a hail of weapon's fire. Each shot hitting their target. Some men fell instantly, some gasping and clawing at their chests as the bullets entered their bodies, tearing flesh and ripping through vital organs. The rest lurched in place before collapsing unconscious. One man, who was sitting behind a desk, dropped out of his chair, taking cover. He wrestled for his weapon as the bodies hit the floor around him. As he drew his weapon, a ghost appeared from the other side of the desk. The man fired, only to be met with a bolt of electricity to the face. His body lurched and fell unconscious, never to see the light of day again.

~Katlyn

She watched the Commander crouch as he moved around the corner, weapon in each hand, not making a sound. As if he were the shadow that followed him instead of the one casting it.

She looked down at the man sharing the stall with her. His mouth slightly open, eyes cloudy and gray. She took a sharp breath and looked away. The man was dead; the Commander killed him. But how? The how still eluded her.

She crept to the end of the half-wall to her left and peeked around the corner. The Commander was crouched low with his back to the sliding barn door. Both arms were up wielding weapons. His head was turned to his right as if listening to the men in the room beyond. His form captivated her; he was an enigma—a regal gentleman. Now a warrior and a killer.

Her breath stuck in her throat when she realized he caught her watching him. His ruby eyes bore down on her. He raised his chin, signaling for her to take cover. She quickly retreated behind the half-wall.

She sat on her legs and hugged the wall next to her, hiding from view, barely breathing. She listened as the Commander fired both weapons in succession. The gasps of dying men stung the air. Then a sudden silence fell over the room. She heard bodies shuffling, then nothing. Was he leaving her behind? She lacked the courage to look, but she didn't need to. Just as quickly as the thought came to her, it was gone when he appeared standing over her. She didn't hear him coming. He appeared as if out of thin air.

"I have found the exit," he said as he holstered his weapon and looked down to her. He reached for her arm, lifting her to her feet and swiftly moving on.

The Commander walked on her right side, blocking her view of the room as they passed through and entered the pitch-black hallway. Katlyn's left hand moved along the wall.

"I can't see where I'm going," she said.

"I am able to see, and I will guide you," he said, still grasping her right arm as they moved through the dark. "We are close."

The door at the top of the steps opened, taking them both by surprise, and two men entered the hallway. The Commander pulled Katlyn behind him while simultaneously firing the guard's weapon, hitting one of the men instantly. The other got off three shots before succumbing to the Commander's return fire.

Katlyn stood frozen behind him. His left arm wrapped around her body, shielding her. His large hand grasped the small of her back. His touch was cool, locked, and made her feel safe. She felt him stagger, and his breath faltered slightly.

The door at the top of the steps was now open. The Commander appeared to listen. Then with his heavy hand still hiding her behind him, they both moved with caution toward the exit, ascending the steps and walking through the door to their freedom.

6. HEALING TOUCH

~Katlyn

The sun fell behind the horizon as Katlyn and the Commander emerged to the surface. Fresh, clean air and an evening chill caressed her face when she stepped out from behind him. He was hunched over, holding his side.

"You've been shot!"

"It will heal," he said. "We must keep moving."

The Commander grabbed her left wrist and pulled her deeper into the forest. She struggled to keep up, as his strides were long and fast. He was running and pulling her along with him. She was barefoot, and the forest's underbrush cut her feet, making it challenging to maintain a steady pace.

"We must find shelter," the Commander said, seemingly frustrated with her inability to keep up.

"I'm trying to keep up with you. I'm sorry. My legs are short, and I don't have shoes!" She attempted to jerk her wrist from his grasp. "You're hurting me!"

The Commander stopped abruptly, turning his head and darting his eyes down to hers faster than she would've thought possible. Finally releasing his grasp, he turned to face her, and gently pushed down on her shoulders as he, too, lowered himself into a crouched position. He brought one finger to his pale lips, hushing her as he appeared to listen. For what, she didn't know.

Katlyn could see his face in the twilight despite the thick forest surrounding them. His thick white hair draped over both shoulders, stopping around his waist. It was parted messily on his left side and covered part of the right side of his face, giving him a rugged, yet mysterious appearance. He was looking right at her. The blacks of his eyes widened as they adjusted to the darkness, the red irises reflecting the remaining light. She inhaled sharply, forcing herself to look away.

"We are not being followed," he whispered. His cool breath caught in her ear. "We may rest if you wish."

"No, you're right," she said as she looked up at him. "We should keep moving, but you need to understand that I can only move so fast."

"I understand." He squared his shoulders and raised his sharp chin. The hair that covered the right side of his face fell back.

"Moving a little slower is better than stopping altogether, right?"

"You are correct," he agreed. "We must still find shelter. It will take time to modify my weapon. Then we must wait for my ship to arrive."

They both stood upright. Katlyn craned her neck to see his face. "How long will it take them to get here?" she asked as they started walking in no designated direction. The Commander looked back at her, raising an eyebrow.

"Minutes or days depending on their current location."

"Great," Katlyn mumbled. "How did you even get here? Is leaving the same way not an option?"

"I do not know where my flier is, and even if I did, that is most certainly the first place the guards will look."

After several long strides, the Commander stopped abruptly, turning again to face her. Hands clasped behind his back, chin level to the earth beneath them. "You may set the pace," he said, bowing his head to her.

Katlyn stammered and her face flushed. She tucked a thick curl behind her left ear. "Okay," she said with a quiet chuckle. "Which direction?"

The Commander righted his head and closed his eyes. He inhaled deeply, lifting his chin as his nostrils flared. His brow furrowed, and he turned his head to the right. He opened his eyes, looking down at her. "We will go to the river"—he pointed toward their intended direction—"that way."

"Onward then," Katlyn said as she began to march dramatically. Twigs and autumn leaves crunched underfoot. "How far do you think it is?"

"Not too far, but not close."

"You can hear it?"

"Yes," he said. "As well as smell it."

Katlyn cocked her head back toward him and raised an eyebrow. "Seriously?"

"Yes, my senses are keen."

His senses are keen, she thought to herself.

She was suddenly embarrassed because she knew that she hadn't bathed since waking up in that cell. That asshole pouring water on her didn't count as a bath. She pushed that thought out of her mind as she trudged along at a steady pace. Faster than a walk, but not quite a jog. The Commander followed closely behind. She could feel him behind her, but he was surprisingly quiet compared to the loud crunches she made with each step.

"I apologize for hurting you," he said suddenly.

"It's all right. I understand that you're in a hurry. Right now, it's mostly my feet that are bothering me."

"We will find shelter soon."

Katlyn figured they walked nearly a mile before coming up on the river. More a creek than a river. The Commander stood on the edge of the natural embankment, and the water was below. He looked around, seeming to assess their surroundings. He had one boot on the edge of the embankment, the other underneath him bearing his weight. He scooped the sides of his coat behind him, clasping his hands together underneath, behind his back. He wore soft black leather pants that hugged his form. His weapon's holster was strapped tightly to his left thigh. He wore snug fitting boots that stopped just below his knee and had black steel buckles along the sides. The collar on his black shirt came up high, which only elongated his already long neck. He was fit but not bulky. He had a commanding presence. As if he could silence a room just by entering it. He was very regal, courtly, and looked like he belonged next to a queen. Katlyn couldn't help but think he was beautiful.

Her thoughts were interrupted when he jumped off the embankment down to the receding riverbed. The low water revealed a path that appeared to follow the length of the river.

"We will move downriver." He walked toward her, stopping just beneath where she stood. "Would you like me to assist you?" he asked, looking up and holding his hand out to her.

The embankment's edge came to the middle of his chest. Under normal circumstances, Katlyn would be able to jump down on her own, but trudging through the forest barefoot left her feet with cuts and bruises. Walking was a struggle.

She hesitated to accept his offer. She wasn't sure why. If he was going to hurt her, surely he would've done it already. She was slowing him down. He could easily leave her behind or kill her, and there's nothing she could do to stop him.

"I'm slowing you down."

He pulled his hand back. "Perhaps, but through no fault of your own," he said as she knelt in front of him.

"Thank you"—she pushed both hands through his soft hair, gripping his shoulders—"for not leaving me behind."

He placed his hands under each arm, lifting her gently off the embankment, and stood her on the river's edge beside him. "You completed your task. Now I must complete mine," he said as he looked her in the eyes. "You will be free of this world. You have my word."

They didn't walk for long before coming up on what appeared to be a drainage pipe. It wasn't large, but was big enough for the Commander to traverse, slightly bent at the waist.

"This will be sufficient. It is dry," he said.

Roots and ivy had fallen over the entrance—no doubt from years of abandonment. The Commander told her that Veda was once heavily populated. With industry and a thriving metropolis. War, hundreds of years ago, left the planet in ruin.

"How does war destroy an entire planet?" Katlyn asked.

"War on a galactic scale can do a lot of damage. There are many here who wish to be the dominant power."

"There's been war here for hundreds of years?"

"My people have been at war for much longer."

She could only imagine why as she leaned back against the wall of the pipe with her knees up, dress covering her legs. The Commander knelt on one knee across from her, working on converting his weapon. His fingers moved over the disassembled pieces. As if caressing a lover.

"How will we know when your ship is here?"

"I will hear them. We should remain here until they arrive."

Katlyn could see him clearly as they sat inside the pipe. The bright light of the moon illuminated his white skin. She watched with interest as he worked. His hands didn't appear as lean as before. His black shirt looked to be silk or satin. The flat collar rested more than halfway up his neck, secured at the base of his neck with a red gemstone button. The collar separated gently in the front, revealing his throat and another tattoo.

When he finished with his work, he placed the modified weapon in his coat pocket, then turned his head toward her. More tattoo peeked out from underneath his collar. She looked away and lowered her legs to sit cross-legged. She placed her hands in her lap, then suddenly noticed the blood along her hands and gown.

She inhaled sharply, rubbing her hands together in a futile attempt to remove the dried blood. Her heart raced as panic set in. The Commander leaned close, gently placing one hand over hers, covering them almost completely. She stopped and looked up at him. He was mere inches from her. A calming sensation washed over her body.

"You did what you must."

"I suppose," she said, gently freeing herself from him and looking out at the water. She chuckled and looked back at him. His head was tilted to one side. "I guess I'm leaving this world covered in someone else's blood after all."

He smiled faintly, revealing a pair of sharp eyeteeth. His red eyes danced in the moonlight. "Yes, you are."

"I'll be right back," she said.

Katlyn stood up and stepped out of the pipe. Moving just out of his view, she knelt at the river's edge so she could wash her hands and face. When she finished, she tucked the gown under her, placing her feet in the water. The sudden chill stung the cuts and made her wince.

"Are you all right?"

His voice was deep, dark, and sounded delicious.

"Yes," she said. "It's just my feet."

She washed off the dirt and debris, then dried them with her gown before returning to the pipe and taking her place opposite the Commander. He was kneeling on both knees, sitting on his legs, hands clasped loosely in front of him, watching her. Katlyn sat with her legs to her side toward him.

"May I help you?" he asked.

"What do you mean?"

He reached toward her feet with his left hand. She jumped and retreated her limbs closer to her body.

"I was merely going to help. I understand if you still do not trust me," he said as he put his hands on his thighs and squared his shoulders.

"I'm sorry," she said. "It's not that... I... just, I can't... never mind," she stammered as she hid her face with her hand and chuckled.

They sat in silence for a moment. The Commander sat slightly behind her. Katlyn's breath was visible in the nighttime air. She shivered and tucked her knees into the warmth of her gown.

"You are cold."

"I'll be all right," she said, failing at holding back the shiver that consumed her.

The Commander removed his coat. "May I?" he asked, holding it out to her like a shield.

"Won't you get cold?"

"I will not."

Katlyn hesitated before accepting his offer. She slid her arms into its warmth, and it enveloped her like a womb. She moaned as she wrapped her entire body inside.

"Oh my gosh! Thank you so much."

"You are most welcome," he said with a gentle bow of his head.

She leaned back against the pipe, looking at him as he looked outside. "What were you going to do with my feet?"

"I have the ability to heal others," he said, meeting her gaze.

She chewed on her bottom lip for a moment as they stared at each other. Then she slowly lowered her legs, sliding her feet toward him. He inhaled deeply, and even though she offered her feet to him, he still asked, "May I touch you?"

Katlyn cleared her throat and chewed on her bottom lip as she nodded.

The Commander wrapped his left hand around her right ankle, lifting her foot off the floor of the pipe, and resting her heel on his upper thigh. With his right hand, he rubbed the bottom of her foot, almost massaging it. Placing his fingers over every scratch and cut, healing them instantly.

Katlyn's arms bolted to her sides as she stifled a moan. His touch sent heat and electricity through her body. *That's only one foot,* she thought to herself as she bit her lower lip. She looked away and held back a smile when he picked up her other foot. She couldn't look at him, and had to push her thoughts aside. Her face was hot with embarrassment as her head fell back and she moaned. She tried to squeeze her thighs together to stifle her arousal, but it was useless.

"Oh God!" she yelped, jerking her foot out of his hand. She swallowed hard. "Thanks," she forced out. The words barely formed. He was watching her and her ridiculous display. She was so embarrassed. She behaved as if she'd never been touched before.

She refused to make eye contact with him. She prayed he couldn't read her mind. She's not sure why, but her mouth moved on its own, and she turned toward him, catching him staring at her. "Is it always like that when you heal someone?" She regretted asking as soon as the words fell out of her mouth. "Never mind! I don't need to know. I didn't even mean to ask."

She curled her legs back up to her chest, wrapping herself with his coat and peered outside. "What the hell was that?" she demanded as she turned to face him again. His hands were back on his thighs, and he was still staring at her. "And why are you looking at me like that?"

"Please forgive me," he said, "but I do not know." He seemed just as confused as she was.

She scowled at him. "How can *you* not know?"

The Commander took a deep breath as he looked past her toward the mouth of the pipe. "It is not always like that," he said. "That has never happened before." Katlyn looked at him, brow furrowed. "I felt it as well. Please do not be angry."

Katlyn sighed, sucking in her top lip. "I'm not mad," she said. "I was just taken by surprise."

"As was I."

Katlyn watched him, waiting for him to look at her. When he finally did, she said, "I'm sorry I snapped at you."

With his hands clasped loosely at his thighs, he bowed his head to her. "You should rest," he said as he righted himself. "I will keep watch."

"Don't you need to sleep?"

"Not the same as you."

Katlyn rested on her left side as the Commander moved closer to the mouth of the pipe. She was exhausted, and her eyes were heavy. She tried to watch him but surrounded by the warmth of his coat, she quickly fell asleep.

~Commander

As he moved to the mouth of the pipe, he could feel Katlyn's gaze upon him. He resisted the urge to turn his head toward her, instead focusing his attention to the outside. His mind went back to their walk through the forest—her coiled hair swaying at her full hips as she walked. The wind billowing her shift about her body. Her scent was musky, but sweet. He closed his eyes and shook his head, attempting to shake the thought from his mind.

It did not take long for Katlyn to fall asleep. He could hear her shallow breathing and steady pulse. When she reached a deep sleep, he stepped outside the pipe and listened. He could not sense any humans besides Katlyn, but he would need to walk upriver to be sure. He did so quickly and listened closely. Perhaps he killed all the guards on duty that evening. Hopefully, he and Katlyn had plenty of time before they were discovered.

He still needed to find a suitable clearing for extraction. The area surrounding their shelter had too many trees overhead. He headed back downriver toward the waterfall that caught his attention earlier. He stopped at the pipe and looked at Katlyn through the vines. He knew she would sleep long enough for him to scout ahead to the waterfall. He would not be so far away that he could not return promptly.

He turned and ran along the river's edge toward the falls, and stood on the edge of a short rocky cliff. He needed to find a safe route down so Katlyn would be able to make the journey. He could see there was a suitable clearing at the base of the waterfall, but the route was exposed. Trees hung overhead along the cliff, but the path down was a clear shot from the base of the waterfall. The enemy could easily fire upon them. Once their captors began looking for them, they would need to be able to take cover. He decided to look for another route.

He turned to his right and trekked along the cliff's edge. After a short, easy climb, the cliff curved around and made a gentle slope down to the valley below. That route was mostly shrouded in trees, and the base had several large boulders that would make for good coverage from all directions. The clearing and waterfall were a short distance from there.

He headed back toward the pipe, and Katlyn, deep in thought about what transpired earlier. He healed humans before. Not many, but the Specter had humans who served them. As well as those who were followers, or saw the Specter as gods. If one were injured, they were healed. What a follower wanted from a Specter was immortality, which was a gift they could give, but it was more personal and intimate than even nourishing one's body.

When the Commander returned to the pipe, Katlyn had fallen into an uncomfortable position. Her left side was against the pipe, and her head slipped forward, bent into an awkward angle, and was affecting her breathing.

He crouched in front of her and roused her awake. She lifted her head and rubbed her neck with a look of discomfort. She glanced at him sleepily. "Is everything okay?" she asked, yawning.

"You appeared to be very uncomfortable."

"Yeah, that's not the best way to sleep."

"You may rest your head on me if you wish," he said.

He sat in front of her, leaning his back against the wall of the pipe. Without hesitating, she laid her head on his shoulder. Her forehead rested in the crook of his neck. She brought her hand up to push the pieces of his hair aside that fell into her face.

"You smell like earth and wood after it's rained." She curled up to him and relaxed into his shoulder.

As he sat with a human female resting on his shoulder, his mind went back to healing her. He did not yet understand his connection to her. For a fleeting moment, he had his suspicions, but brushed it off. She was human, after all, and he did not believe imprinting on a human was possible. He never heard of such a thing. For her sake, he hoped he would be able to get her home. She did not belong here, but part of him desired to keep her close.

This is absurd, he said to himself, hissing under his breath. He was a warrior, and he served great women. He was Doyen and commanded one of the Queen's fleets. He oversaw thousands of men who respected and honored him with their unwavering loyalty. Humans were victuals! Yet, there he sat, next to a human female whose warm body was curled up to him sleeping peacefully.

He exhaled deeply, turning his head toward her. His chin rested against the side of her forehead; her skin was warm and comforting. More comforting than he expected it to be. He savored the scent she exuded. Despite being in a cell for several days, her scent was stimulating. He could still smell her arousal from when he touched her feet. *What are you doing to me?* he said to himself. He rested his chin against her forehead, closed his eyes, and fell into an observant slumber.

7. VICTUALS

~Katlyn

"Mom, Natalie!" James said with an excited tone as he walked through the door. "Guess what?"

"What?" they both asked in unison.

"I got assigned a new duty station."

"Okay," Katlyn said.

"Where?" Natalie asked.

"Get this," he began, "are you ready?"

"Yes," Natalie said as Katlyn nodded her head.

"I can't tell you!" James said, laughing.

"What do you mean?" Natalie asked, scowling at him.

"It's classified!"

"You're kidding!" Natalie scoffed.

"I totally believe it," Katlyn said, beaming with pride. "I mean, it's the Space Force. Most anything having to do with outer space and aliens *is going to be classified," Katlyn said as she began laughing.*

"Mom! Why do you say aliens like that?" James asked.

"Because! Why in the hell would we need a Space Force? We have NASA for space exploration. The only reason we need to militarize space is if there are aliens. I'm not stupid," she said, rolling her eyes.

"Mom, stop it."

"Well? I'm not so naïve or self-righteous to believe that humans on Earth are the only intelligent life. Give me a break," Katlyn said, laughing.

***

Katlyn woke up to the sound of morning. The birds were chirping, and the sun was shining. The warmth of its rays crept up on her. She opened her eyes and realized her head was no longer on the Commander's shoulder. She slipped down to his chest sometime during the night, and his soft hair brushed against her forehead. She caught a hint of honeysuckle that mingled with the woody earth scent that his body exuded. He sat quietly, unmoving with his legs stretched out and crossed in front of him. His right arm was underneath her, hand on his hip. His heartbeat thumped rhythmically, and she felt the rise and fall of his chest with every breath. The urge to look at his crotch right in front of her was overwhelming. Instead, she put her arm under her to brace herself as she sat up, stretching and yawning.

"You slept well," he said.

She rubbed her eyes. "Yes, I did, actually," she admitted with a smile. "Thank you!"

"You are most welcome."

"I'm assuming we aren't being chased yet?" she asked as the Commander righted himself and put his arms on his now bent knees.

"Not that I can tell, though I am sure the guards have been discovered by now. Hopefully, my ship arrives soon," he said, looking at Katlyn as she peered outside.

"What's going to happen to me once we get off this planet?" Her voice trembled.

"I do not know. I expect you will stay on my ship until we find a more suitable situation for you."

"Is that wise or safe?" Her concern was legitimate. The Commander was the only Specter she had met, and she knew they consumed humans.

He gently pulled her chin so she would look at him. The blacks of his eyes narrowed in the morning light. "You will be my guest under my protection. My Regent will be grateful to you for aiding in my escape. You need not be concerned about your safety."

Katlyn squeezed her eyes closed and opened them again. "This is just a big culture shock for me."

"I understand," he said, resting both arms on his knees again.

"Sometimes, I still feel like I'm dreaming. Like I'm in a coma, and I'm going to wake up any minute, back on Earth, and this is a crazy dream that I tell my kids about repeatedly until they get tired of hearing it."

"I assure you; this is not a dream."

"That's exactly what you'd say in my dream," she teased, grinning at him.

The Commander inhaled deeply, the right side of his mouth a faint smirk. "Please remain here," he requested as he stood up and stepped out onto the riverbank. "I must listen for movement."

~Commander

The Commander walked upriver, following the path along the river's edge. He needed to listen as far as he was able. The sound of the rushing water would mask the humans' movements. He knew using the clearing at the base of the falls was risky. The enemy could easily flank them there, but it was a calculated risk. Surely Bry'aere, his Lodestar, would send reinforcements to the planet once they confirmed his location. His men knew what to do. They had all been trained well and served together for many generations. He was confident in their abilities.

When he reached a point where the waterfall was not a distraction, he jumped up to the chest-high embankment. He crouched down, closed his eyes, and inhaled deeply. Smelling and listening for any humans in the vicinity. He could detect them in the direction of the bunker. Their heavy boots crunched on the forest floor.

Humans are terrible hunters, he chuckled to himself. *They are very heavy-footed.*

As he listened, some men were receding, while others were maintaining their current distance but moved briskly parallel to the river. Possibly in the direction of the falls. He hissed through his teeth, dropped down to the path below, and moved quickly downriver.

~Katlyn

Katlyn sat just inside the mouth of the pipe, still wrapped in the warmth of the Commander's coat. Her mind reeled with recent events when she suddenly needed to pee—something she had been doing in a hole for the past week.

She carefully removed his coat, laying it against the wall of the pipe. It was made of soft leather. Soft with a satiny feel, but definitely a leather of some type. Not like his pants, which were smooth and shiny, and more a tactical leather for ease of movement. The coat was a heavier leather, but lightweight—a beautiful noble man in leather.

Katlyn rolled her eyes and scoffed loudly as she slapped her forehead with her hand and rubbed it along the side of her face. "Stop it, Katlyn!" she said aloud. "What the hell is wrong with you?" she huffed, then stood up and stepped out of the pipe.

The Commander was nowhere in sight. She turned in the direction he sprinted, but still nothing. She looked on the embankment, but she couldn't see over the top.

"Commander?" she called out; voice elevated. "I'm about to pee. Please don't watch me or sneak up on me," she pleaded into the emptiness.

She spotted a secluded bush on the opposite side of the river. For a forest, there weren't many bushes close by, or trees big enough for her to hide behind. The trees she could see were all skinny. Very tall, but not significant. The bush that caught her eye sat next to a tree. She knew she would be reasonably hidden there.

Not far upriver, stones protruded from the water. Steppingstones perhaps? She went to investigate, and sure enough, there were smooth rocks that jutted out of the clear water. They were placed sporadically from one shoreline to the other, appearing almost intentional.

All this just to pee, she thought to herself. She balanced on the stones as she made the trek across the water. *That was easy enough*. One quick jaunt to the bush, and back across the river, and she'd be good.

She squatted at the bush, making sure there were no snakes or men to take her by surprise. When she finished, she made her way back across the river. About halfway, she noticed the water wasn't very deep. "I should just get in, cause if I fall..." Her voice trailed off when she heard footfalls and looked up to see the Commander sprinting alongside the river toward her.

She gingerly placed her right foot on the next stone, praying that she didn't fall in. A gust of wind caught her off guard, blowing her dress up. In her panic to regain her composure, she, very predictably, slipped on the rock, falling toward the frigid water, screaming as she flew in slow motion.

Why is this happening to me? she thought to herself as her body was consumed by ice.

Just as she suspected, the water wasn't deep, but falling in drenched her completely. If she had walked in the water, only her legs would be wet. She bolted upright and refused to move. Her hands were fisted at her breasts as the water floated her dress around her. She sat on the river bottom with her knees slightly bent; her hair clung to her head and neck as the water lapped at her shoulders. She shook her head as the

Commander approached, attempting to stifle any conversation he may be compelled to start as she sat in the frigid water with her dignity floating downriver.

~Commander

As the Commander neared their shelter, he spotted Katlyn on the opposite side of the river. She was walking from behind a bush and began to tread carefully among some rocks. *What is she doing?* he asked himself as he watched her walk warily across the water, balancing on the rocks. About halfway across she looked up and noticed him. The wind caught her shift. She grabbed around it in a failed attempt to reclaim her dignity, only to slip on a stone and fall into the water. A hasty screech escaped her lips before she disappeared under the surface.

He increased his pace to reach her quicker, and she righted herself into a seated position. Her hands fisted at her breasts, and her lips turned a light lavender color as she looked up at him, shaking her head.

He stepped in the water, holding his hand out to her. "Are you all right?" he asked. She said nothing, only continued to shake her head from side to side as her jaw shook. "What were you doing?"

She rolled her eyes and turned her head to the left. "I... ne—needed pri—privacy," she stuttered through chattering teeth.

"I do not understand." He cocked his head.

She exhaled, her breath a vapor in front of her. "I ha—had to pppee," she forced out, chin shaking strenuously.

He pulled his head back when he realized what she meant. "I see," he said, looking down at her.

She pulled her legs closer to her body, repositioning them under her. She sat up on her knees and took his hand, looking at him as she pulled herself out of the water. He maintained eye contact with her but could not help but notice that her shift clung to her body. The water made it transparent, and it revealed every curve of her breasts and hips as if she were not clothed at all. He looked away quickly. She jerked her hand back and screeched.

"I will not look," he said as he continued to look downriver.

The wet fabric resisted her as she pulled at it, attempting to free it from her body. He continued to look away when she retook his hand, and they exited the water together.

Through chattering teeth, she told him where his coat was. He suggested that she should wring her clothing out while he walked to the pipe to retrieve his coat. Once his coat was in hand, he kept his back to her as she approached. He took her shift, and she took his coat.

"I'm covered. Thanks for being such a gentleman."

He turned to face her. Her face and neck were flushed crimson, but still, she laughed and smiled, gently shaking her head. "I've been clumsy my whole life. I don't know why this surprises me," she chuckled.

"Accidents happen," he said as he laid her gown over some branches to dry in the sun.

They both sat down inside the pipe. Katlyn, with her legs crossed, the Commander kneeling on one knee at the opening. He stared outside; his eyes darted back and forth.

"They are searching for us," he said, "but they are not close."

"Great," she said, devoid of enthusiasm. "Nothing of your ship yet, I guess."

"They will come. We merely need to stay hidden until they do. When they arrive and are able, they will send reinforcements."

"You sure about that?"

He looked at her, cocking his head to one side. "I am."

Katlyn raised both eyebrows and looked outside the pipe. "Okay," she said.

"They are my men. I trained most of them personally. They have served under my command for generations. I am confident in their abilities," he said, chin raised as he looked back out toward the trees.

"You said you would hear them. What will it sound like?"

"You will not hear it. The reaper frequency is too low for humans to hear."

"Reaper?" she asked with an elevated tone.

He looked at her, hesitating. "Are you sure you would like to know?"

Katlyn drew her head back. "Probably not," she said, looking away from him.

The Commander continued looking at her as she watched the trees. Would she have been so kind and trusting under different circumstances? If she had grown up knowing of his kind. Was her escape the sole reason for her demeanor toward him? She was no longer afraid of him, but she was all too aware of what he was, what he was capable of, and what he had done thus far.

"I cannot help what I am."

She glanced at him. "I know."

"When we reach maturity, we are allowed to choose. Some choose death rather than a life consuming others." Her jaw clenched, and her eyes darted away. He was sharing with her things that were not shared with humans. Things that were not even discussed among his kind.

Katlyn chewed on her bottom lip, then asked, "Why did you make the choice you made?"

He raised his chin as he took a deep breath. "I should not be sharing this with you," he said with stoicism.

"Why are you?"

"I do not know."

The silence between them was deafening as they looked beyond each other at the forest in front of them.

"If I made another choice, you might still be in that cell," he finally said.

Katlyn looked at him sharply. "You might be right. I would still be in that cell, having been assaulted by that pig, but my freedom isn't worth the innocent lives you've taken since making that choice," she said with obvious contempt.

"Those humans would be dead anyway!"

Her jaw dropped, then she looked back outside the pipe.

"Perhaps moirai may have a different plan for you."

She sighed. "I don't know what that is," she said. "It sounds like a name I've heard before, but I don't know what it means."

He looked up, searching for a translation. Then finally said, "Something predetermined."

"Destiny or fate?"

"Yes."

Katlyn scoffed. "Are you trying to say that fate or destiny has something to do with this?"

"I do not know," he said, looking down at the water. "I made my choice because humans would die regardless. Whether I lived or took my own life, those I have killed would still be gone. If not by my hand, then by another." He remembered his mother's words so many millennia ago as he continued to share with this woman, things she may not want to hear, but she needed to—he needed her to understand. "At my hand, they do not suffer. I take their life quickly and ease their pain. They go peacefully. Many do not offer such solace." He took a deep breath. "Many Specter hunt for pleasure. I do not; I hunt because I have no choice. Many of my people desire peaceful coexistence, but how do hunter and prey live peacefully together?"

"There has to be another way?"

"As of yet, there is not." He shook his head. "In all my years of life, this is the only time I know of when hunter and prey have worked side by side, sharing a common goal." Katlyn inhaled sharply; her neck was visibly tense at his words. "We have humans who serve us, yes, but they still fear us. We could take their life when they no longer serve their purpose."

"You could do the same to me."

"Yes, but I will not."

"Why? The only thing I've done for you is kill a man and hand you some keys."

"I have given you my word, and you are different from any human I have ever encountered. I cannot explain it," he told her in disbelief of his own words. "The humans who serve us do so only for their benefit, to save their own lives. They would never risk their life as you have. Even when you discovered what I am, you still assisted me. No other human has ever behaved as you have."

"Maybe that's because I'm not from here."

"Coming from an intact world should make you more fearful of me."

Katlyn shook her head gently. "You haven't given me a reason to be afraid of you."

"My existence should be reason enough," he said matter-of-factly. "I take the lives of humans to extend my own. Humans are victuals, nourishment; nothing more!" The words stung even his own ears as they slipped past his tongue, making her breath catch, and her eyes dart away from him. She shook her head as she chewed on her bottom lip and looked at the river.

He regretted the words as soon as he spoke them. She was the only human who ever showed him kindness or compassion, but the words were said, and once the words were said, they could not be unsaid.

8. SACRIFICE

~James

"It's been several weeks, James! Who could possibly have taken her?" Natalie sobbed.

"We don't know if someone took her—"

"You must be joking? Please tell me you're kidding. You think she'd just up and leave?" Natalie snapped.

"Of course not!"

"Are you still leaving? You're really going to leave me here to deal with this all by myself?"

"Daniel is here. You know I can't just take time off. What I'm doing is important," James said.

"More important than finding mom?"

"No, but I can't just... mom would understand. She understands how important this is to me. She would want me to go," James tried to reassure his sister.

"Mom isn't here!" she reminded him heatedly. "She's missing, and you're just going to run off and do whatever it is you do in only God knows where!"

"Natalie, look—" he was interrupted by a knock on the door. He grumbled as he stood to his feet and hurried to answer it.

"Commodore!" he said, puzzled. "Please come in. This is my sister, Natalie." He waved his hand toward his sister, who stood in the middle of the room with her hands crossed at her chest.

"Pardon the intrusion, Captain, but this couldn't be said over the phone. I came straight here after receiving this information," the Commodore said, holding out a file.

James took the classified file and glanced at his sister. "Sir, my sister is here."

"This involves her, too, unfortunately."

"What are you talking about?" Natalie snapped.

"I'll say what I can. We received a data burst," he began, looking at James. "We know who has your mother."

"What!" Natalie shouted and headed toward them.

"I can't go into great detail with you, I'm sorry," he said to Natalie. "All I can say is we know where she is, and we can attempt to retrieve her."

"How in the hell does the military have anything to do with her missing?" Natalie asked.

"I can't tell you that," the Commodore said.

Natalie lunged, attempting to grab the file out of James' hand, only to be met with his other hand outstretched, preventing her from reaching it.

"Natalie, I'll read this, and I promise that I'll tell you what I can. Which probably won't be much more than what the Commodore told you. At least now we have some answers."

"You can take your clearance and shove it up your ass. Tell me where mom is!" she shouted at him.

"I'm sure this has something to do with me personally," James said to both. "Why would anyone kidnap *my* mom unless I pissed someone off."

"Why did it take this long to find out anything?" Natalie asked.

"I can't tell you that. Just stop asking questions. You know as much as you're able to know," James said.

"You can leave as soon as you're ready, Captain," the Commodore said.

"Now, can I go? Or would you rather I stay here and help you deal with this?" he asked Natalie sarcastically, who slapped him across the face.

"This is all your fault!" she screamed through sobs. "You better find mom and bring her back, or I never want to see you again!" she yelled, then stormed out of the front door.

~Commander

As the sun neared zenith, Katlyn's shift was dry, and she was clothed again. She offered his coat to him, but he refused. Telling her she should keep it—the only words they spoke to each other since the harshness of their previous conversation.

Katlyn sat in the pipe while he sat on the dry riverbed, both avoiding conversation with each other. The last thing he said to her was harsh, bitter, and very unlike his previous demeanor toward her—the words even took him by surprise.

It was well past midday when he heard the faint hum of a reaper; his ship finally arrived. "Katlyn! My ship has arrived. We must move now," he said, looking down at her sitting alone in the pipe. She jumped up, her heart rate picked up in her neck, and her body became noticeably tense. "I scouted ahead and found a suitable clearing for extraction, but we must attempt to make our way there undetected. I do not know if the guards are waiting for us. The waterfall would mask their movements," he said as he began walking downriver. She spoke not a word, following closely behind him despite his long strides.

As they neared the waterfall, and the path that diverged along the cliff's edge, the Commander motioned for Katlyn to get down while he peered over the edge of the falls. He could not see anyone down below, but that did not mean no one was there. He turned abruptly, grasping Katlyn's upper arm, and guided her onto the path he chose for them the night before. He moved quickly, yet gracefully, urging her along next to him. She fumbled to keep up, but she did not resist. His coat flowed gently behind her; it barely seemed to contact the ground even though its size devoured her.

The two of them moved from tree to tree as they made their way around the curvature of the cliff. The boulders at the base were just within sight when he froze. He crouched low and pushed Katlyn behind him. He heard footfalls and could sense humans were near—at least three men.

"We have been discovered," he whispered to Katlyn as she crouched behind him. He grasped her arm and quickly moved from tree to tree. Finally, stopping at a large tree surrounded by bushes that provided ample cover for them both. "They block our path." His voice was low. "I must eliminate them before we are able to continue," he said as he released Katlyn's arm. "Remain here."

With Katlyn at his back, the Commander began to leave the safety of the bushes, when a hand grabbed his right arm. He paused to look back and saw Katlyn staring up at him. Her hand grasped the crook of his elbow. Her eyes were wide, and her mouth opened as if she wished to speak. She snapped it shut, appearing to change her mind as soon as he looked at her. She started to retreat her hand, but he brushed his on top of hers before rising out of the bushes and leaving her behind.

~Katlyn

Katlyn hunkered down as close to the ground as she could, waiting for the Commander to come back and retrieve her. The silence was broken by the sound of what seemed to be a rapid-fire weapon, like an assault rifle. Pull the trigger once for a hail of bullets, type of weapon. She knew the Commander killed a room full of guards before, but he caught them by surprise. They weren't expecting him, but these men came prepared. Katlyn didn't know what type of injuries the Commander could sustain. She knew he had been shot escaping the bunker, but the injury didn't seem to bother him for long. And if he was able to heal others, what about himself?

The bullets rained down just beyond her. Followed by scuffling, then the sound of what she only assumed were bones breaking, then nothing. Then again, more weapon's fire, scuffling, and breaking bones. Then silence. The silence felt like a vice gripping her throat as she waited. What would pull her from the bushes? Human or Specter? Did it matter which? Were both her enemy? What kind of life awaited her from here?

She finally decided to peek out from the safety of the bushes. She raised her arms in surrender as she stood up, expecting to meet gunfire, only to hear and see nothing—nothing, except white hair in the distance. She could see the Commander's head, but he wasn't moving. He appeared to be kneeling in the shrubbery.

As if her feet had a mind of their own, she ran toward him. Her body moved in slow motion; she could see herself bolt across the forest frame by frame. The Commander's thick hair moved in the wind as his head fell back. When she reached him, his body wavered as he knelt next to two dead men.

~Commander

He left the confines of the bush, and Katlyn, to nothing. There was nothing in front of him. He knew the humans were close. He could smell their fear and taste the metal of their projectile weapons that damaged flesh and killed men with a single shot.

Such a waste, he said to himself.

He took several quick long strides, creating a reasonable distance between him and Katlyn when suddenly flashes of white light blinded him. Heat pierced the right side of his body as the humans fired their weapons. He moved like a bullet in the direction of one of the humans, snapping his neck with one hand. The Commander was injured, but he would heal.

From the safety of the dead human's covert position, he was able to get a bearing on the next closest target. Two males sheltered together not far from him, both seemed to have the same type of weapon. He was already injured. If both humans were able to shoot him, he would quickly succumb to his injuries. He needed to subdue at least one of the men so he could take their essence.

Moving like an apparition and faster than the wind could carry him, he swept down onto both men. They were more prepared than he expected, both getting several shots off before he could kill them. He dropped to his knees beside the dead humans, dark ichor pouring from his mouth and chest. He looked up at the sky through the canopy of the trees, wheezing, then seeing a woman approach. She called out, and her hands reached for him. Her image was blurry as his vision faded. His life was trying to escape his body.

~Katlyn

"Commander!" Katlyn cried as she reached out, catching his collapsing body before he hit the ground. She tried frantically to stem the bleeding; his black blood soaked her clothing. He was gasping and struggling to breathe. Blood was pouring out of his mouth. His eyes were open, looking at her but through her.

"What can I do?" she cried, covering his wounds with her hands.

"I..." he wheezed with a forced breath. The air in his lungs escaped through the holes in his chest, and his eyes began to close.

"No!" Katlyn screamed at him. "You can't die!" she shouted as she shook him back into consciousness. His eyes opened, looking at her. "Tell me what to do! How can I help you?"

"You... cannot," he stammered, coughing up blood as he spoke.

"Yes, I can!"

"I will not..." his voice trailed off. Katlyn's fear turned to anger. She grabbed fistfuls of his hair on each side of his head, pulling his face within a hairsbreadth of hers. "I will not hurt you," he choked. His cool breath wafted over her face.

73

"You gave me your word that you would get me off this planet!" she screamed into his face. "You take what you need to keep your word!"

Tears ran down her cheeks as she sobbed.

"Even if I'm dead when I leave here"—she sobbed—"at least I'll be off this planet!" She dropped her head onto his chest. "You do what you have to do. One of us should get out of here alive," she pleaded into his bleeding chest.

The Commander's hand reached up, grasping her chin and pulling her face up, leaving behind a streak of black blood. He took a struggled breath. "I... cannot ease the pain for you," he forced out. "Too weak..." he said on an exhale.

"I don't care!" Katlyn said through her sobs. "*Please*! We can't both die here!"

The Commander wrapped his right hand around her throat. His breath shook as he exhaled, and with clear fatigue consuming him, he pulled her over his body, onto the ground beside him and rolled toward her. His head fell onto hers, forehead meeting forehead, and she grabbed both his shoulders. She still didn't understand what he needed or what he would do.

He inhaled deeply and looked at her. The blacks of his eyes constricted to almost nothing. "This will not be pleasant," he said with a dying breath. His left hand cradled the back of her neck. She forced her eyes closed as her body was consumed by fire.

Heat. Every nerve in her body was on fire and were being pulled out through her nose and mouth. The fire started at her hands and feet and consumed her limbs up to her core. Her organs convulsed as if being punched with so much force, they could explode. Her lungs burned like she had inhaled the flame of a blowtorch. Then calm, followed by aching—every muscle in her body ached. The muscles in her arms and legs spasmed. She gasped for air, but her lungs refused to work. She opened her eyes, but her vision was blurry. She could see the Commander's silhouette. His hand was still on her throat, but his grip loosened, and his forehead rested on her chest. She could hear him, his breathing had eased, and he was no longer wheezing or struggling to breathe. His breaths became more even, while Katlyn's were more sporadic and restricted like there was fluid in her lungs.

Slowly, the Commander began to move. His right hand released her throat and dragged down her body, stopping on her hip as he tried to balance himself. His head was still resting on her chest. After a moment, he sat upright. Her vision was still blurry, and his face was only a white shadow in front of her. Her breathing was shaky and irregular, but the air came more naturally with each heave of her chest.

~Commander

Katlyn was motionless as he sat over her. The essence of her life returning his strength and healing his wounds. Her breathing was irregular, and her eyes were cloudy, but she would live. Briefly, but long enough for him to give back what he took from her—something he had never been in the position to do for a human. He would forever be in her debt.

He sat next to her with his arms resting on his bent knees. Katlyn moved slowly, visibly fighting her body. She let out painful moans as she sat upright. "We have to keep moving." Her breath faltered, and her voice was hoarse.

His head shifted, acknowledging what she said, but he refused to look at her. "I gave you my word that I would not harm you." He could not hide the shame and regret his tone carried.

"You also gave your word that you'd get me off this planet," she said shakily, her voice raspy. "You can't do that if you're dead."

He took a deep breath and lifted his chin parallel to the ground, then rose to his feet. He looked down at Katlyn. She was hunched over, barely able to sit up on her own. She looked up at him, eyes cloudy, mouth agape, struggling to breathe. He crouched down in front of her and reached under both arms, lifting her off the ground. He carried all her weight, and she had to lean on him to steady herself.

When Katlyn's legs were finally able to bear weight, they both began walking down the cliff's edge toward the boulders below. Katlyn stumbled, even though his strides were small and slow. He grasped her left arm, so she did not fall.

They took cover behind the boulders when they entered the valley. The waterfall was loud enough to provide concealment for anyone who approached. The Commander's strength had not fully returned, so he could not yet tell by listening whether anyone was beyond the tree line. Then suddenly, a heavy voice called out to them.

"You're trapped. Surrender now, and we won't kill you. We'd prefer to take you both alive."

The Commander crouched with his back to the voice; Katlyn sat on the ground next to him. She dropped her head onto his knee. "This isn't happening," she said. "If they have explosives, we're dead. All they have to do is toss one over here, and it's over for us." Katlyn was breathing heavy as her body shook. "Can you tell how many there are?"

"Perhaps, if they are close enough," he said, then he closed his eyes and listened for the sound of their breathing. "There are four, maybe five."

"Great," Katlyn said, rolling her eyes. "Would you be able to take them out if I can distract them?"

He looked at her with one eyebrow raised—a hint of a smile formed on his lips. "If I am able to sneak up on one, then yes. I will use him as a shield against the others."

"Okay, I'll distract them this way"—she pointed to the right—"then you can go around the other way using the boulders as cover. But don't come out right away. I'm going to try to convince them I'm alone. Maybe it'll be easier for you to sneak up on them."

"I'm giving you to the count of three!" the boisterous voice demanded from the other side of the boulders.

"I'm coming out!" Katlyn hollered, looking at the Commander and removing his coat.

"Are you positive you are not a warrior?" he asked her with pride.

She scoffed and shook her head. "This is the act of a desperate woman," she said as she raised her hands.

~Katlyn

Katlyn moved cautiously away from the safety of the boulders. "I'm coming out. Please don't shoot!" Her vision was still blurry. She kept her eyes down on the ground so she wouldn't trip. "Please don't shoot," she said again as she moved around the side to draw their attention in her direction.

"Where is the Specter?" a man asked. She couldn't see his face; only shadows as she looked in his direction without lifting her head.

She shook her head and started to cry, then pointed to the top of the cliff where the Commander had been shot moments before. The men must have believed her because they seemed to let down their guard. She could see several shadows approach her.

"You've become quite the problem," one of them said. "We lost a lot of good men. The Director is beginning to think you aren't worth the trouble."

"Why am I here?" she asked shakily as she continued to move slowly in the opposite direction of the Commander.

"It doesn't matter."

Katlyn continued looking at the ground as a dark shadow leapt out from behind a tree, taking the farthest man by surprise, grabbing him, and snapping his neck with a single movement. The Commander fired the dead man's weapon, using him as a shield. The other men turned around and started firing their guns, only to hit their fallen comrade.

Searing pain tore through Katlyn's body as the man in front of her fired his weapon prematurely. She was knocked back and fell violently to the ground, clutching at the wounds in her abdomen. She could feel warm blood coating her hands as she heard more men and the scuffling of feet. Then suddenly, a ghost appeared above her. Her already blurred vision continued to diminish. She could feel the ghost's arms slide under her, lifting her as if she were weightless. He carried her close to his body; his soft hair brushed across her face. Her head rested comfortably in the crook of his elbow. She looked up as light surrounded them, then she drifted into unconsciousness.

~Commander

The Commander shot and killed two of the humans as several of his men appeared out of thin air just outside the tree line. All of them spread out in the clearing. The ones closest to him fired their weapons at the other two humans, incapacitating them.

"Clear the area!" his Lodestar shouted. Several men fanned out around the clearing, taking on fire from humans hidden throughout the valley. "Sir! We came as soon as we detected your precise location."

The Commander acknowledged him with a quick nod of his head as he marched over to Katlyn. She was holding her side and struggling to breathe. Her eyes fluttered opened and closed. He gently scooped her up and cradled her in his arms, then walked into the clearing.

"We have neutralized all the threats," his Lodestar said. "Sir?" he asked with a curious tone when he saw the human female cradled in the Commander's arms.

"This woman saved my life."

"Of course, Commander," he responded with a quick bow of his head. "We have gathered the remaining humans and are ready to return to the ship. On your command, sir."

"Very well. Return to the ship," he commanded.

While others loaded onto a reaper, his Lodestar activated the transport. He and the Commander were engulfed in soft light as they were transported back to the ship.

9. RENEWED

~Katlyn

She drifted in and out of consciousness as her body moved, under no volition of her own. She felt as if she were floating, being carried by an ethereal being. Her vision came and went, so she saw momentary flashes of soft light, followed by darkness surrounding the figure above her. His shadowy silhouette being the only constant in front of her. Soft wisps of satin caressed her face. Her body ached and was an inferno. Earth and wood soothed her as delicate tendrils encompassed her body.

Suddenly, she was no longer floating but sinking, sinking as if settling in for a long nap. Was she settling into the earth, perhaps? Was she dead? Her body was numb, but she knew the ghost caressed her shoulders. She couldn't respond to him. She was lifeless as he clenched her throat. She couldn't move her body, then she fell back into unconsciousness.

DOYEN

~Commander

"Welcome back, Commander!" the bridge's second centurion greeted him enthusiastically. "You have been missed."

The Commander stepped off the transfer platform ahead of his Lodestar. "Not presumed dead, I hope."

"Absolutely not!" The centurion bowed his head sharply. As he righted himself, he tilted his head to the side when he saw the human cradled in the Commander's arms. "What is this?" he asked, raising an eyebrow and waving his hand toward Katlyn.

"You need not concern yourself," the Commander retorted as he hurried his way out of the room. "I will be in my quarters. I am not to be disturbed, and send Nia in right away."

"As you command," the centurion said, lowering his eyes.

The Commander left the transfer room and turned right down the dimly lit corridor. Passing warriors along the way who acknowledged his return with gentle head bows and welcoming gestures. They paid no attention to the bleeding female at his breast. That, or they chose not to question their Commander. The bridge's second centurion was bold to have asked. His Lodestar being his second in command and longtime friend, was another matter.

He came to a junction in the corridor. To his left was the hangar bay, straight ahead was more of the same passage that was behind him—private quarters for his men—as well as the Regent's gathering hall and private quarters. To his right, the corridor opened to another gathering place with storage rooms. That was where the humans on board congregated for various reasons.

He turned right at the junction. His private quarters were through the gathering place and down another short corridor. As he approached his quarters, the doors detected his presence before he reached them, and opened smoothly. He entered, overlooking the fact that there were no conscripts present. Two conscripts always guarded his quarters.

The room before him was a sitting room for his private gatherings or personal guests. There were a couple of tables

80

about the room with comfortable chairs. The tables were for games, meetings, or just lounging. He never did have much time for mere lounging, though.

On the opposite side of the room was a large window with bench-style seating on each side. Various pillows were thrown about—exactly how he left it. To the left of the sitting room was his bedchamber, and to the right was another bedchamber for personal guests. That room was rarely occupied; he rarely had time for guests.

He turned to the right and pushed the button beside the door with his elbow. The door slid open, invitingly, and he stepped inside. The darkened room awoke upon sensing his presence, and the lights raised just enough that was comfortable to his eyes.

He approached the bed opposite the door and gently placed Katlyn down. The bed was bare and without linens— only being prepared for guests. He did not have time to announce a guest.

Katlyn was unconscious. Her chest barely moved, struggling with each haggard breath. Her shift was torn from the shots entering her body and was covered in black and red ichor; hers and his vital fluids mingling together.

He grasped her shoulders and shook her gently, attempting to rouse her, but she was unresponsive. He reached for the front of her neck with his right hand, and the base of her head with his left, placing his face above hers. He must breathe life into her before healing her wounds. The projectiles must be extracted so she could heal properly, and in her weakened state, her heart may not be strong enough. But the Commander himself was barely strong enough to give her life.

He grasped her delicately, closing his eyes as he took a deep breath. He tightened his grip around her and exhaled slowly over her open mouth and nose. He gave her what life he was able to spare. Just as he began to stumble, Nia entered the room.

"Commander!" she said. "It's good to see you. You requested me?"

"I need you to control the bleeding. I need nourishment if I am to heal her," he said with faltered breath, staggering slightly.

"Who is she?" Nia asked, then winced. "My apologies, Commander. That's not my business."

He snapped his head in her direction, looking down without shifting his head down toward her. "No! It is not your business. Just do as I ask."

"Yes, Commander!" She bowed gently at the waist.

"I will return shortly," he said, then walked out of the door.

The Commander left his private quarters with haste. Not running, but not walking down the corridor. If he was going to save Katlyn, he must act quickly. The life he gave was not enough to sustain her for long—she was dying. A human sacrificed herself to save his life, and he must do what he could to save hers in return. He would do nothing less for anyone else.

He approached the junction in the corridors. His Lodestar and lifelong friend, Bry'aere stood before him. He caught the Commander's hand in his for a private conversation.

'Commander,' Bry'aere's mind projected devotion, loyalty, and strength. *'Our Regent wishes for an audience.'*

'Of course,' the Commander responded. *'Please tell her I am in the debt of a woman who saved my life. With such, I must try to save hers. She will die if I do not act quickly.'*

'I will inform her.'

'She will understand. That I am certain,' the Commander projected. *'Where are the humans from the planet?'*

'They have all been relocated to holding cells.'

'Thank you,' the Commander responded. *'Please give our Regent my apologies, and I will be there straightaway,'* he projected. Then pulled away and turned the corner, immediately stepping into a darkened stairwell, the tails of his coat flowed gracefully behind him.

He followed the stairs down two levels to the holding cells. He walked along the dark corridor, passing conscripts guarding cells, and saw the faces of humans looking back at him. Some in defiance, others in anger, but all were afraid. They knew why he was there.

"Where are the humans who have just recently arrived?" he asked. Not directed at any single conscript, but all at once.

Three cells down, a conscript stepped into the corridor, drawing his attention. In a few long strides, his coat rippling behind him, he reached the cell and peered inside. Seven humans were lying about the room; all dressed the same. All still unconscious from the Specters' weapon's fire.

The Commander brushed his hand over the control panel on the corridor wall behind the conscript. The crystalline door retracted, allowing him entrance. He bent down to each human, extinguishing their life one by one and leaving nothing but empty, cloudy gray-eyed shells behind.

~Bry'aere

Bry'aere waited for the Commander to disappear before retreating to deliver his message to their Regent. He turned on his heel and walked down the corridor, turning right at the next junction.

"I must see our Regent," he informed the conscripts standing guard at the door. Both moved aside while one brushed their hand over the door control, opening the double doors. Bry'aere moved through, and both doors shut briskly behind him.

The gathering hall was opulent. Beneath Bry'aere's feet was veined marble with dark sapphire, emerald, and violet hues. They mingled together like oil floating on water, much like the sky above their homeworld. Above his head hung vines with an assortment of colored leaves surrounded by stringed lights that cast a gentle glow throughout the room. In the center of the room on a double platform, also of marble, sat a long table carved from a solid piece of buloke, an exceedingly rare wood that was difficult to find. It was not found on most worlds. The wood was coated with a lacquer to give it a glistening finish that enhanced the grain. Surrounding the table were chairs carved from the same type of wood but inlaid with alabaster. On each side of the room were crystalline doors that opened to short corridors. On both sides of each corridor were quarters for the Regent's private escorts, centurions, and personal guests. Opposite where Bry'aere stood was another set of double doors. Conscripts stood guard on each side. The Regent's private chambers, only a select few were allowed in there. Bry'aere not being one of them. To his immediate left, the Regent's drone sat on a bench leaning up against the wall. Eyes closed; arms crossed against his chest. His long soft leather coat folded about his legs.

"Please inform our Regent that I wish to see her," Bry'aere said.

The man rose and moved around the room, activating the door control, and entering her private chambers. The doors closed quietly behind him. Merely a breath later, they opened again, and out glided their Regent. Bry'aere bowed deeply at the waist as she approached him. Her long black hair flowed down her back. Her white silk gown dropped over her shoulders, revealing porcelain white skin. The fabric flowed over her body, accentuating every curve, ending at her ankles where it moved about like a gentle tide.

"Domina," Bry'aere addressed her as he took her hands, lowering his forehead to caress the tops. *'The Commander sends his regret that he is currently unable to come—'*

'Why?' she projected. Her mind felt like a harsh winter—cold and bitter.

Bry'aere righted himself, but kept his head bowed to her as he held her hands. *'He brought someone with him. He informed me that this woman saved his life, and in doing so, became injured herself. He is attempting to save her life in return.'*

'A woman saved his life?'

'Yes, Domina,' he responded. His mind was closed to her without being too obvious; he did not want to reveal too much. He did not see her being pleased that a *human* woman stole her commander's attention just as he returned.

She pulled her hands back, seeming to sense his hesitation. "What are you not telling me, Lodestar?"

"Domina," he looked her in the eyes despite his head being bowed, "she is human."

"What!" Her voice was elevated. Her brow furrowed as she looked at her drone, who appeared just as confused. "Tell the Commander I demand to see him as soon as possible!" she snapped.

"Yes, Domina. I will inform him," Bry'aere said, bowing deeply before leaving the room.

~Katlyn

She was motionless. Her body no longer an inferno, but she ached. Her left side hurt, and there were sharp stabbing pains with every heave of her chest. Breathing was a struggle. The ghost was no longer there. He was replaced by something else. But what? What now hovered over her dying body? Was it a wraith? A smaller, darker image replaced the ghostlike apparition. One that squeezed the fire at her side, as if trying to rip her soul from her body. Katlyn struggled to open her eyes. The figure touched her hand and spoke to her in hushed tones. It was not a wraith, but a woman. Her voice was soft and calming, caressing Katlyn's ears, but still, she touched, squeezed at her side. Katlyn's breath wavered as she forced her eyes open. She could see the woman sitting next to her, but the image was fleeting as she lost the ability to hold her eyes open.

Her mind was reeling, dreaming. She couldn't decipher what was real and what was a fantasy. She saw her kids' faces one minute, then the next she saw the ghost, touching her body and massaging her. Then, a bolt of electricity. Passion and fire, but no pain. Pleasure. She had no control over her body and could hear herself moaning at the ghost's touch.

She was calm, at peace. Then the ghost touched her again, but he was not massaging. He was digging, clawing at her insides. She tried to resist him, not because he was hurting her, but because he was touching her. Why was he clawing and digging at her body? A sound escaped from her when she grabbed at him. Her eyes opened, her vision was no longer blurry, and she could see the ghost clearly; he was a man. She recognized him but couldn't find his name. She stopped resisting as warmth and electricity once again passed through her body.

She could feel the ghost caressing her, looking for something. He found what he was looking for, and was touching her again. She wanted to resist, but at the same time, she desired it, longed for it. Again, he dug, but that was not why she resisted him. She resisted because she *wanted* him to touch her, but knew that she shouldn't. Her eyes were still heavy, but they opened suddenly. Seeing the man, she grabbed at his hands and tried to kick him off her, only to be met with resistance from another. She was trapped. Her hands wouldn't obey her. She could see both the man and the woman pinning her body. She couldn't fight them as the ghost dug into her flesh.

Then calm, followed by an intense wave of euphoria. Katlyn was free of pain, and the weight that was stabbing her lungs and stole her breath. She opened her eyes for a fleeting moment and saw the Commander. A beautiful regal man leaned over her and touched her. Then she passed out.

~Commander

The Commander returned to his quarters quickly. Fully regenerated and better able to help Katlyn.

"This room will need fresh linens," he said when he entered the guest quarters. "I do not know how long our guest will be staying."

"Of course, Commander," the young human said as she rose from the side of the bed. "The bleeding has slowed, but so has her breathing, and her pulse is weak. She also opened her eyes for a moment," she informed him, stepping away as he approached. He was in top physical condition, the holes in his silk shirt being the only evidence of any injury. "Would you like me to find your attendant?" Nia asked as he sat on the edge of the bed.

"Yes, please. I do not know how long this will take. Have him wait in my bedchamber."

"Yes, Commander." She bowed her head before leaving the room.

The Commander sat on the bed next to Katlyn. He tried again to wake her, to no avail. Her life was fading fast. He grasped her neck and head again, bringing her face close to his, and breathing life back into her. She inhaled his gift deeply but still struggled to breathe. Her pulse was weak, no doubt from the injuries she sustained.

He laid her back down and began moving his hands delicately along the curvature of her body, searching for her injuries. Rather than removing her shift altogether, and exposing her, he tore through the material to reveal the wounds. There were three wounds, and two of them still had shrapnel inside.

The single wound that was a clean shot was at her waist, just above her hip. It did not appear to have hit anything but muscle upon entering and exiting. He placed his left hand on the front of the wound, and his right hand behind her on her back and gently massaged them. Katlyn inhaled sharply and moaned. Her head fell back as she responded to him. The Commander again felt what he felt the first time he healed her. The wounds closed quickly, leaving only faint bruises behind.

The other two wounds would require him to extract the metal inside before closing them. He began with the one in her lower abdomen, placing his right hand above it, with the hole positioned in between his thumb and forefinger. He would need to ease her pain as much as possible as he extracted the metal.

Using the claw and forefinger on his left hand, he reached into the wound, feeling for the projectile inside. He pierced her already tender flesh, searching for the invading piece, and she yelped suddenly, grabbing his hand. Her eyes opened briefly, then fluttered shut, and her hand fell back to her side. He was able to extract the piece, and tossed it onto the floor at his feet.

At that moment, Nia entered the room, carrying a large wicker basket filled with clean linens, a blanket, and heavy plush pillows. She also had a fur draped over one arm. The Commander paid her no attention as he massaged Katlyn's wound, eliciting another gentle moan from her. The electricity coursed through both their bodies as he touched her. He was all too aware of Nia watching him from the center of the room.

As his hands moved delicately up the side of Katlyn's body, searching for another wound, he turned sharply to Nia, which made her jump. She looked away and placed the basket down on the floor by the window.

"Your attendant is waiting. How else may I be of service?" she asked, not meeting his eyes.

"She will need to be washed. I am almost finished."

The final wound was below Katlyn's left breast. The shrapnel may have nicked her lung, which could be contributing to her staggered breathing. The Commander gently placed his right hand just above the wound in the same manner as before. Unable to avoid touching her breast, and aware that Nia was still watching him.

He searched for the invading metal. Katlyn inhaled sharply, her breath faltering as she attempted to push him away. Her knee came up and pushed against his chest. Her eyes opened again as she grabbed for his hands.

"Nia, hold her arms!"

Nia did as he commanded and grabbed Katlyn's wrists, holding them above her head while he pushed her leg back down and repositioned himself above her waist. He worked quickly, trying to extract the piece, her eyes opening and closing while she struggled.

"Why is she in pain?" Nia asked. It was a fair question. Nia was aware that Specter had the ability to ease pain.

"She is not. She is fighting the touch. She is fighting me," he answered. "I must remove this to heal her properly. It has damaged her lung."

He was finally able to extract the piece and tossed it on the floor with the other. "You may release her," he said. Nia promptly complied and picked the pieces up off the floor, placing them in her pocket.

The Commander once again focused his attention on Katlyn, gently massaging the wound. Her eyes opened again, and she looked at him as he leaned over her. He gazed at her with longing as she moaned, and her breathing normalized. Then she quickly fell into a deep healing sleep.

Once he healed her, he hesitated to remove his hands from her body. Then he quickly looked at Nia, who averted her eyes.

"I should not need to tell you to never repeat what you have seen here," he said in earnest.

"I will not." Nia obediently bowed her head.

"I will lift her so you can prepare the bed. I cannot replace the fluid she has lost. She will need to rest."

"Yes, Commander," Nia said as she reached into the basket for the bed linens.

He picked Katlyn up, cradling her against his chest while Nia made the bed, then placed her down after Nia finished. "Wash her and stay with her until I return. I must see my Regent."

"Yes, Commander."

***

"Commander! It's good to see you. Welcome back!" Rory said when the Commander entered his bedchamber. "I have fresh clothes prepared."

Rory was lean and stood at the Commander's chin. His eyes were the color of grass, and his round face was surrounded by shoulder-length hair that was the color of fire. He kept it pulled neatly behind his head, secured with a leather tie at the base of his skull.

He wore a tan-colored long-sleeved single piece tunic with no ties or buttons, and stopped just above his knees, with matching trousers. The material was a type of linen. Easy to come by, easy to clean, and it allowed ease of movement. Most of the bound serfs dressed similarly; it was simpler that way.

The Commander walked across the room and removed his coat, draping it over a chair, then peeled off the tattered and bloodstained silk shirt. "Dispose of this," he said as he handed it to his attendant. Rory took the shirt, placing it in a basket.

"I will be quick," the Commander said, then he pulled back the curtain that covered the entrance to his lavatory. He quickly washed the dried blood off his body. Then stepped back into the room where Rory waited patiently with a pristine shirt.

As the Commander stepped into the center of the room, Rory said, "Your Lodestar came looking for you. He delivered your message to the Regent. She demands to see you as soon as possible."

"Yes, I am going to see her straightaway."

The Commander dressed quickly, opting for his satin knee-length formal coat rather than the ankle-length he had been wearing. He stood in front of his full-length mirror, smoothing over the front of his shirt and coat as Rory smoothed the back. Then Rory combed his hair, pulling the sides above his ears gently to the back and securing it with a ruby-encrusted hair clip. He must be presentable for his Regent, especially since he did not see her immediately upon his return.

"That is acceptable." He squared his shoulders and raised his chin.

"Would you like your timepiece, Commander?" Rory asked as he reached into a small trinket box inside the wardrobe.

"Yes, thank you."

He was fortunate to have not had the piece with him when he went hunting so many moons ago. The humans would surely have enjoyed acquiring it. The piece belonged to his sire and was incredibly old.

After Rory buttoned his coat, the Commander clipped the end of the long silver chain onto a jeweled button and slipped the device into an adjacent pocket. The ruby lavaliere dangled gingerly in between.

"Very nice, Commander," Rory said as he ran his hands quickly over the front of the Commander's shoulders. Then stepped to the side, out of his way. The Commander took one last quick look over before leaving his quarters.

The corridors were bustling with Specter and humans. Everyone greeted him with elation and welcomed him back warmly. He nodded his head in acknowledgment as he passed them. Though he did not show it on his face, his mind was overjoyed by the sounds and feelings of the others.

He rounded the corner at the junction and walked down the corridor toward the Regent's gathering hall.

"I am here to see our Regent," he announced to the conscripts standing guard. They both moved while one activated the door control. Both doors opened invitingly, and the Commander stepped inside.

The large room was empty except for two more conscripts standing guard at her private chambers. The Commander walked around the double platform in the center and approached the doors. Both conscripts stood aside, then he activated the door control. The doors opened smoothly, and the Commander stepped into the room.

The Regent's private chambers were just as elaborate as the previous room. Like the gathering hall, the room was circular, with marble floors, colorful vines, and soft lighting throughout. The furniture in the center was covered in plush velvet fabrics, with heavy pillows strewn about. The shelves along the walls on both sides were covered with books and trinkets that his Regent collected over the years.

Besides the Regent's drone sitting motionless in a chair against the wall to his left, the room was empty.

"Is our Regent in her bedchamber?" he asked the drone.

"Yes, she is expecting you," he responded without moving or opening his eyes.

The Commander crossed the room to the other side, approaching the single door. He activated the door control and crossed the threshold, entering another circular room. The door shut quickly behind him.

Only the Regent's handmaid, consort, the occasional lover, and the ship's commander, if she did not have a consort, were allowed in her private sanctuary. Not even her drone was allowed, but he only had one purpose, and his use was hardly an intimate affair.

The Regent was reading a book with her feet up in the bed, back resting against the alabaster headboard. She dropped her book onto the silk linens as soon as the Commander entered the room.

"Domina," he said, bowing deeply at the waist.

She rose from the bed as if carried by a gentle breeze, and approached him, reaching both hands out to him. He took them eagerly, holding each hand in his own, and brought his forehead down to rest on the tops of them. His hair fell neatly over his shoulders.

'I came as soon as I was able,' he projected to her fondly.

'Yes, the Lodestar told me what kept you busy.'

'Yes, Domina. She was dying. I am in her debt.'

'A human no less,' she responded with skepticism.

He held her hands affectionately in his as he looked up at her. She pulled her hands out of his grasp, and he slowly righted himself, head still bowed down to her. He squared his shoulders as he clasped his hands tightly behind his back. Then he raised his head to meet her gaze.

"Yes, Domina. A human woman saved my life," he said with sincerity, despite the stoic look on his face.

"I am grateful to have you safely returned to me."

"As I knew you would be, Domina," he said as he gently bowed his head again.

"Why?" she asked.

"Domina?"

"Why would a human save your life?"

"Domina, she did not merely save my life; she sacrificed her own life."

She drew her head back, cocking it to one side. "What do you mean?"

"I was gravely injured and dying. She allowed me to use her to heal myself. Not knowing whether I would take her life or not." The Commander raised his chin parallel to the floor and looked at his Regent with earnest. "She did not know about my ability to return her life to her. She was willing to die for me."

"It seems to me that you respect this human."

"If I may be so bold, Domina, I do respect her. She is strong and has spirit. I owe her my life. I would not be here standing before you without her help."

"I see," she said. "I would like to meet this *human* female who has brought you back to me. I am curious why a human would do such a thing. I must ask her myself."

"Of course, Domina. When she is well, I will bring her to you," he said, bowing briefly.

"Until then, please entertain me with the story of your capture and this daring rescue that injured you gravely and nearly took the life of your rescuer," the Regent requested as she returned to her bed. She sat down and gently patted on the bed next to her. "Sit with me."

He approached her bedside and sat obligingly. He caressed her hand while he showed her the events of the last several cycles, and of the woman who dared to defy their captors. She was enthralled with his tale and the images he projected to her. His mind was fervent and fierce. His emotions were of passion and admiration as he spoke of the human female who saved his life.

10. COULD IT BE?

~Katlyn

"Mom, wake up!"

"What?"

"You fell asleep on the tree swing again."

"James?" she asked, rubbing her eyes.

"Yes, mom. It's time to wake up," he said, chuckling.

Katlyn sat up lazily, and the swing beneath her moved gently. She could hear Natalie snickering in the background. "Mom, we came by to check on you. You weren't answering the phone," Natalie said.

Katlyn opened her eyes and smiled at the familiar sound and faces of her children, both standing in front of her. "How long have I been asleep?"

"Several hours I'd imagine," James chuckled. "You started on the yard this morning. It's early evening."

"Oh, wow!" Katlyn said, brushing the hair out of her face.

"You always take a nap on the swing after you finish mowing," Natalie reminded her.

Katlyn reached out to caress her son's face. "What's wrong, mom?" he asked her.

"I had the most bizarre dream!"

"Dream?" he asked, tilting his head to the side.

"Yes!" she said. "I dreamt I was on another planet—"

"But mom—"

"A man and I helped each other escape," she said.

"Mom!" James said.

"What?"

"You need to wake up, mom," he said.

"I am awake. I'm telling you about this crazy ridiculous dream I had," she said, furrowing her brow at him.

"But, Katlyn—"

"Why are you calling me that, James? What's going on?"

"You're dreaming now, mom."

Katlyn's breath caught in her throat, and she pulled her head back. "No, this is real. The other was a dream."

"I assure you, that was not a dream," he said in a voice she recognized, but it was not her son's voice. "Wake up!"

***

Katlyn's eyes opened to a dimly lit room. The faces of her children were lost to her, replaced by the face of a woman she didn't recognize. The woman was sitting next to the bed, watching her.

"James," Katlyn said sleepily.

"Mistress," the woman whispered.

"Where am I?"

"You are safe. You should rest." The woman caressed Katlyn's hand.

"Where am I?" Katlyn asked again.

"You're in the Commander's private guest quarters."

"Commander..." Katlyn drifted back to sleep.

~Commander

95

The Commander rose from the side of the bed, holding his hand out to his Regent. She accepted it and rose gracefully.

"Thank you for seeing me, Commander."

"Of course, Domina," he responded, bowing gently. "I do have other duties I must attend to since my return," he informed her.

"Yes, and check on your... guest."

"Yes," he said, bowing his head again.

The Commander activated the door control, turned around again to face her, and bowed deeply. "I will take my leave now, Domina." His tone and expression were warm. He truly was glad to be home. "I am pleased to have returned to you."

He righted himself, turned on his heel, and left the room. The door closed swiftly behind him.

As he left the Regent's quarters, he thought about his guest, and he wanted to get back there quickly, but he had yet to visit the bridge since his return.

He walked to the junction and turned left. To his immediate left, along the same corridor leading to his private quarters, was a storage room. Across from there were a few steps leading up to a platform with a table, and another storage room. Past the table, down another short corridor, was the bridge.

He ascended the steps and walked past the table, acknowledging the humans who welcomed him. He then turned left down the corridor that led to the bridge. The conscripts activated the door control, and he crossed the threshold.

"We are pleased for your safe return, Commander," the bridge's first centurion said warmly as the Commander moved to the center of the room.

"Thank you," he responded.

"What of the human?" he asked.

The Commander jerked his head sharply to the second centurion standing on the opposite side of the room, the man who first greeted him in the transfer room, who quickly looked down at his console.

"I told only our Regent, Commander," Bry'aere said.

The Commander inhaled deeply. "I suppose I cannot keep our guest a secret for long," he said. "I received assistance in escaping the planet. A woman. A *human*. Not only did she aid in my escape, but she saved my life. I am in her debt." The Commander looked around the bridge at his men, all of them listening intently. "She is my guest and under my protection. She is not to be harmed. Do I make myself clear?"

"Yes, Commander!" the men responded in unison.

The Commander walked slowly but deliberately toward the second centurion. Back straight, chin level to the floor, hands clasped gently behind his back. The centurion spun around to face him, squaring his shoulders, and leveling his chin, and said, "Please forgive me, Commander," he began as the Commander approached. The Commander backed the centurion up against the wall. They stood so close that they shared the same breath.

"We do not entertain idle gossip," he snarled, looking down at the centurion. "I said you need not concern yourself with my business. That was not an invitation to speak about it amongst yourselves."

"Yes, Commander!" the centurion said sharply. "Please accept my regret." He attempted to bow his head, but the Commander's proximity impeded the gesture. "It will not happen again."

"No, it will not!" the Commander demanded, then he stepped back.

"I understand this is an extraordinary situation," he said as he moved around the room, weaving between the men, "and some of you, as well as the men under you, may not be accustomed to being cordial to humans, but I expect nothing less than the utmost civility." He stopped just short of the doors and turned to face his men. "When I say she saved my life, I do not mean she simply helped me escape. I was near death, and she sacrificed herself to save me. I would not be here amongst you if not for her. She will be treated as anyone else who may have done the same for any of you."

"Is she well?" Bry'aere asked.

"She will be. I returned what she gave and was able to heal her wounds, but she lost a lot of fluid that I am unable to replace. She is resting. Nia is with her," the Commander said. "I will be in my quarters if anyone should need me. Our Regent has already been made aware of the situation. Please make everyone else aware, Lodestar. I do not expect there to be any problems."

"Of course, Commander," Bry'aere said.

"I will need a data node with all the star charts we have at our disposal," the Commander said to the first centurion.

"Right away, Commander," the centurion said.

"Please join me," the Commander said to Bry'aere.

"Yes, Commander."

The Commander acknowledged the men with a gentle nod of his head, then he activated the door control and disappeared down the corridor, Bry'aere followed closely behind.

Nia was sitting in a chair beside Katlyn's bed when the Commander entered the guest quarters.

"Any change?" he asked.

"She woke up briefly, asked for James and where she was," Nia said as she rose from her seat. The Commander inhaled deeply and approached the bed. "I told her where she was, and then she seemed to ask for you, but I'm not sure. She fell right back to sleep."

The Commander cocked his head and raised his brow as he glanced at Nia. "You may go now. Please return in the morning."

"Yes, Commander," she said, then she bowed her head and retrieved the chair. Then she left the room.

When Bry'aere entered, the Commander sat on the edge of the bed, gazing at Katlyn.

"May we speak as friends?" the Commander asked.

"Of course."

The Commander looked out the window beside the bed. He took a deep breath, then looked at Katlyn lying next to him. "I am not sure where to begin," he admitted as he brushed her cheek with the back of his hand.

"It is always best to start from the beginning," Bry'aere suggested as he sat on the window seat.

He shared with his friend everything that transpired, beginning with Katlyn first entering her cell. He did not fail to mention what occurred when he healed her. When he told the tale to his Regent, he left out certain details he felt she did not need to know or were unimportant, but he asked his friend to listen, to counsel him. So, he left nothing unsaid.

"That is quite the tale," Bry'aere said.

"I am not sure what to think or how to feel, except weak. I feel like a weak boy. A youngling..." He sighed. "I do not know."

They sat in silence for a moment. "I hope you remember that our Regent intended to make you consort at some point?" Bry'aere reminded him. "She spoke of it before you disappeared."

"Yes, I remember. What does that have to do with this?"

"We are speaking as friends, yes?"

"Yes," the Commander said, furrowing his brow.

"I mention it because it sounds to me as though you have imprinted on this woman." The Commander drew his head back and bolted up from the bed. "And more than imprinting, you may even have a passionate affection for her."

The Commander grabbed his friend by the shoulder, pulling him to his feet. Then led him out of the room. He was angry and did not wish to wake Katlyn.

"That is not possible!" he responded fiercely as soon as they entered the sitting room.

"You asked for my counsel, as friends. Do not get angry with me when I tell you something you do not wish to hear."

"What you say is not possible."

"Why do you believe that?" Bry'aere asked.

"She is human."

"I do not think that matters."

"Why do you think it *is* possible?"

"We have human DNA. I am a scientist, old friend. I do believe that I understand a little better how this works. Perhaps that is why you asked for my counsel," Bry'aere said.

"No, I asked to speak with you as friends. Not for you to suggest something unnatural."

"Perhaps it is unnatural, but it is not forbidden."

"It should be!" the Commander said coldly as he crossed his arms at his chest and paced the room. "To suggest that I may have passion for her is preposterous!"

"Okay, I am wrong," Bry'aere retorted with obvious sarcasm in his tone. "Perhaps you feel affection for her because she saved your life. You would not be so offended by my suggestion if you did not believe it to be true." Bry'aere paused, waiting for his friend to respond. "You said that you were willing to protect her before she even opened her eyes."

"No," the Commander lied as he paced. His mind was angry and confused. "I am not a weak boy chasing a female!" he snapped at Bry'aere.

"No, you are not. Imprinting can happen to anyone or no one. You cannot control it. Most go their entire lives without it ever happening. They are still able to join and have families; they just never imprint. Nor do they bind themselves. No one—not even you—can control who they have affection for."

"You may be confusing curiosity for passion," the Commander suggested. "I am curious about her."

"Perhaps."

"What kind of leader can I be if what you suggest is true?" the Commander asked in earnest, waving his hand in front of him.

"This has nothing to do with your leadership. It can, however, affect our Regent. I would imagine this would make her terribly angry. I do not wish to be in your position," Bry'aere said.

"I refuse to believe this is possible. Perhaps I am just beyond grateful for what she has done for me. I have never given life to a human before. It is feasible that it is affecting my judgment."

Bry'aere shrugged his shoulders and cocked his head to one side. "Perhaps, but I do not believe that is the case."

"You are not helping at all with this ridiculous nonsense!"

"We have been friends since childhood. Sometimes I know you better than you know yourself."

"What does that have to do with this?"

"I have seen you with women," Bry'aere said. "Never have you behaved in the manner that you behave with this woman. If what you have told me is true anyway, and by observing you with her. I suspected it when I saw you with her on the planet."

"No!"

"Again, you would not be so offended if it were not true." The Commander hissed in defiance. "There is nothing to be ashamed of," Bry'aere said.

"There is everything to be ashamed of! I cannot imprint on a human. This is absurd!"

"I am sorry, but you cannot fight it—no one can. Once imprinting occurs, it cannot be undone. Wishing it away will not make it so. I recommend finding somewhere for her to go. Our Regent will be very offended if she knows her favorite has imprinted on a human, even if it is beyond your control," Bry'aere said. "I am surprised you did not think of this yourself."

"I did, but rejected the idea immediately because I do not understand how such a thing could be possible." The Commander sighed as he continued pacing the room.

"Allow me to ask you a couple of questions," Bry'aere suggested.

"Go ahead," he said, waving his hand toward his friend.

"You would do anything for our Regent, yes?"

"Absolutely! What kind of question is that?"

"Bear with me."

"Continue," the Commander said.

"Would you kill this human if our Regent commanded it?" The Commander's breath caught in his throat, and he hesitated as he looked at Bry'aere. "There is your answer," Bry'aere said. "You have imprinted on her. As for possibly loving her, such a thing can increase your desire to protect her. You do not need to have passion or affection for someone you have imprinted on, but if you do, that is rare indeed, and usually culminates with bonding at some point."

"This cannot happen! Please go back to the bridge and find a suitable world for her. Preferably one that is in our territory," the Commander demanded.

"I will do as you ask, but to be honest, where she goes should not matter. Your desire for her to be safe in our territory is confirmation."

"She saved my life," the Commander reminded him. "Despite what you say or how I feel, I am indebted to her. If I am unable to return her home, I owe it to her to put her somewhere safe."

"I understand. I will do as you ask."

The Commander walked back into Katlyn's room. Bry'aere stood in the doorway while the Commander paced, glancing at Katlyn sleeping in the bed.

"What kind of man would I be if I allow this to happen?" he asked his friend solemnly. "What would I become? What would *we* become? Why would she even consider such a thing? She knows what I am."

"Those are questions I am not able to answer, but I know your men, and they would follow you anywhere. Even if you did have a human by your side."

"I will concede to having imprinted because my desire to protect her is great, but I draw the line there," the Commander whispered through clenched teeth. "I could not possibly have passion for a human. The mere suggestion is outrageous."

He was despondent, and his mind was in turmoil. He agreed with Bry'aere one minute but was insulted the next. "Our Regent would surely kill her," he said, shaking his head. "How could this have happened?"

"You cannot control it any more than you can control what you are," Bry'aere said. "I do not doubt it has happened before. Albeit rare, and most likely nothing came of it, or they were killed."

"That is *very* reassuring," the Commander said sarcastically.

Bry'aere chuckled. "You, we, a lot of us have always desired peace. But, how could such a thing be possible? Perhaps this is how?" Bry'aere said as he waved his hand toward Katlyn. "Perhaps this is moirai. This woman could be the catalyst for peace. What are the odds that *she* would be thrown into a cell next to *you*? Of all Specter and human? The two of you ended up together. And now this?"

"Why are you encouraging this? You know the Regent would kill her. This is impossible."

"Because you are my friend, and I can see and feel your mind, the passion you have when you look at her. You cannot deny what you know to be true, but I will do as you ask, and find a safe world for her."

"Our Regent can never find out about this. Please forgive me for laying this burden on you. I cannot expect you to lie or hide anything from her. I will understand if you do not."

"You know I am loyal to you above all. So are your men," Bry'aere said. "Everything will work out as it should."

"Yes, it will," the Commander responded flatly. "We will never speak of this again." His tone was dispassionate, but his mind conveyed a different emotion.

"As you wish," Bry'aere said with a gentle bow of his head, then left his friend standing alone in the middle of the room.

The Commander sensed his friend was watching him, but he was drawn to Katlyn. His shoulders softened as he took slow, quiet steps toward the bed and sat down gently next to her. She was resting under a fur, her arms and shoulders bare. He caressed her arm. "What is this?" he whispered to her. "This cannot happen. I cannot ask you to live this life." He sighed with regret.

11. UNFAMILIAR TERRITORY

~Nia

Nia sat at the window, sewing. She had a small mobile light to see by; she didn't want to disturb the Commander's guest. She was very curious about the mysterious woman. The Commander rarely had guests, but he had never been so accommodating to a human. Of course, he was affable. He was always more pleasant and polite than other Specter, but to take a human guest and aid her in such a way was unusual—even for him.

She looked up when she heard the woman stir and laid her project in the basket at her feet to approach the bed. She stepped close to her so the woman could see her face.

"My name is Nia," she said. "I serve the Commander."

The woman blinked and furrowed her brow. "The Commander? Where am I?"

"You're in the Commander's private guest quarters. I will notify him that you're awake—"

"Wait!" the woman said as she grabbed Nia's arm.

"Do not be afraid. You're safe here," she said, attempting to calm the woman. She was clearly distressed. She shook her head and clutched tighter onto Nia's arm. "The Commander will want to know you're awake." Nia tried to free herself. "Mistress, please," she said, forcing her arm out of the woman's tight grip. "I will return quickly." Then she hurried from the room.

"Commander, she's awake." The commander was sitting at a table with a portable console in his hand. Nia could tell he was looking over star charts.

"I will be right there."

"She seems very frightened, Commander."

"She is disoriented. Before she was injured, I—" The Commander placed the console on the table. "She is disoriented, that is all. I will be right there."

"Yes, Commander," Nia said, then turned to go back into the room.

"She allowed me to draw strength from her, to heal myself," the Commander said.

Nia stopped, giving the Commander a side-eye glance. *That explains why he is so accommodating to her,* she said to herself. "I see," she said aloud. "I will tell her you will be in shortly."

"Thank you," he said, then turned away and went into his bedchamber.

~Katlyn

Katlyn was very disoriented and felt out of place when she woke up. She was vaguely aware of the woman sitting in the room. She knew they exchanged words before the woman scurried away, but she couldn't remember what was said.

She sat up slowly on the side of the bed. As her feet touched the cold metal floor, whatever covered her body fell, and Katlyn realized she was naked. The room was dimly lit, so she couldn't see well. She felt frantically on the bed for something to cover herself. Her hands brushed a soft furry material. She grabbed it and wrapped it around her body just as the woman came back into the room.

"Why am I naked?" Katlyn blurted out. The woman stopped just inside the door. "What is going on? Who are you?" she demanded as she grabbed her forehead. She felt lightheaded, and her stomach hurt from hunger.

"My name is Nia. I serve the Commander. He will be here shortly, and he will explain everything," Nia said as she approached the middle of the room.

"I want to see him right now!" Katlyn hollered, just as the Commander entered the room, carrying something over his arm.

"She is angry, Commander," Nia said.

He stopped short of the middle of the room and looked at Katlyn. Her face was heated, and she was scowling at him.

"I can see that," he said.

"Why am I naked?" she hissed. "How long have I been out? Where am I?" Her voice shuddered, and she pinched her forehead. "Why am I lightheaded? What did you do to me?" she demanded.

The Commander squared his shoulders and leveled his chin as Nia backed away. The shock was visible on her face as she watched the drama unfold in front of her.

"Please allow me to explain. I will answer all of your questions," the Commander said as he crossed the room, kneeling on one knee in front of Katlyn. "You are on my ship. You were gravely injured. One of the men on the planet fired his weapon, hitting you. You lost a lot of fluids. That is why you are lightheaded," he told her. "You also have not had a proper meal in some time."

"My vision was blurry..." she trailed off.

"Yes, I returned what you gave. That is why your vision has cleared."

"You returned? What?" Katlyn's mind was cloudy, muddled. She was confused and hungry.

The Commander took a deep breath. "We are able to return, or give life. You saved my life. I merely returned what you gave."

Katlyn thought about what he said. "Did you have to kill someone to do that?"

The Commander sighed, lowered his head, and gazed at her in a way that made her heart skip a beat. "Yes, I took the life of those who imprisoned you."

Katlyn took a sharp breath and glanced at Nia, who had her back against the wall watching their conversation. "Please don't ever do that to someone again to save me," Katlyn said, looking at the Commander. "Just let me die." She choked back tears and covered her face.

The Commander leveled his chin to her. "I will not apologize for saving your life," he said flatly.

Katlyn dropped her head into her hands and began sobbing. "I don't want anyone to die because of me," she whispered. Then, she blurted out, "Why am I naked!" right into his face, making him draw his head back. Nia jumped on the other side of the room.

"I did not see your unclothed body. I simply tended to your injuries. I only observed what I needed in order to heal you. Nia"—he pointed to the visibly terrified woman across the room—"washed you in private after I left."

Katlyn's face softened, then she dropped her head back into one of her hands. "I'm sorry for being so nasty. I just... I don't know. I'm sorry," she said, turning her head in her hands just enough to look at Nia.

"You have no reason to apologize. You have been through quite an ordeal," he said.

"How long have we been here?"

"We arrived yesterday. You have been asleep for over a day," he told her as he stood up and gave Nia what he had draped over his arm. "I will leave you now so you may wash and dress. I will be waiting just outside." He pointed to the door on the opposite side of the room.

Katlyn finally noticed how he was dressed. Very elegantly. His shirt was the same as before but in immaculate condition.

His unbuttoned coat was shorter and more formal, with red gemstone buttons along the front and red embroidery on the cuffs and collar. His hair was groomed and swept up above his ears, secured in the back, allowing full view of his face.

He's even more beautiful... She gently slapped her forehead at the thought, eliciting a curious look from the Commander and Nia. "I'll be quick," she said aloud.

"Please take your time. There is no reason to hurry," he said, then activated the door control and left, leaving her and Nia alone.

Katlyn sighed and looked at Nia. "I'm really sorry for snapping at you."

"It's fine, I assure you. No harm was done," she said as she approached the center of the room.

"First impressions are important," Katlyn chuckled.

"Perhaps, but these are extenuating circumstances," Nia said with a smile.

As Katlyn watched Nia, she was reminded of her daughter, Natalie. The two young women could be sisters. Nia's appearance was so similar to Natalie, that her presence was comforting. They were both young, early twenties. Both stood about the same height as Katlyn with brown eyes and blond hair. Nia's hair was long and tightly braided down her back. Natalie's was shorter though, and curly. Both had fair skin and freckles along their nose and cheeks. Nia wore a tan wrap style dress with elbow-length sleeves, and the hem went to her ankles. The material reminded Katlyn of muslin.

"I will run you a bath," Nia said when Katlyn stood to her feet.

"A bath!" Katlyn said. "Will it be warm?" she laughed.

Nia cocked her head to the side. "As warm as you'd like for it to be," she said with a serious tone.

"The last time I was in the water, it was the river, and it was cold. I fell in because I'm clumsy."

"Oh, I see. Yes, your bath will be warm. I assure you," she said with a smile as she pulled a dark curtain aside on the left side of the room that Katlyn hadn't noticed until that moment. She then disappeared beyond the opening.

Katlyn could hear the water running and got excited. *A bath!* She pulled the fur as much around her body as it would go as she turned around the room. The walls and floor were dark—the lighting above recessed into the dark ceiling. At the head of the bed was a large window with a window seat. Outside, nothing but stars. She was not prepared to look outside the window into nothingness, so she turned the opposite direction.

At the foot of the bed, against the wall, was a wardrobe. She opened the doors, but it was empty. It had hooks along the back and shelves on the side. A full-length mirror was on the inside of one of the doors. Beside the wardrobe was a table with a tray. The tray had linens, a bottle with a thick liquid, a natural sea sponge, and a wooden comb. Katlyn opened the bottle and brought it to her nose. It smelled like honeysuckle and reminded her of the Commander.

"That is a cleanser," Nia said, suddenly standing beside her.

"Oh." Katlyn placed the bottle back on the tray.

"This is for your bath, which is ready." She stood to the side and motioned toward the doorway.

"Oh... okay!" Katlyn said excitedly. "Thank you so much!"

"It is my pleasure."

Katlyn stepped into the room. It was a full-service bathroom. Not big, but it had all the essentials. The sink and tub were both shaped like bowls and appeared to be carved from the same material. Marble, maybe, and both were black. Everything in the room was black except for the fixtures, which looked to be copper, or something similar. The tub was not big enough to stretch out in, but it was deep enough that the water would cover her up to her shoulders.

I've never had a bath that was deep enough to cover my knees and boobs at the same time, she laughed.

"Would you like assistance?" Nia asked from the doorway, holding the tray.

"Uh... no," Katlyn chuckled. "No, thank you. I can manage."

"Very well." Nia placed the tray on top of the sink. "I'll be right outside the door if you need anything."

"Thanks."

When Nia stepped out of the room, Katlyn removed the fur, placing it on a hook on the bathroom wall, and carefully stepped into the tub. It wasn't as hot as she usually liked her bath, but it was far better than a shocking dunk in the river. She sank into the water up to her ears. She must have made a sound because Nia came in to check on her.

"I'm fine!" Katlyn chuckled. "I just haven't had a warm bath in a while."

"Are you sure you don't need help?"

"Uh, yes, I'm sure. I've been bathing myself for a long time. Thank you, though."

"Just making sure. The Commander instructed me to assist you with anything you may need. I am at your service," she said, then stepped back into the bedroom.

Katlyn dunked the rest of her head under the water. Then washed her hair and body with the cleanser. When she finished, she wrapped up with linen and stepped back into the bedroom.

"Is this as bright as the lights get?" Katlyn asked Nia, who was waiting patiently by the bed, where a blue dress was laid out.

"This is how they are coded automatically because the Specter prefer low light. I can adjust them manually," she said as she walked to the console by the door. "How bright would you like them?"

"Just a little brighter. Not much," Katlyn said as the room filled with light. "Thank you."

"The Commander brought this for you to wear," Nia said, walking back to the bed.

"Oh, he did?"

"I can find something else for you if this is unsatisfactory."

"No, this is fine. I'm his guest. It's fine."

Both women stared at each other for a minute; Katlyn in nothing but a towel like linen, and Nia unwavering by the bed as if awaiting further instructions. Then Katlyn slowly raised her eyebrow, looking to the side, not sure what to say next.

"Uh..." Katlyn mumbled.

"I can help you dress if you'd like," Nia finally said.

"No!" Katlyn said sharply, followed by a quick smile. "I can dress myself, thank you."

"You are not accustomed to having a handmaiden, are you?" Nia asked. "I'm sorry if that's not my business."

"A handmaiden? No. No, I'm not. I don't need someone to wait on me."

"I am a bound serf and at the Commander's bidding. He has requested I attend to you. If you would prefer I didn't—"

"What is a bound serf?" Katlyn interrupted. Nia hesitated like a deer caught in headlights. "Never mind," Katlyn said. "You don't need to answer that. This is all new to me. I'm sorry. I come from somewhere that has never heard of the Specter before."

"Really?" Nia's head drew back. "How is that possible?"

"That's a good question. I still have no idea how I got here. Or where 'here' even is. I woke up in a cell next to the Commander," Katlyn said, shaking her head. "I still can't believe I'm not dreaming."

"I see. I will turn my back if you prefer to dress yourself. If I leave the room without you, the Commander will wonder why."

"Okay?" Katlyn pondered. "Are you afraid of him?"

"You're not?"

"No. I'm not," Katlyn said. "I guess I'm afraid of what he's capable of because I've seen it firsthand. And I let him..." she hesitated, "but I'm not afraid of *him*, no."

Nia looked at Katlyn with a look of astonishment. "I know of no humans who don't fear the Specter."

"In my defense, he is the only one I've met so far. I might feel different after I've met more."

"I don't think you have to worry about that here. The Commander has made it clear you aren't to be harmed and to be treated with the utmost respect," Nia said. "I would imagine he'd be very unhappy if anyone disobeyed his orders."

"Well, that's reassuring," Katlyn said, puzzled. "Why do you work for him if you're afraid of him?"

"Perhaps I'm more afraid of what he's capable of. It is complicated. I really shouldn't be having this conversation with you. The Commander might be displeased."

"Don't worry about it. Our conversations will be private. I promise," Katlyn assured her.

"Thank you," Nia said as she stepped away from the bed and turned to face the window.

Katlyn dried off then slipped the dress over her head. It was dark blue and made of silk with delicate beadwork and pearls along the low neckline that showed just a hint of cleavage. The top of the long and flowy sleeves barely sat on her shoulders. It may have been designed to set off the shoulders or worn either way. The bodice cupped her breasts with long fabric pieces at the center, meant to be tied in the back. The form-fitting bodice flowed gently from the waist down. The skirt wasn't tight, and although it was flowy like the sleeves, it still seemed to cling to her body, showing all her curves. The hem fell softly around her feet. It was obviously made for a taller woman.

"I'm dressed," Katlyn said, "but I could use help tying this if you don't mind." She held up the long pieces.

"Of course," Nia said when she turned around.

Katlyn walked to the wardrobe with the full-length mirror. She opened the door as Nia began tying the fabric behind her. "Wow!" Katlyn said, astonished, rubbing her hands along the dress and chuckling.

"It's almost as if it was made for you," Nia said.

"Yeah, that's kinda weird. I'm sorry. He didn't see me naked, but he knows what size I wear," she said, laughing and shaking her head.

"It seems that the Commander has good taste," Nia said, eliciting a raised eyebrow and awkward look from Katlyn. "Now, let's comb your hair." She walked toward the bathroom to retrieve the comb.

After combing her hair, Katlyn pulled all of it over her shoulder and braided it loosely down the front. Then she and Nia walked into the sitting room.

The Commander laid a tablet-looking device on the table when Katlyn walked into the room. He squared his shoulders when he stood up, and lowered his chin gently. Katlyn noticed he buttoned his coat and had what appeared to be a pocket watch chain dangling from his pocket. It had a delicate looking piece of gemstone jewelry attached to it.

He definitely looks like he belongs next to royalty, Katlyn said to herself with a chuckle.

~Commander

He cleared his throat as Katlyn walked toward him. "You look..." he started as he gazed at her. She looked better than he imagined she would. The dress did not fit her as snug as it was designed to, but it still hugged and accentuated the fullness of her curves. Her form standing before him affected him more than he thought possible, and for a moment he forgot Nia was in the room.

"She has not had a meal in some time," he said as he clasped his hands behind his back, righting himself and looking at Nia.

"Yes, Commander," Nia said with a quick bow of her head. Then she left the room.

Katlyn and the Commander stood silent in the center of the room for a moment. He lowered his chin to look at her while she looked at everything *but* him.

"Thanks for not eating me," she said, stifling a chuckle when she met his gaze.

He chuckled lightly; the side of his lip curled up. *Technically, I did,* he said to himself but did not dare remind her of the unpleasant experience.

"I know what I said before about letting me die, but thank you for helping me. I really do appreciate it. And you got me off that planet like you said you would."

"We had an arrangement," he said, then he bowed gently at the waist, "and you saved my life. I am in your debt."

"And thanks for... the dress... that fits a little too well. It's kinda weird how well it fits," she said, laughing.

"It belonged to my mother. She was taller and... I presumed it would fit well enough."

Katlyn raised an eyebrow. "And what?"

The Commander inhaled deeply and squared his shoulders. "She had wider hips."

"Oh!" Katlyn's face and neck flushed cerise. "You've looked at my hips enough to know they're not as wide as your mother's?"

He exhaled as his mouth came open slightly. "Humans are smaller than my kind," he said.

"Thanks again for the dress. I'm honored." She stifled a chuckle, and her faced flushed again.

"The only other option was something of Nia's, but you are my guest. I would not expect you to wear her clothing."

"Speaking of Nia, I have to ask," Katlyn said. "What is she? Like, what does she do? What is her purpose? I just wasn't expecting to see a human here working for you after what you said to me."

He remembered the last conversation they had before his ship arrived, about humans being nothing more than nourishment. He took a deep breath, regretting what he said to her.

"Nia is a bound serf. She is attached to my house."

"What is a serf?"

The Commander looked up, searching. "To serve," he said.

"She's a servant?"

"Yes."

"Bound? Meaning... forced? Like a slave?" Katlyn asked, raising an eyebrow.

"She was not forced, but she is bound. She bound herself to my service of her own volition."

"Why would she do that?"

"To purchase her safety and the safety of any young she may have."

"Is she free to leave anytime she wants?"

"Not exactly," he said.

"What do you mean? Is she paid for her service?"

"She does not receive a stipend. She serves until such a time as I see fit to release her."

"So, she's a slave."

"Yes."

"You keep humans as slaves?" Katlyn asked with contempt in her tone.

"Do you not have slaves on your world?"

"Where I'm from slavery was outlawed a long time ago. And rightfully so. People aren't beasts of burden," she said flatly, crossing her arms at her chest.

He cocked his head to the side. "They are only human."

Katlyn's jaw dropped in visible shock. Her face distorted into a scowl, and she was clearly offended. "I'm human! Why do you have such a blasé attitude toward humans? Especially after some of the conversations we've had."

"You are different," he said, raising his chin.

"You only say that because I saved your life," she said, raising her voice slightly.

He squared his shoulders. "You did not merely save my life. Saving a life is easy. You were willing to sacrifice your own life. To die to save mine."

"I just wanted off that planet."

"No. I may have been near death, but I remember the words you spoke to me before you insisted—" Katlyn took a sharp breath. "I knew you were different from any other human the first moment I laid eyes upon you."

"What do you mean?"

"I cannot explain it. The words come to my mind, but I cannot find them to speak them aloud," he lied. He knew what it was. After the conversation with Bry'aere, he was sure what it was. He imprinted on her. This human he would die to protect, but he could not tell her that.

Katlyn walked to the window and peered out into the vastness of space. "So, we're on your ship?"

"Yes," he responded as he approached the window to stand behind her.

"What will happen to me now, Commander?" she asked with a trembling voice, then turned back to look at him. He was looking up again, searching.

"Kel'ardent," he said as he looked at her.

"What?"

"My name. Kel means decisive and resolute. Ardent means passionate, fervent, and fierce."

Her breath fluttered, and her face flushed again. "Thank you for sharing your name with me."

"You may call me Kel, Ardent, or both," he said. "Kel is the name my mother gave me. Ardent is the name I received when I matured."

"Did that happen to have anything to do with that choice you told me about?"

"We are able to communicate with each other telepathically through touch. Ardent is what my mind projects. It is my temperament."

"Your temperament is passionate and fierce?" she said as a broad smile formed across her face, and her skin flushed a dark crimson.

He lowered his chin. "You seem to be of a similar temperament."

She whimpered quietly and began to fidget with her hands. "Which would you prefer I call you? Surely you have a preference?"

"I do not. No human has ever spoken those names before."

"You've never told a human your name?"

"I have never had a reason to. Humans have always called me by my title."

"Why would you share something with me that seems so personal?"

Her question caught him off guard. He looked away, his eyes darting about as if watching a small winged insect flutter by. "I do not know," he lied.

But he did know.

"So, back to my question," Katlyn said. "What's going to happen to me?"

He walked to the table, where he laid the handheld device. "I have been searching star charts," he said, "but I have yet to find any worlds called Earth."

"I doubt it would be called that on your charts," she said as he held the device up to her.

"You are probably correct. Unless you know the pattern of stars in your sky, then I am not sure how to find your world," he said with regret. "Please walk with me. I will take you to the bridge. Perhaps it will be easier to see the constellations on a larger console."

Katlyn hesitated when he activated the door control. "You do not need to be afraid," he assured her, holding his hand out to her.

"I'm not afraid!" She straightened her shoulders and walked toward him.

He smiled when she brushed past him with enthusiasm, blue dress caressing her full hips and flowing gently on the floor behind her as she moved into the corridor. It was difficult indeed not to notice her when she walked. She moved with purpose, as if she knew exactly where she was going and what lay before her. She was passionate, enthusiastic, and fiery. She was like him—ardent. Perhaps that is what drew him to her.

~Katlyn

Katlyn stopped at the steps leading up to the bridge. Kel was following closely behind and stopped next to her as she waited.

"I don't know where I'm going," she said.

"Please follow me." He ascended the steps, hands clasped loosely behind him, passing humans scurrying about who welcomed him with gentle nods and quick head bows.

Slaves, Katlyn said to herself with disgust and rolled her eyes as she followed him up the steps.

"Hello, mistress," Nia said from the doorway of a room on the opposite side of a table. "I will have your meal ready soon."

"Thank you—"

"Take it to my sitting room," Kel interrupted as his cold finger brushed Katlyn's arm to get her attention, then he motioned her down the next corridor. She couldn't help but notice everyone staring at her as if she had two heads.

"Why is everyone looking at me like that?" she asked Kel from the privacy of the corridor.

"There has never been a human in your position on this ship before today."

"My position? What does that mean?"

"A position of authority."

"I do not have authority over anyone but myself," she said sharply.

"You are my guest, and as such, you are in a position of authority. You may disagree, but that is how it is," he said matter-of-factly as they reached the end of the corridor.

Two men were standing at the door, and they both moved aside as Kel approached, one activating the door control. Katlyn stopped when she noticed them, realizing that two exactly like them were standing at the main doors to Kel's quarters. Their skin tone was the same as Kel's, white, but their hair was solid black. They were both dressed in a simple leather type coat that appeared to zip from mid-neck to waist, although the length of the coat went to the knee. They wore black leather pants and knee-high boots, and both were clearly armed. She could tell they had holstered weapons on each thigh. She must have had a look of confusion on her face because Kel stopped just short of the now opened door and stepped back toward her.

"They are conscripts."

She looked at him, puzzled. "They look exactly the same as the other two."

Kel chuckled. "Perhaps I will explain another time. I will tell you now that you will not be able to communicate with them. They are not capable of speech and only take commands from another Specter."

"Okay, so how will I get into your quarters?"

"They have already been informed to allow you access."

"Alrighty then," she chortled as he bowed gently and waved his hand toward the door.

"Shall we?"

When Katlyn walked through the door, there were four white faces and eight red eyeballs staring at her. She suddenly felt like she was going to faint. She took a deep breath and exhaled slowly as she followed Kel to a large console in the center of the room. She chewed on her bottom lip and tried to ignore the eyes burning through her. Kel cleared his throat, as if to send a message, then everyone swiftly averted their eyes.

"Katlyn, this is my Lodestar"—Kel waved his hand toward the man approaching him—"he is my second in command."

The Lodestar was shorter than Kel, the top of his head came to Kel's eyes. His face was soft but devoid of expression. He didn't seem surly, just indifferent. His hair was past his shoulders, the top pulled to the back and secured with what looked to be a leather tie. He didn't wear a leather coat like the others. His was a more delicate fabric, possibly silk. *They sure seem to like their silk.* It closed at his right shoulder rather than the front and had embroidery along the front edge. The hem stopped past his rear. Like the others, he was armed.

"Mistress," he said to Katlyn, nodding his head slightly, then turned to Kel. "Commander, I looked into what you requested." He passed a small tablet-like device to Kel, then nodded again at Katlyn before walking away to stand at a console behind them.

Kel slipped the device into his pocket, then tapped on the large console in front of them. Maps of stars with varying sizes of solar systems appeared on the screen. Countless suns and planets danced before her. She felt lightheaded and grabbed the side of the console to keep from falling over.

"Are you all right?" Kel asked.

"Yes, I just felt lightheaded all of a sudden," she said as she rubbed her forehead.

"We can do this another time. You still have not eaten."

"No, we're already here," she said, her voice trembling.

"Very well. Where shall we begin?" he asked, waving his hand over the console.

"I know what my solar system looks like, but there are thousands here." Katlyn felt a wave of anxiety wash over her.

"Millions," Kel said. "We will look through all of them if that is what it takes."

"It would probably help if I knew anything about constellations or things like that. This is my son's area of expertise. I've never been into this kind of thing, unfortunately," she said, leaning gently over the console. "Could we possibly narrow these down? Like, solar systems with inhabited planets? Or those with a specific number of planets? Cause I do know that the solar system my planet is in only has one inhabited planet."

Kel nodded. "Yes, I can eliminate uninhabited solar systems. As well as those with more than one inhabited world." He began moving his hands about the screen. Katlyn was shuddering as she breathed, and Kel turned his head slightly to glance at her.

"How many stars, or suns, and planets are in your solar system?" a voice asked from the other side of the console.

"Well," Katlyn chuckled, "that's debatable actually. Eight planets with a dwarf planet, I believe. The dwarf planet being constantly debated on whether it's classified as a planet or not... and one star."

Kel touched the screen again, eliminating solar systems with more than one star and nine planets. "There are still thousands here," he said.

"Maybe..." Katlyn started, "could you possibly give specific parameters? For example, the third planet from the sun is inhabited. I know that might be too specific."

"Commander," the same voice said, "are you certain her world is in this galaxy?"

Kel drew his head back slightly and steepled his hands to his lips.

"What would that mean?" Katlyn asked.

"These charts are for this galaxy. We do not have intergalactic travel, so we have no use for star charts beyond our reach," Kel said. "If your world is in another galaxy..." he paused, "I would not be able to return you."

Katlyn exhaled sharply and pinched the bridge of her nose. "I refuse to believe that I could be in a completely different galaxy!" she snapped. "The fact that I'm here at all is still tough for me to accept." She choked back tears and her body trembled.

Kel looked at his men around the room and nodded his head toward the door. Everyone left without a word.

"I'm sorry. I didn't mean to snap at you," she said. "This is very overwhelming. There are still thousands of solar systems here."

"I am sorry, but your world is unknown to us, and we are unknown to you. You most likely did travel here from an unknown galaxy. There is still a chance, however, that you came from a world in an outlying solar system. Traveling that far, for us, can take many cycles. We seldom go there."

"Why are you just now telling me this? That it isn't likely I'm even from this galaxy?" she said as she began to weep.

"I did not want you to lose hope," he said. "There is still a chance. I must be honest with you. Even if I could return you to your world, I would not."

"Why?" she asked, furrowing her brow.

"Your world is intact. You do not know of our kind. If I returned you, then your world would no longer be safe."

"You'd really do that!" she hissed at him. "You're saying my world wouldn't be safe from *you*?"

"No, I would not choose to reap your world, but I do not speak for my Regent."

"I don't understand."

"If my Regent or any Regent knows of an unspoiled world, that world would no longer be safe. I did not tell my Regent of your world," he admitted quietly. "I did not tell anyone except for my second in command that you did not know of my kind before we met."

"How would I get back home then?"

"I do not know. I will still do what I can. I will ask if any new traders have made their presence known. I will also speak with those on Veda," he said as Katlyn's balance wavered.

"I don't feel so good," she said, suddenly feeling weak.

"We will go back to my quarters. You must rest and eat," he said as he turned around, gently grasping her arm to steady her.

As Katlyn turned to leave, she felt dizzy and nauseous. The room began to spin, and her vision tunneled. She quickly lost her balance and collapsed into Kel's arms.

12. BLOOD

~Katlyn

Katlyn opened her eyes to the dim lights of the guestroom. Kel sat on the side of the bed, wiping her forehead with a cold, wet cloth.

"You collapsed," he whispered. She covered her face with both hands as she sobbed. "Nia brought your meal."

She sat up on her elbows, trembling. "I'm not quite sure what to say." Her voice faltered.

"You collapsed because you have not eaten."

"No, it's more than that. I just... I don't see how I'm ever going to get home. I was overwhelmed with everything. I don't even know how I got here or how long I was out before waking up in that cell. Being hungry isn't helping, of course."

"You should eat." He stood up and held his hand out.

Katlyn looked up at him and hesitated before finally accepting it.

Kel led her into the sitting room where a food tray was placed on one of the tables. He walked to the chair and pulled

123

it out, inviting her to sit down with one hand. Almost as if he read her mind several days before, when she thought to herself that no man ever did such a thing for her. She smiled and thanked him as she sat down.

"I will leave you to your meal," he said, bowing gently at the waist.

"Do you have somewhere else you need to be?" she asked, then immediately apologized. "I'm sorry. That's not my business."

"I assumed that you would prefer to eat in private."

Katlyn cocked her head with a puzzled look on her face. "Not especially, if I'm being honest."

Kel righted himself, still looking down at her. "Then, I will stay if that is what you wish."

"If you wouldn't mind, but if you have something else you would rather do, I understand."

"There is nothing," he said, then turned on his heel and walked toward the window.

On a tray in front of her was a bowl of steaming hot stew with meat and vegetables, bread on the side, and a glass of water as well as another glass of what appeared to be red wine. Katlyn inhaled the aroma of the first real meal she'd had in a while. Kel stood at the window with his back to her.

"You're welcome to sit down," she said before taking a bite.

Kel turned his head slightly in her direction, acknowledging what she said, but still hesitated to move.

"What's wrong?"

"I presumed eating was private."

Katlyn scoffed quietly. "It appears there are things you don't know about us, just like humans don't know things about you. We don't normally eat alone," she said as he turned around and approached the table. "Please, sit down. Unless me eating in front of you makes you uncomfortable."

"Not at all. I am curious to hear about your customs." He pulled the chair out and sat down across from her.

"You mean to tell me that you have humans all over your ship, but you've never seen any of them eat?" she asked.

"They tend to avoid us when they can. I would never expect them to invite us to dine with them."

"Would you dine with them if they invited you?"

Kel tilted his head to one side as if to consider her question. "I do not know."

"Would you dine with me if I asked?"

"Perhaps."

"I know you can drink water. What about eating food?"

"We are still able to consume human food, but what would be the point?"

Katlyn shrugged a shoulder as she took a drink of her water. "Because food tastes good," she said. "We usually eat the food we enjoy, but avoid foods we don't like."

"I see."

"You said 'still able to.' What does that mean?"

Kel looked at her and hesitated.

"If I'm asking, it's because I'd like to know. I think I have a fairly good idea of how this works now."

"Very well," he said. "Before we reach maturity, we do consume food the same as you, for nourishment. The ability to consume it never changes; however, getting nourishment from it does. It no longer sustains us after..." he paused, leveling his chin to the ground as he continued looking at her.

"After you're mature enough to suck the life out of a human," she finished matter-of-factly.

"Precisely," he said with indifference in his tone.

"At first, I thought you were a vampire," Katlyn said, chuckling as she took another drink of water.

Kel pulled his head back. "I do not know what that is," he confessed.

Katlyn stifled a laugh and bit her top lip. "Well, they're basically folklore or legends. Stories that people tell each other. They're usually nocturnal and drink blood," she said, snickering. "They're portrayed as rising from the dead, sleeping in coffins, or something equally ridiculous," she continued laughing. "I know it sounds idiotic."

"Not entirely."

"What do you mean?"

"We do consume blood," he said with a slight smirk on his face.

Katlyn scowled at him with her mouth agape. "You're kidding," she said. "Aren't you? Are you teasing me?" she asked with a broad smile forming on her face.

Kel started chuckling. A tiny smile formed on his lips revealing sharp canines, but not fangs like you'd expect with a vampire. Maybe sharp enough to break the skin. Katlyn found them intriguing, and pulled her head back in surprise when the tip of his tongue grazed one.

"Oh, you have jokes now?" she said, laughing.

"No, I am not teasing. We do consume it on occasion."

Katlyn's jaw dropped in disbelief. "Why?"

"Because it tastes good," he said with an amused look on his face.

Katlyn scoffed, then burst into laughter. She laughed for several minutes as Kel sat across from her with a smirk on his face. She finally asked, "Are you being serious? I can't tell if you're teasing me or being serious because of the look on your face."

"I find it enjoyable that you appear to be so amused by this. Any other human would not desire to have this conversation," he said. "I am being truthful. We have been known to consume human blood."

Katlyn grimaced, stifling an awkward chuckle. "Okay, is it really because it tastes good, or are there other reasons?"

Kel took a deep breath and placed his clasped hands on the table in front of him. His nails were perfectly manicured and he had a ring on his pinky. The metal was black, and it looked like delicate filigree with red gemstones scattered throughout the design.

"We do enjoy the taste, yes, but it also gives a..." he paused, "a pleasurable feeling. I would imagine it to be comparable to when humans consume spirits." He looked briefly at the untouched glass of wine on her tray.

"I have to admit that's strange that you get nothing from human food, but blood affects you. Maybe Earth has seen your species after all," she joked.

Kel cocked his head. "What do you mean?"

"Well, the legends of vampires came from somewhere. There are people who really believe vampires are real. The undead going around, sucking humans dry. Maybe they're partly right," Katlyn said in jest.

"Perhaps," he said with a light chuckle. "We do not 'suck humans dry,' as you say."

"Oh?"

"We do not take from the source."

Katlyn's head went back suddenly, and she burst into another fit of laughter. "I can't even think straight enough to know what the hell you mean!"

Kel stared at her with a look of curiosity. "We have never taken blood straight from a human."

"Oh, I see what you mean," she said, covering her mouth with her hand, still giggling. "Why not?"

"We only consume what is withdrawn. Biting another signals bonding. We only bite the one we have bound ourselves to," he said.

"Why does biting signal bonding, but drinking blood doesn't?"

"When a Specter bites their mate, a fluid transfer occurs. Creating a bond— I should not be telling you this," he said abruptly.

"Why?"

"It is very intimate and personal. I have already shared too much with you."

"Okay, if you don't take directly from someone, how do you get it then?" she asked.

"Humans have volunteered to withdraw it, and store it for us."

"Okay..." Katlyn said, looking away and clearing her throat.

They both sat in silence as Katlyn continued chuckling and giggling, shaking her head in disbelief. Her face and neck flushed periodically as she thought about this beautiful man before her, sinking his teeth deep into her jugular. She stifled a moan as it escaped her lips and brushed her hand roughly across her neck as she thought about it. Swallowing hard and licking her lips.

"Why does your skin continue to flush?" Kel asked.

Katlyn rolled her eyes. "Please don't tell me you can read my mind. I know you're telepathic with each other, but if you can read *my* mind, I might just jump out of an airlock or something," she said, snorting and covering her face.

"I am not able to read your mind in this way," he said. "We are only telepathic with each other if we are touching, but what are you thinking that you would not want me to see?" he asked, raising an eyebrow, the right side of his lip curling slightly.

Katlyn froze wide-eyed, shaking her head. "Nothing!" she said quickly. "It's nothing. What does 'in this way' mean?" she asked.

"I would be able to read your memories, but it would require touching you, and I would never do so without your consent. It would be very unpleasant if performed against your will."

She finished her meal, stifling the random awkward giggles.

"What do you find so amusing?" he asked.

She shook her head. "I can't believe I'm going to say this, but if it didn't involve this bonding you didn't want to elaborate on, I might have volunteered..." she trailed off laughing with a big smile on her face. "Since you've been so nice to me and all," she chortled.

He squared his shoulders and straightened his neck as he said, "I would have found that to be most agreeable." The blacks of his eyes widened, and the ruby irises glistened in the low light. His mouth formed into a smile as he gazed at her.

Katlyn's neck and face flushed again with embarrassment and she snickered to herself.

Both sat quietly as Katlyn drank the glass of wine. *Maybe drinking this isn't such a good idea,* she thought to herself. *I might end up volunteering after all!* She shook that thought out of her head as the main doors to Kel's quarters opened suddenly, causing Katlyn to jump. She looked up as a woman walked into the room, accompanied by two more of the same men she had seen at the doors. Conscripts Kel called them.

Kel stood quickly but gracefully as the woman walked toward them. Katlyn sat her glass down and stood up just as Kel bowed at the waist.

"Domina," he said. She lifted her hands gingerly toward him, which he took, and touched them to his forehead. Katlyn straightened her back and lifted her chin respectfully while she watched them.

"You were to bring her to me when she woke, Commander," the woman said, looking down at him.

"Domina, she is still unwell. She collapsed not long ago and needed nourishment."

After a moment, the woman, who Katlyn assumed was the Regent, looked at her, eyeing her from head to toe. "So, this is the human who has returned you to me," she said to Kel.

He righted himself, still bowing his head. "She saved my life. I am in her debt, Domina."

"As am I, it would seem," the woman said. "Thank you for aiding in his escape. As well as saving his life."

"You're welcome. He saved my life as well, so it seems we are indebted to each other," Katlyn managed to say.

"Indeed," the Regent said flatly, raising an eyebrow. "I must ask why you would do such a thing?"

"I'm sorry?" Katlyn asked, confused.

"Why would you save the life of a Specter? And apparently, not only save his life but risk your own, nearly dying in the process," she said coldly. "Such a thing has never been done before. Please excuse me if I need to know why you would do this."

Katlyn took a sharp breath, then scoffed. When she glanced at Kel, he was looking at neither of them. Instead, his eyes appeared to look in between them.

"I was desperate," Katlyn said. "I was at a point where I felt like I had nothing to lose. I had two choices: die in that cell, or take a chance and trust him." She motioned her head toward Kel, then met the woman's gaze, who was several inches taller than her.

"That explains why you trusted him to escape, but it does not explain why you risked your life, allowing him to gain strength from you," the woman said accusingly.

"If I was going to die, I wanted to die fighting. There was no way I was going back to that cell," Katlyn retorted. "When he was injured, I was trapped, backed into a corner. One of us needed to escape, but I couldn't do it on my own. I was willing to die so he could escape. My only other choice was to be recaptured; that wasn't a choice I was willing to live with," she said boldly.

"What world do you come from?" The woman squinted her eyes at Katlyn.

Katlyn had to think fast. She knew that Kel didn't tell the Regent where she was from, but she couldn't lie to her. She had a feeling that would end badly. So, she decided to answer the questions honestly but leaving out specifics.

"I still don't remember very much from before I was put into that cell. Nothing actually. All I remember is waking up in there, and not knowing where I was or how I got there."

That was true enough, she hoped.

"I don't know how to get home from here, I'm sorry."

Also, the truth.

"I see," the Regent said, raising her chin slightly, looking down at Katlyn. "If she is going to stay here, she will need to be useful, Commander," she said, looking at Kel.

"Yes, Domina," he said, bowing his head. "My Lodestar and I are considering all options, and he has looked into possible worlds to relocate her."

Come again? Katlyn thought to herself.

"Very well," the Regent said. "Thank you again for aiding in his escape so he could return to me," she said to Katlyn, then turned abruptly toward Kel. "Come to me later," she told him. He bowed deeply at the waist and held it until the woman turned to leave. She floated out of the room as if carried by a cloud.

Katlyn let out the breath she was holding, then inhaled deeply, exhaling slowly out of her nose.

"You did fine," Kel said.

"I remembered you telling me that you didn't tell her where I'm from. I did panic for a minute there."

"I could not tell."

"If my world is in a different galaxy, which you wouldn't be able to reach anyway, what is the harm in telling her? Why would you choose to keep that from her?"

"At the time, I did not consider your world to be in a different galaxy," he said. "It still could be closer than we think. If she knows it is intact, I assure you, your people will not be safe."

"But if it is in a different galaxy, you can't even travel there."

"No, but someone in this galaxy *is* able to travel there. She cannot know this. It is better this way."

"Why does it matter to you? They're only human," Katlyn said coldly, crossing her arms with indifference on her face.

She could hear his breath catch when she repeated his own words to him. He squared his shoulders, walked up to her, and almost touching her, said, "I already told you, you are different."

Katlyn took a step back so she could look up at him. "I just don't understand why you're willing to keep something from her. This seems like a pretty big secret."

Kel sighed. "You are very persistent," he said, shaking his head. "Some things are better left unsaid."

Katlyn scoffed dramatically. "Which I tend to say things that are better left unsaid!" she retorted, then stormed off toward her room. "My mouth tends to get me into trouble."

Kel squared his shoulders again and clasped his hands behind his back. "I believe you."

Katlyn scoffed again and stormed into her room. If she could slam the door, she would have.

13. TOO FAMILIAR

~Kel

"Commander!" the Regent welcomed him when he entered her bedchamber. He bowed gracefully before joining her at a table.

"Your guest does have spirit. She was very bold," the Regent chuckled.

"Yes, indeed, Domina."

"I can see why she draws your attention," she said, smirking at him.

"Domina," Kel smiled, "I am simply curious about her. She is unlike any human I have ever encountered."

"Yes, she is almost fearless to stand before me as she did. No matter. That is not why I have requested you see me. We have possibly encountered a new enemy, Commander."

"Have I missed an epic battle?"

"Not yet, but you may have had you been imprisoned much longer. It is advantageous that you returned when you did," she said.

"I look forward to hearing about our new enemy. What can you tell me?"

"Not a lot yet, except they appeared several months ago, not long after you disappeared. Apparently, they traveled from a distant star that is unknown to us."

Kel's head shifted back, and an eyebrow raised slightly.

"I have piqued your interest, Commander?"

"You have, Domina. I wish to know more."

"I am sure your Lodestar will apprise you of pertinent details. For now, I wish to play a game. Will you sit with me for a while?" she asked. "I have missed your company."

"I will stay if you wish. I am at your leisure," he said as he bowed his head.

~Katlyn

Katlyn sat in the window, looking out at the vastness of space and the alien world in front of her. She didn't know much about the subject, but the images always fascinated her. Seeing pictures of Earth from the International Space Station were awe-inspiring. She had never been so self-righteous to believe that humans on Earth were the only sentient beings in the universe. Still, she was not prepared to wake up in a completely different solar system – galaxy, altogether, next to an alien. Maybe her longtime willingness to believe there was intelligent life elsewhere, was how she had been able to better accept her current situation.

She lounged back into the corner of the window, reflecting on the past week's events. She was tired, confused, and angry. Hearing Kel mention relocation robbed her of the joy she felt during dinner—the only real joy she experienced at all since waking up on a cold brick floor. Just out of nowhere, without consulting her, he decided what was going to happen to her. She felt her face and neck flush with anger, but the feeling was fleeting. She couldn't be mad at him. She didn't belong on his ship, but she didn't really belong anywhere. What little hope she had was fading fast. Why?—the one question that continuously ate at her. Why her? There were almost eight billion people on Earth; why was *she* taken? Only to be dumped in a cell on some distant world in a galaxy that she knew nothing about.

She suddenly felt exhausted. Kel told her that she still needed to rest, that she hadn't fully recovered from her ordeal. She decided she would sleep, maybe her kids' faces would come to her in her dreams.

As she stood up, she realized that she had nothing there; no clothes except the dress she was wearing. She went to the wardrobe in the hopes that someone would have considered that, only to see nothing inside.

She removed the dress Kel provided for her, folded it, and placed it on a shelf in the wardrobe. *Guess I'm sleeping naked,* she thought to herself. It wouldn't be the first time.

~Kel

It was late when Kel left the Regent's quarters. As he walked to his quarters, he thought of Katlyn. She was visibly upset with him after her meal. She did not understand why he would keep a secret from his Regent. Only Bry'aere was aware of the imprinting. Kel did not understand it himself. If he imprinted on a Specter, there would be no doubt in his mind, but he still did not understand how he could have imprinted on a human. How could he make Katlyn understand? If his Regent knew Katlyn's world was untouched, she would do everything within her power to find it, and Katlyn would not be safe. He could not allow that to happen.

He stood in the corridor leading to his quarters for a moment, hesitating. He would need to be prepared to speak with her if she were in the sitting room. He hissed lightly to himself when it occurred to him that he was avoiding his own quarters because of a human. He straightened himself and strode to the doors; the conscript activated them as he approached. When he crossed the threshold, he saw that the room was empty. He glanced at her door, half tempted to buzz her, but the thought escaped him as quickly as it entered his mind.

He walked into his bedchamber and quickly disrobed. He was tired and had not slept well in some time. Even though he spent the past several moons in meditation, he still preferred doing so before turning in for the night. So, he knelt in the middle of his room, steepled both hands at his chest, and attempted to relax.

Katlyn occupied his thoughts, and he hissed at himself in irritation. His mind was restless; meditation brought him no comfort. He chose to lie in bed instead, hands steepled at his waist, looking at the dim light inside his bed alcove. He closed his eyes, and when he opened them again, some time had passed. He woke to a clear mind—nothing occupied his thoughts. For a moment, he achieved vacuity.

~Katlyn

Katlyn tossed and turned. Sleep would not come to her. She figured she was in bed for a couple of hours when she finally decided to sit up. Was it nighttime? She had no idea what time of day or night it was. She assumed it was night, only because Kel told her they'd arrived after midday, and she'd been asleep for over a day. She guessed that her meal was dinner. There was no way to tell from looking out the window.

She put her feet on the floor and stood up. She wrapped the sheet on her bed around her body, tucking it into itself high on her chest, then paced the length of her room. She wanted to leave, but do what? Where would she go except into the next room, especially at night? She assumed she could leave Kel's quarters but didn't want to leave bad enough to get dressed again. So, she decided to go into the sitting room.

After dinner, when the Regent showed up, she asked Kel to go to her, so Katlyn assumed that's where he was. She felt comfortable roaming around the sitting room, half-naked. Naked actually, covered in a bedsheet.

The room was dimly lit, but she could see well enough. She didn't know what she was going to do anyway except sit in a different window with the same view as hers. So that's what she did.

The window in the sitting room was more significant than hers. Her entire body could fit in the nook. She curled up, looking out into space at the beautiful blue and green planet in front of her, and without even trying, she quickly fell asleep.

***

"Mom!" Katlyn could barely hear her son's voice over the lawnmower. She released the bar and walked onto the patio to join him. He was so handsome in his sharp dress uniform. His light brown hair was in a crew cut. He had a rugged but soft appearance to his oval face; friendly and masculine. He was several inches taller than Katlyn, and lean. They embraced when she stepped up on the patio.

"How's it going?" she asked.

"I needed to see you before I left."

"Well, I'm happy you're able to do that." She smiled.

"I'll be leaving for a while, and you know that's all I can tell you," he said.

"Yes, I know."

"I probably won't be able to email you or call. I don't know how long I'll be gone," he said with a serious tone.

"I understand."

"I don't know how you do it, mom. How did you do it with dad?"

"It was easier with him," she said, looking up at James with a smile.

"Why?"

"Because he wasn't my son."

~Kel

He rose from his bed and opened the door to his bedchamber, ready to step into his sitting room, but the scent of a female inundated his senses, and he retreated into his room, promptly closing the door.

He was not accustomed to having guests. After waking, he forgot that Katlyn was there. How he could have forgotten, escaped him. He thought nothing of entering his sitting room unclothed. That is until he scented her.

He did not wish to get dressed just to step into the next room, so he retrieved his robe, tying it snug on the side, then opened his door again.

The lights in the sitting room had not been elevated. He could see Katlyn coiled in the window, but her breathing was shallow, and she did not seem to detect his presence. As he approached, he could tell she was asleep. She coiled herself onto the window seat, and her head rested in the corner against the window. He stood over her, watching for a moment. Her scent was sweeter now, and she was curiously wrapped in bed linen.

He took a deep breath, closing his eyes as his nostrils flared, and his mouth opened slightly. Then he reached down to tap her shoulder, rousing her awake.

Katlyn took a sharp breath as she woke. She rubbed her eyes with one hand, then opened them and jumped when she realized he was standing over her.

"Uh... I'm sorry," she stammered. "I didn't mean to fall asleep here," she said as she turned to put her feet on the floor. Kel stepped back to give her room. She looked back up to him, her gaze fell on his neck momentarily, and her face flushed. He imagined the stammering and flushing cerise occurred when she was nervous or embarrassed.

"I apologize for disturbing you, but this does not seem like a good place to sleep."

"I didn't know you were here," she said, still rubbing her eyes.

"Where else would I be during the night hours?"

Katlyn stood up quickly, pulling her top lip into her mouth. A move she often did when she was nervous or embarrassed.

"Well, I just assumed—"

"Assumed what?" he interrupted as he drew his head back.

"Well, the Regent asked... so I just figured that's where you were tonight," Katlyn said, stumbling over her words.

Kel suspected that Katlyn thought he would stay the night with the Regent. He smirked without meaning to. "Oh?"

She tucked a thick curl behind her ear and looked to the side, avoiding eye contact with him—another quirk that indicated nervousness.

"I always did imagine you next to a queen," she said, stifling a chuckle.

"I see," he said, squaring his shoulders and clasping his hands behind his back. "I am not her companion."

Katlyn's body stiffened. "That's not my business!" she yelped, catching him by surprise.

"You assumed I would spend the night with her."

"Well, she kinda asked you to go see her, and I knew it was late... but like I said, that's not my business," Katlyn said as she fumbled with her hands.

"She and I are not intimate. I am her Commander, nothing more."

Katlyn exhaled sharply, then scoffed. "I don't know why you're telling me this. It isn't my business."

"I do not wish for you to form an improper opinion of me."

"Why does my opinion even matter?"

She seemed to be cross with him still.

"Why were you cross after your meal? Even now, you appear to be troubled," he said as he lowered his chin.

Katlyn sighed and turned back toward the window. "I'm afraid," she admitted. "My fear tends to manifest as anger. I'm sorry. I have no reason to be upset with you." She crossed her arms in front of her and glanced at him over her shoulder. "Not much of a warrior, am I?"

Kel relaxed his shoulders and took a step closer to her. "Fear does not make you weak. You can be afraid *and* brave. You have been very brave," he whispered affectionately.

"Are you really going to dump me on a planet somewhere?" she asked. "I guess that's what got me upset after dinner. I wasn't expecting to hear that."

He lowered his head and averted her gaze. He felt ashamed for choosing to relocate her so soon, but her presence was a distraction he could not afford. "We are at war. This is a ship of war. You will not be safe here," he said. That was not entirely a lie, but he could not tell her the truth.

"You told me I would be."

"You are safe among *my* men, but we could be thrown into battle at any moment. You do not belong here," he said quietly.

"I don't belong anywhere."

Kel took a deep breath as he watched her. She was looking out the window again, leaning up against the corner with her hands behind her back. The linen hugged her form intimately. He could see her pulse beating steady in her neck, and he hissed quietly through his teeth. Katlyn turned her head to look at him.

"Why are you wrapped in bed linen?" he whispered as he took a step closer. He reached down, gently grasping the open edge below her breasts.

She straightened up and grabbed the top as if to prevent it from coming open. "I... uh..." she stammered, "didn't have anything to sleep in, and I didn't want to sleep in that dress," she said, then she pulled in her bottom lip and chewed on it.

Kel took another step toward her, still holding the front of the linen. His hand pushed into her, and she leaned back, her head stopping abruptly along the corner of the window alcove. She looked straight ahead and took a sharp breath, holding it as her pulse quickened. Kel closed his eyes as he stood over her. He could feel her breath flutter at his chest as she released it. He inhaled her scent, her hair moving gently on the top of her head as he exhaled. Their bodies were not touching but were close enough that he could feel her warmth.

We are becoming too familiar, he said to himself.

He stepped back, releasing the linen, and turned his back to her. "I will speak with Nia tomorrow about more clothing," he forced out as he walked to one of the tables. "I may have news for you," he said, then sat down.

Katlyn hesitated for a moment before joining him. Her breathing was heavy and staggered, and her sweet scent had become faintly musky. He suspected she was aroused like she was at the river. He felt shame for putting her in such a precarious position. It had become increasingly difficult to be around her. Her physical presence overwhelmed him; he had never had such a reaction to any female.

She avoided his gaze and clutched at the linen with both hands as she sat across from him.

"We have acquired a new enemy since my capture. They come from a distant star that is unknown to us," he said. Katlyn looked up at him wide-eyed. "Perhaps they are your people or know of them."

"Maybe," Katlyn said, looking down at the table.

"I will look into it. In the meantime, we will take you to a settlement that is in our territory. We trade with them occasionally. You should be safe there," he said with more harshness than he intended, then rose from the table, turning his back to her to retreat to his private room.

"Why can't I stay here?" she asked. "At least until you find something out." Her voice broke as she spoke. He paused, then stepped toward his room again. "Kel," she whispered.

The sound of his name caressing her lips pulled at him more than he thought it would. He stopped, but kept his back to her, inhaling deeply and closing his eyes. Turning around concerned him. If he looked at her at that moment, he worried how he might react.

"You cannot stay here." He breathed in as he squared his shoulders. "You cannot. I am sorry." Then he quickly walked through the door to his private room, leaving her sitting alone.

~Katlyn

She sat at the table, clutching the sheet around her, staring at Kel's door as it shut behind him. What did she do to make him want to get rid of her? She had to remind herself that he was no ordinary man—he was an alien. Not only that, but he was a species that consumed humans. She experienced it firsthand, but unlike most humans, she lived to talk about it.

She wiped the hurt off her face and pulled herself up from the chair. She walked to her room, where she collapsed into the bed. Naturally, she wasn't tired as she stared at the ceiling.

She touched along the open edge of the sheet where Kel touched, and her mind reeled back to him standing over her. His heavy hand pushing against her, his breath on the top of her head. She could smell the woody earth that his body exuded. She never imagined the smell of wood, earth, and rain would be so arousing—but it was. It didn't help that he was barely dressed. She figured he was probably naked under the robe. She could see his feet and ankles, as well as the top of his chest and neck. Her mind wouldn't allow her to stop thinking about him. Every time she closed her eyes, she felt him in front of her, his hand pushing into her. She found herself becoming more aroused as she thought about him.

She bolted up from the bed and went into the bathroom to take a hell water hot bath. Thinking about him pissed her off and excited her. A hot bath would help her sleep, and she regretted not thinking of it sooner. She could have avoided the entire situation that just occurred.

14. REALIZATION

~Kel

"Commander?" the bridge's first centurion seemed surprised when Kel walked onto the bridge. "What brings you here during the night watch, sir?"

"Where is Bry'aere?"

"He left not long ago. He didn't say where he was going," the centurion said.

"Very well," Kel said, unmoving.

"Is your guest well?" the centurion asked.

"Yes." He walked to the console in the center of the room. "Make a heading for this planet," he said as he brought up a star chart. "This is where we are taking her."

"Did you find her people?"

"No, but she cannot stay. She does not belong here," Kel said heatedly as he turned around and walked briskly from the room.

It was quiet as he walked through the corridors of his ship—his home. He was finally home, and he could sense his comrades. Even in the stillness, while most of them slept, he could sense their presence.

He would have preferred the company of his friend, but instead of going to Bry'aere's quarters, he got into the lift and went up two levels to the recreation room. As he stepped out of the lift, he could hear the commotion of the night sentries. He turned the corner abruptly from the lift. Not many men were there at that hour. Most of them were on reserve in case they were needed for fliers.

"Commander!" He could feel their eagerness as they greeted him. He had not been home long and had yet to see most of his men.

"It is pleasant to see you, Commander," one man said, and others nodded in agreement.

He acknowledged their greetings as he walked around the room, not quite sure what he was looking for.

"May we help you with something, sir?" one of the men asked.

"Have you seen Bry'aere recently?"

"No, sir. If he isn't on the bridge, he's most likely with the analyst or in his quarters."

"Thank you," Kel said, then turned to leave the room.

He took a right when he stepped into the corridor. To his immediate right was the primary analyst's lab. He approached the door, and a conscript activated the control, allowing him access.

The room beyond had lab consoles of varying types. Kel was not sure whether the analyst would be awake at that hour, but he went in anyway.

"Commander!" the analyst said eagerly from the corner of the room. He approached Kel, offering his hand to him, which he accepted.

His primary analyst was calm, and his mind was a flash of light.

'To what do I owe the honor of your visit at this late hour?' Roe'lys projected fondly when they touched.

Kel sighed, careful to keep his mind closed. *'I am not sure. I could not sleep. I did not think you would be awake.'*

'I could not sleep either,' Roe'lys said. *'Perhaps my mind knew you were restless.'*

"Perhaps," Kel said, pulling his hand back. "Since I am here, I am interested in some information."

"Of course. What can I help you with?"

"I would like... and I expect you to keep this between us," he said, raising an eyebrow.

"Absolutely!" Roe'lys said with a bow.

"I would like information about imprinting."

Roe'lys rested his chin on his thumb and forefinger as if searching. "What is it you would like to know? Anything specific, or just in general?"

"I am not sure exactly. I suppose in general for now. I am mostly interested in what causes one to imprint on another, but any information you are able to provide would be appreciated."

"There is still a lot we don't know about imprinting, but without researching, I can inform you from memory, that it is a chemical reaction. It is surprising how little we know about it, to be honest, sir. We have no control over it. A male can imprint on a female, a youngling, or even another male," Roe'lys said.

"What causes it? Why does it occur? And what exactly does it mean?"

"Well, sir, as I said, there is a lot we still don't know. There is never a way of monitoring when or if it will happen. So, we can't exactly monitor the brain's reaction when it occurs. We can only study the before and after."

"I see."

"I can also tell you that it has nothing to do with intimacy. Imprinting on another does not mean you're attracted to them intimately. It merely means they are significant to you in some way, and you are bound to protect them."

"Why would a parent not imprint on their own young?"

"We do not know that, sir. I'm sorry. I know I'm not being extremely helpful."

"No, this is sufficient. Someone who has imprinted is not necessarily intended to bond or mate with the one they have imprinted on?"

"No." Roe'lys shook his head. "As I said, a male can imprint on a youngling or even another male. That does not mean that either will be your mate."

"I see."

"However, if a male does have a passion or love for the one he imprints on, it can increase his desire to protect them. It could even cause irrational behavior. Most males who have passion for the one they imprint on end up bonding with them."

"Is there any record of a male imprinting on..." he hesitated. "Please do not get the wrong impression when I ask this."

"Of course not, sir! But before you ask, a male can imprint on anyone for any reason. There is no explanation as to why it occurs. There is a lot we don't know about it. The brain is still a mystery."

"Is there any record of a male imprinting on a human? Is such a thing even possible?" Kel asked.

"I don't recall seeing any record of it, but that doesn't mean it's never happened. I don't see why it wouldn't be possible."

"Would it not be considered unnatural?"

"I don't believe so. We are humanoid after all, and possess human DNA."

"This is true."

"Also, we nourish our bodies with their bodies. Imprinting on a human is not beyond the realm of possibilities. It would only mean the male would have a strong desire to protect that human. Just because we nourish ourselves with them doesn't mean we can't be fond of them or have affection for them," Roe'lys said. "I am quite fond of my human, to be honest, sir."

"How so?"

"He is good company. I would almost go as far as to call him a friend. Although I wouldn't necessarily trust him with anything sharp." Roe'lys and Kel both laughed.

"Has a Specter ever mated with a human?" Kel's question seemed to catch Roe'lys by surprise. He pulled his head back sharply as he cocked it to the side, then furrowed his brow. "Would such a thing even be possible?"

Roe'lys took in a sharp breath. "I don't see why it wouldn't be, but *that* would be considered unnatural. Or at the very least, unusual. I think it may depend on the circumstances." After a long pause, Roe'lys said, "I have heard of males assaulting human females with disastrous results."

Kel looked at him with disgust. "If any of my men have ever done such a thing, I expect to be informed about it. Any male who would do that does not deserve to live!" His tone was elevated. He became angry at the thought of any of his men committing such an atrocity.

"Of course, sir! I mentioned it because you asked if mating would be possible. I know anatomically we are similar enough, but we are so much larger than humans, as well as stronger and more powerful. I am not sure if a human female would be able to undertake such a venture... for lack of better words, sir. The humans who were assaulted did not survive long from what I understand."

"Similar enough? Please elaborate."

"It is my understanding that human and Specter females differ slightly. Not enough that mating wouldn't be possible, but there are subtle differences. I'm sorry, I don't know much more than that."

"Please forgive my unusual questions," Kel said. "These are the rantings of a man who has been imprisoned for many cycles." He laughed.

"It is fine, sir. These are not the most unusual questions I have been asked. I am an analyst, after all. Men come to me quite frequently with bizarre requests and strange questions."

"I do have one more question," Kel said. "Why would a Specter feel pleasure from someone while healing them?"

"Only two reasons for that, sir. Imprinting or bonding. When one is being healed, they find pleasure in it. I'm sure you have experienced pleasure while being healed."

"Yes." He nodded.

"Whoever is on the receiving end of healing or being given life feels pleasure or joy. Even humans experience a type of euphoria during the process. If a male has imprinted on someone, he will feel what they feel. There is a transference of energy. The feeling is increased with bonding."

"Thank you for entertaining my curiosity. I will take my leave now," Kel said. "Have a good night."

"Thank you, sir. You as well." Roe'lys said as he bowed his head gently.

Kel left the lab and took the lift down to the main level. He took the corridors as if he were going back to his quarters, but still wished to speak with Bry'aere, so after passing the steps to the bridge, he took a left down another corridor and tapped the door control. It did not take long for his friend to open the door.

"Hello, Kel'ardent. What has you up at this hour?"

Kel sighed and hissed as he took a seat in the corner of the room next to the faux window that was backlit with soft blue lighting.

"I could not stay in my quarters, Bry'aere."

"I see," Bry'aere said, cocking his head to the side.

"I have chosen a planet for her, and we are en route there now."

"Ready to be rid of her so soon?"

"She cannot stay here. We are becoming too familiar. Her presence is a distraction. It is inappropriate, and I know our Regent senses something."

"I thought you did not wish to discuss this further?" Bry'aere asked.

"Listen or do not. It does not matter."

"Would you like to tell me what happened?"

"How could I have let this happen?" Kel asked, not expecting, or even wanting an answer.

"You cannot control imprinting. You know this."

"Not that!"

"Then what?"

"I do not wish to discuss it," Kel retorted.

Bry'aere gave an annoyed sigh and rolled his eyes. "You are in turmoil, friend. Perhaps you should bed her and get it over with," Bry'aere suggested sharply.

"Have you lost your mind?" Kel bolted out of the chair, making Bry'aere jump.

"Not more than you at this point," Bry'aere snapped back. "That is exactly what I would tell you if we were discussing any other female."

"This is not just *any* female," he barked. "I do not know why I came here. I should have known better. You have always been a terrible influence."

"She is a beautiful woman, Kel'ardent. I do not know what more to tell you."

"She is human. I cannot believe we are even discussing this again. She will be gone in less than two days, and that will be the end of it," Kel said with irritation.

"Something tells me that is not true," Bry'aere said.

Kel sat back in the chair and crossed his arms sternly across his chest.

"You may sleep here if you wish."

Kel growled quietly, then hissed.

"Or sit there and sulk. I do not care. I am going to bed. I cannot believe you are behaving this way because of a woman." Bry'aere shook his head.

"She is not—"

"I know!" Bry'aere snapped as he turned on his heel and disappeared through the curtain on the opposite side of the small sitting room, leaving Kel to seethe in private.

~Katlyn

Katlyn woke up to Nia nudging her shoulder. She was carrying a basket full of clothes. The Commander told her to gather a few things for Katlyn to keep.

As she put her feet on the floor, she glanced toward the window. The stars and planet were gone. The window was dark with faint white streaks passing by. She pulled her head back and gave Nia a puzzled look.

"We are in star drive. We are traveling, going somewhere. I'm not sure where, though."

Katlyn huffed and rubbed her face with her hands. "He's taking me to some planet."

"Oh? Are you certain? He didn't seem to be in a hurry—"

"Yes, I'm sure. He told me last night," Katlyn said, flustered.

"Oh, I see," Nia said quietly. "I'll take my leave so you may dress," she said, turning toward the door.

Katlyn rummaged through the basket, looking at what Nia brought. A couple of wrap-style dresses, a nightgown, and what looked like a slip style dress. A shift she assumed. She put that on first. It was open in the front and cinched just below her breasts. The top did offer a little support, thankfully. The sleeves came just above the elbows, and the hem stopped just above the knee. Both dresses were the same and closed like a robe. Easy on, easy off. Pretty easy to make, and one size fits all. After slipping on sandals that were also in the basket, Katlyn walked to the sitting room and found Nia waiting with a man.

"Mistress," he said as he bowed his head.

She recognized him from the bridge. He was the second in command.

"Morning," Katlyn said, apathetic.

"I came to notify you that we will arrive at our destination tomorrow after midday."

"Okay, I guess I'm being dumped off somewhere sooner than I expected," Katlyn responded, indifferent.

The man cocked his head to the side. "You should have known that you could not stay here."

"The Regent implied that I could. I'd just have to be useful."

"I see," he said, righting himself. "The Commander must believe this to be a better option," he told her kindly.

"So, I'm just at his whim then? I get no say as to what happens to me?" Katlyn snapped, causing Nia to stiffen, and the man to pull his head back. "Why are you telling me, and not him?"

"He is occupied with other matters. He requested that I inform you."

Katlyn looked away toward the window, chuckling softly. "So even you, the Specter, are not above sending someone else to do your dirty work?"

"Nia, please leave us," the man said. He stood silent until Nia left the room. "I should not be telling you this—"

"Then don't!" Katlyn said as she looked him in the eyes.

"I feel you need to hear it."

"Please don't tell me what I *need* or what you, or Kel—" she stopped abruptly, shaking her head, "the Commander feels is best for me."

The man squared his shoulders and chuckled softly, curling the side of his lip.

"Why are you laughing at me?"

"I am not laughing at you, mistress," he said, smiling. "I am fascinated."

"What do you mean?" Katlyn asked, furrowing her brow.

"You most certainly are a unique woman," he said with a tone of admiration.

Katlyn rolled her eyes and scowled. "You just aren't used to humans talking back."

"Perhaps," he said with a light chuckle, "but it is more than that. If you were Specter, you would make a great Regent," he said, bowing gently. "I will take my leave."

As he reached the door, Katlyn stopped him. "Is the Commander going to say goodbye before I leave? Or is he planning on avoiding his quarters until I'm gone?"

"I do not know. If you wish, I will inform him that you asked," he said before activating the door control and disappearing.

~Bry'aere

As he exited Kel'ardent's quarters, he could not help but think about how this woman, this human woman, may be exactly what his friend needed. Perhaps he *was* a terrible influence, just as Kel'ardent said. It was vulgar to entertain such an idea, after all. No Specter had ever done such a thing, but Kel'ardent was just the man to do it, and he had an obvious affection for her. As for Katlyn, she was clearly cross with him. Something must have happened between them for Kel'ardent to have avoided even his own private room all night.

For a moment, he almost told Katlyn about Kel'ardent having imprinted on her. Perhaps that would ease the tension between them, and she may understand why he was behaving out of the ordinary, but in hindsight, he was glad she interrupted him. That information was not his to share.

Something told him that Kel'ardent would not be able to stay away from Katlyn. She may be going to a planet soon, but she would not be there for long.

15. PASSION

~Katlyn

Katlyn sat in the window watching the stars pass by as she pondered her uncertain future. After the last conversation she had with Kel, she was restless and didn't sleep well. She was dozing off curled up in the window nook, vaguely aware of Nia entering the room.

"You don't have to stay in here," she said. "I'll be preparing the midday meal soon. You're welcome to join us."

"I'd love to get out of here and do something. I don't even care what it is," Katlyn said as she put her feet on the floor and stood up.

They both left Kel's quarters together, passing two conscripts who stood on each side of the door.

"Kel said he was going to explain them, but never did," Katlyn said to Nia, motioning her head toward the conscripts.

"Who?" Nia gave a puzzled look.

"The conscripts."

"No, the other name you used."

Katlyn stammered when she realized she used Kel's name, and he told her he never shared it with another human. "Never mind," she whispered.

Nia stopped about halfway down the corridor, whispering to Katlyn, "Did the Commander tell you his name?"

Katlyn swallowed and licked her lips. "He did, but I didn't mean to call him that," she confessed. "It slipped out. Which is really stupid because I've only said it out loud two other times."

"I have been in his service for many years, and I don't even know his name."

"It's actually Kel'ardent, but you didn't hear it from me!"

"Oh, don't worry. I would never call him by his name—even if I had known it," she said. "We'll go in here." Nia led her through a door on the right that was just past the steps leading to the bridge. "This is where we prepare and eat our meals."

The room was lit brighter than the rest of the ship and had counters along two walls, and food crates with various fruits and vegetables along another. Jars with dried goods and dishes sat on the counters. There even appeared to be a stove for cooking.

"I'm assuming only humans come in here?" Katlyn asked.

"Yes," Nia said as she gathered ingredients to make bread. "This is about the only room we can go where we have total privacy. The Specter have no reason to be in here."

Katlyn gawked. "Really? You don't even have privacy where you sleep or bathe?"

"We do, but it isn't guaranteed. Any of our masters or the Regent can enter at any time, for any reason. They typically don't, but they could if they need us," Nia said as if it were normal to be treated in such a way. Katlyn supposed that for her, it was normal.

"Slavery is illegal where I'm from. People shouldn't be treated this way. I'm sorry you have to deal with this," Katlyn whispered.

Nia chuckled. "I chose this. Any children I have will be safe. That's something I can live with. Serving the Commander isn't so bad. He isn't abusive, and he respects females. So, he doesn't mistreat me or allow anyone else to. Sometimes he can be abrupt, but otherwise, it isn't so bad."

Katlyn sighed. "People aren't property. No matter how you try to justify it."

"It beats the alternative if I'm honest. Living your whole life in fear, and dying in such a way. From what I understand, you know what the alternative is like."

"I see your point," Katlyn said ruefully. "I can honestly say I never want to do that again. I don't recall any other pain quite like it, but I can also say that I'd rather die that way than to live under someone's boot. I *was* willing to die that way rather than be captured again. There's no telling what they would have done to me after I killed one of their guards."

While Katlyn and Nia visited, a few other women came into the room. They greeted Katlyn and each other as they grabbed various foodstuffs. Then everyone sat at the table in the middle of the room so they could visit and prepare the meal together.

"Is there anything I can help with?" Katlyn asked as she sat across from Nia. "I don't want to just sit here and watch."

"Sure!" a woman said happily, then she handed Katlyn a knife and some carrot looking things. "Just cut them into bite-size pieces."

"Are you sure that's a good idea?" another woman asked with a worried tone.

"What do you mean?" Katlyn asked.

"Well, you're the Commander's guest," she reminded her. "He may be cross if he knew you were helping us."

Katlyn resisted the urge to roll her eyes. After all, this life was normal to them, and Kel was basically their owner or in charge of their owners anyway, but that didn't stop her from the dramatic sigh she released before she spoke again.

"I offered. Nobody asked for my help. That's what I'll tell him if it comes up."

All the women cut vegetables, kneaded dough, and told stories. For a moment, Katlyn felt happy and content—like she finally belonged somewhere. The stories these women told were full of intrigue and humor. Katlyn hadn't laughed so hard in a long time.

As the women sat over the uncooked food, telling each other about their families and friends, stories Katlyn was sure they'd all shared with each other before, the room suddenly grew quiet. Katlyn looked up at everyone, and she immediately knew there was a Specter in the room, which Nia said never happened. Katlyn glanced over her shoulder to see Kel standing just inside the door, staring at her with a stoic look on his face. He was dressed the same way he was when they first met, and his arms hung rigid at his sides.

"What are you doing?" he asked as Katlyn swiftly rose to her feet.

"I'm helping, and we're visiting."

A scowl briefly formed on his face, then he went stoic again as he moved his head to look at the women sitting quietly behind her. Before he could accuse them of anything, she moved to block his view, so he was looking at her again. "I offered to help," she said.

Kel raised an eyebrow and cocked his head to the side. "Why?"

"Because I'd like to be useful for the short time I'm here."

"I would prefer you not help in this way," he said as he stepped farther into the room.

"Why?" she asked boldly.

"We will discuss this elsewhere." Katlyn could have sworn he was gritting his teeth when he spoke.

"Mistress—"

"Please stop calling me that!" Katlyn interrupted Nia. "I am no one's mistress. My name is Katlyn," she snapped. She was suddenly annoyed. Not at Nia, but at Kel for being so surly toward her for no reason whatsoever.

"You are a guest," he reminded her.

"Okay"—she opened her hands in front of her—"am I not free to move about as I please? Or do I need your permission to leave my room?" she spat with more disrespect than she intended. "And doesn't the host normally visit with their guest? Or do you always treat guests this way?"

Kel leaned forward, lowering his head and squinting just enough for her to notice. The blacks of his eyes narrowed as he looked at the other women in the room, his gaze finally resting on Katlyn. "Your mate must be a very patient man," he murmured through clenched teeth.

Katlyn's jaw dropped, and she inhaled sharply. She and Kel never discussed her late husband. He had no idea that she was a widow, but that did not matter. Whether her husband was dead or alive, the beast standing in front of her had no business bringing him up.

She lost all composure as she drew her arms back and stood on her toes so she could get as close to his face as possible. "My *husband* is dead, and he was never threatened by me. Don't you *ever* mention him again!" she shouted, her voice breaking as the words fell out.

Kel righted himself, and his face softened as she seethed in front of him.

"Why are you being so mean to me all of a sudden?" she asked as her lip quivered, trying desperately not to cry. Kel squared his shoulders and raised his chin, then grabbed her arm and pulled her out of the room.

"Let go of me!" she wailed. "You're hurting me!"

Her pleas went unanswered as she yelled profanities at him. It was as if he were a different person as he pulled her down the corridor and into the sitting room of his quarters.

~Kel

The way Katlyn spoke to him, fearless and fiery, ignited something in him. He felt terrible for mentioning her mate, but when he discovered she was unattached, he wanted to take her into his arms. His position would not permit it, especially surrounded by others, but the passion he felt for her at that moment would not allow him to simply walk away.

He released her arm upon entering his sitting room but turned his back to her. He knew she was upset with him. She yelled and cursed at him as they hurried through the corridor.

She stood behind him weeping. "Are you trying to make me hate you?" she cried. "Cause if you are, it's working!"

Kel did not know or understand what came over him. He was not angry, quite the opposite. His feelings were passionate, but his reaction was fierce, nonetheless. He turned around to face her, moving so fast she had no time to react. He grasped the side of her neck firmly with his left hand and her hip with his right as he picked her up and laid her down onto the table beside them. He moved with such speed that anyone else would have thought he was violent with her, but he was not.

She clawed at his hand and cried out as his wide hips pushed into her. Her dress and shift both came open, exposing her left thigh and part of her hip. He grasped her neck, but he was not hurting her. He just held her there. The leather of his coat rubbed against the tender skin of her inner thighs.

"Do it!" she screamed. "Please kill me and get it over with!" she pleaded between sobs as she clawed at the hand and arm that held her down.

He stood frozen. The look on her face was familiar to him. It was an expression he saw many times on the faces of humans who knew they were about to die. Katlyn believed he wanted to kill her, but taking the life of the woman before him was not what he wanted to do. What he wanted was something he should not. He desired her. He did not wish to harm her. He wanted nothing more than to please her; to make love to her, but she was afraid of him. Something he hoped would never happen.

He did not understand the feelings he had. How could she be expected to understand?

He stood over her, unmoving, gazing down at her as she trembled beneath him. He was confused and not sure how to behave. He suddenly felt compelled to touch her affectionately, to right the wrong he had done.

He released both hands from her, moving his left to her shoulder. Her arms hovered over her body, as if to protect herself, and her chest heaved. She continued to sob and pulled her hands up to cover her face. He embraced her exposed hip with his right hand as the doors to his quarters opened, and Bry'aere entered the room.

"Commander!" he called out.

Katlyn lay on the table sobbing as Kel stepped away from her. He reached for her arm to help her up. When her feet touched the floor, she pulled her hand back over her shoulder and struck him across the face with such force that he stumbled back into the wall behind him.

"Don't ever touch me again!" she screamed at him with an anger that he felt to his core. He could not move, and even if he could, what would he do?

He watched in horror as she bolted away, pushing Bry'aere to the side, then activating the door control to her room and disappearing.

~Katlyn

Katlyn was angry at Kel for mentioning her husband, but at the same time, she wasn't. He had no idea. They never talked about her husband, and she never thought to tell him, but the comment he made still hurt her all the same. He caught her off guard, and she was already on the defensive, which only made her angrier at his remark. That didn't compare to how hurt and confused she was about his behavior in the sitting room, though. She didn't understand why he was so hostile to her, why he was so short and callous. Why he was behaving so feral and manhandling her. She knew he wouldn't hurt her, but for a moment she doubted even herself.

As much as she wanted to stay, she was ready to leave. To try to build somewhat of a life on a planet that she knew nothing about, with people who feared a creature she had an unexpected affection for but was quickly learning why she shouldn't.

She collapsed into the bed, pulling a pillow close. Her head throbbed from the tears that forced their way past her eyelids and soaked her cheeks. She cried herself to sleep, wanting nothing more at that moment than for this to be a horrible nightmare.

~Bry'aere

He watched with trepidation as Katlyn struck Kel'ardent in the face with such force he lost his footing. He did not know if it was the physical or emotional pain that caused his friend to stumble. Clearly, there was a miscommunication between them.

He watched, unsure of what to say as Kel'ardent paced the room. His hands were fisted at his sides, and his breath chuffed with every step. His friend was filled with a rage and fury that he had never seen before. The heat of his anger clearly visible on his face without the words needing to be spoken.

"Kel'ardent—"

"Do not!" he spat, then stomped toward his bedchamber, activating the door control, and rushing inside. Bry'aere followed closely, shutting the door behind him.

"Brother," he said as Kel'ardent stormed to the opposite side of the room, "somewhere there has been a miscommunication between you two."

"I do not know what you mean. She made it perfectly clear that she hates me and wishes for me never to touch her again," Kel'ardent retorted.

"What makes you believe she hates you?"

"She told me as much before you entered the room!"

"I do not believe that to be true." Bry'aere shook his head.

"Why would you believe it to be untrue?" Kel'ardent snapped.

"I spoke with her this morning—"

"What!" Kel'ardent snarled with gritted teeth.

Bry'aere raised one hand defensively. "She does not fear you. She has been wounded."

"You did not see the look on her face! She was terrified of me. Even if only for a moment, at that moment, she saw me for what I am. She believed I wished to kill her. She begged me to end her life," Kel'ardent said, clearly despondent as he recalled the memory.

He continued to pace the room. His chest heaved, and his eyes looked at the ceiling as he moved from one side of the room to the other. "I do not wish to harm her. I desire to please her," he confessed. "My desire to please her is even more powerful than my desire to please our Regent"—he shook his head—"but all I have done is push her away. I do not know how to behave." He breathed in deep as he ran both hands across the top of his head. "I have never had such strong emotions toward a female. I do not understand what is happening to me."

"You have never been in love before, Kel'ardent. I suspect any one of us would act in a similar way toward someone we are drawn to, but should not be with."

"I cannot accept that I have passion for a human!"

"You are in denial, which is understandable, given your position. It is easy for me to encourage you. I do not carry the burden, the station you do. I am sure the Queen would prefer you not be with a human, but I cannot say. You know her better than any other."

"I honestly do not know how she would feel about such a thing. We have always been close, but," Kel'ardent hesitated, "any daughter I were to sire..." his voice trailed off as he approached his window. "Why did you come when you did?" He turned to Bry'aere.

"I heard her yelling and cursing. Why was she so upset with you?"

"I searched for her to apologize for my behavior last night. I found her helping Nia and the others, and I behaved inappropriately. The situation escalated, and now I must apologize for even more foul behavior!"

"I see no reason you cannot enjoy Katlyn's company until she is able to return home. Perhaps you should allow her to stay—"

"No!" Kel'ardent snapped. "She cannot stay. She would not be safe. One moment I wish to," he paused and shook his head, "make love to her. The next moment, I know that I cannot. Our Regent would never allow it. Especially since she has her sights set on making me consort."

Bry'aere knew his friend. He knew him better than he knew himself, and he was not concerned with reminding Kel'ardent of that fact. He knew being tied to their current Regent would not make Kel'ardent happy.

"Do you believe you would be happy as her consort?"

"My happiness is irrelevant."

"That is not entirely true. You say that as Commander, not as Kel'ardent."

"I am both!"

"Your station, your lineage, allows you to refuse her proposal. You know this."

"I cannot refuse her because of a human. Even under my emblem, Katlyn would not be safe. This cannot be. I wish for you to take her to the planet when we arrive. I cannot."

"I would do anything for you, brother, but I will not do that. You chose to relocate her. She would be even more wounded if you assign the task to me," Bry'aere said as he shook his head. "You will have to order me publicly. I am sorry."

Kel'ardent hissed at him before retreating to his lavatory.

"I will take my leave," Bry'aere said, then he activated the door control and left.

Bry'aere knew Katlyn was hurt, not afraid. He may not have seen her face before he entered the room, but he saw her face as she stormed away from Kel'ardent, after she struck him. Her outburst toward him was out of pain, not fear. Kel'ardent had wounded her. She believed his aggression toward her was out of anger, and Kel'ardent believed her hostility toward him was out of fear. Neither realized that the other's aggression was because of passion. They each desired the other but did not know it or understand it. Both were passionate and fierce. If Katlyn were Specter, they might have even shared a name.

16. GOODBYE

~Katlyn

Nia's gentle nudging awakened Katlyn. "It is time for the evening meal," she whispered.

"I guess I slept right through lunch. Or was the Commander punishing me for my insolence?" Katlyn asked sarcastically.

"He and I both checked on you, and you were sleeping. He told me not to disturb you," Nia said. "I left some fruit in case you woke up." She pointed to a bowl on the table by the wall. "I felt it wise to wake you for this meal."

"Oh... thanks," Katlyn said shamefully as she stood up.

"You're welcome to join us, or I can bring your meal to you."

Katlyn swallowed hard. "I don't know. I'm a little embarrassed. The way he acted was humiliating. He wasn't anything like that when we were on that other planet. He was such a gentleman, very polite. I don't know how to explain it, but he was nothing at all like how he acted today."

"You have nothing to be ashamed of. The Commander's behavior since his return *has* been peculiar. He even came back into the kitchen and apologized to all of us, and that is something he would never have done before. Please do not take offense, but perhaps you are the reason he has been acting this way," Nia said.

"I can't begin to imagine why."

"You saved his life, and he returned your life back to you, which he has never done for a human before. I don't know a lot about it, but I do know that usually they only do such things amongst themselves, for each other."

"Yeah, I don't know." Katlyn was skeptical. She felt there was more to Kel's behavior than her saving his life. He should be more grateful to her, not acting like a brute, dragging her down the hall and throwing her on tables.

"Will you join us this evening? The other ladies would love to sit with you for a meal. They've never seen anyone stand up to the Commander or any master. Not even his men have done that," she whispered. "We were all hoping you'd join us, but I will bring your meal if you'd rather."

"I'll join you. Thank you. I'd prefer not to eat by myself."

"Great!" Nia said with a smile, then turned toward the door.

Except for the conscripts, the sitting room and corridor were quiet and unoccupied. The kitchen, however, was bustling with conversation. Everyone greeted Katlyn with enthusiasm and curiosity. Asking questions about who she was, where she came from, and how she ended up on the planet she and the Commander were rescued from. They were especially interested in where she came from, maybe due to her demeanor and boldness regarding the Commander, or for other nefarious reasons. She knew the Regent was curious where she was from, so when others asked her, she was careful not to reveal too much. These people may be bound servants, but they still served the Specter. She had to be cautious with the information she revealed to them.

The meal was pleasant, meat and vegetables followed by more of that red wine she had the previous night, which was pretty stout. It only took four glasses before she was snort-laughing inappropriately. Very undignified and not ladylike at all. Everyone was equally tipsy. Nia told her that the evenings were their personal time. So, they were able to indulge after dinner.

Katlyn figured it was late when she decided to stagger her way back to Kel's quarters. As she approached the doors, a conscript activated the control, allowing her access. She stood in the open door for a moment staring at them. She wanted to ask Kel about them but figured she wouldn't have the opportunity now.

She stepped through the doors, waiting for them to close behind her. She walked to the window to watch the stars pass by but couldn't stand there long without feeling woozy. She shook her head as she stumbled, then turned around to go to her room. When she glanced over at Kel's door, she noticed it was open. She took a few steps toward it, her curiosity getting the best of her, but stopped when he appeared. She spun around to head to her own room.

"Please forgive my behavior. I am not accustomed to interacting with humans in this way," he said quietly.

Katlyn scoffed, then turned to face him.

"I am aware that is not an acceptable excuse," he said as he meandered across the room.

"You should never have mentioned my husband," Katlyn said, trying to maintain her composure. "I know you didn't know he was dead, but you still had no right mentioning him at all."

"You are correct. It was inappropriate, and I apologize." He bowed his head, then looked at her in a way that she noticed he only did toward her.

"You shouldn't have put your hands on me like that either!"

"No, I should not have. I do not know what came over me. Please forgive me. It will not happen again."

"No, I guess it won't because I'm leaving tomorrow." She crossed her arms in front of her and looked away from him.

When he looked at her as he did at that moment, it made her feel weak, as if she would collapse into his arms, but the last thing she wanted right then was to be anywhere near him. She was hurt and angry at the sudden change in his demeanor. He was acting worse than a prepubescent tween, amicable one minute, piss and vinegar the next. She raised two children through adolescence. Putting up with a grown-ass *alien* behaving that way was more than she wanted to deal with.

"I could not allow you to leave angry with me."

Katlyn scoffed and rolled her eyes. "Why do you care if I'm mad? I'm food! And don't give me that shit about me saving your life. One minute you're nice, and..." She exhaled heavily when she recalled the memory of him touching her while she was wrapped in the bedsheet. "Then the next, you're being cold and callous and telling me you're dumping me on a planet as soon as possible. Then, throwing me on tables and shit. Either be mean and stay mean or be nice like the man I met on the planet. Personally, I'd prefer you didn't act like a dick, but whatever," she snapped.

Kel pulled his chin back and furrowed his brow. "I do not understand."

"What part of that long ass rant don't you understand exactly?"

"Your reference to a dick."

Hearing him say dick was funnier than she expected it to be. She wasn't sure if it was the alcohol that made it more entertaining, but she couldn't stifle the snort and laugh that escaped her.

"I'm sorry," she said as she waved her hand in front of her face, still laughing. "You don't know what that is?"

"I am aware of the literal translation."

"Okay," she said, trying to stifle her laughter. "Calling a man that is basically calling him mean, hateful, and stupid." She stared at him with a stoic expression on her face. He *was* acting like a dick. That was a perfect description for him lately. "I can be even more disrespectful when I've been drinking."

"My behavior has been out of sorts."

165

"Well, I am sorry for snapping at you in front of your *slaves*," she said, rolling her eyes. "I wouldn't want them to revolt against you. Actually, maybe I would because owning people is really shitty, and even though you've been mean to me for no damn reason I can think of, I still feel like you're above owning people, but whatever. Maybe it's best that I do leave. I'm a terrible influence." She began to laugh and snorted lightly.

Kel chuckled as he stood with his hands clasped behind his back and his chin lowered slightly toward her.

"Can I go to bed now?" Katlyn asked, looking away.

"I am aware that my behavior has been puzzling, and for that, I apologize. I value your opinion."

"Why?"

"I do not expect you to understand."

"Maybe you can try helping me understand," she said, annoyed.

"I cannot," he said, squaring his shoulders and leveling his chin. "I will take my leave. Goodnight." He bowed gently at the waist before turning around and disappearing into his room.

"I cannot," Katlyn mocked before activating her door control and going into her room where she collapsed into bed.

***

Katlyn was thankful that she wasn't saddled with a hangover the next morning. Just a little dry mouth, but nothing serious. She looked out the window to see whether they were still traveling or if they reached her new home—a temporary home she hoped. The window was still dark, with white streaks flickering by. She got up and went into the bathroom and ran a bath. For all she knew, it was the last one she'd have for a while. She got into the tub and sank in up to her ears. She had no idea how long she was there, but long enough for the water to cool and Nia to check on her, telling her that breakfast was ready.

Katlyn got out, dried off, and got dressed. She gathered what few things she had that Nia gave her. She could easily carry everything in her arms. As she was leaving the room, she remembered the dress that Kel gave her to wear. She took it off the shelf of the wardrobe, carried it out of the room with her, and placed it on the bench seat next to his door. She then sat down and ate her breakfast. When she was finished, she picked up the tray and took it to the kitchen.

"I would have gotten that," Nia said when Katlyn entered the room.

"I didn't want to sit in there by myself. Do you mind if I hang out with you? I feel like I'm awaiting my execution in there alone."

Nia happily agreed. They visited while Nia kneaded the dough for lunch. While it baked, she took another round loaf of bread, fruit, and cheese, and wrapped everything in a large cloth, then placed it in the bottom of a burlap bag.

She handed the bag to Katlyn. "This is for you. The clothes I gave you should fit in there, too."

"Thank you," Katlyn said despondently, then walked toward the door. "I'll go pack, I guess."

"Everything will be okay. You'll see," Nia said with a friendly smile.

"I hope so. Thanks for everything. I appreciate it."

"It's been my pleasure."

Back in Kel's quarters, Katlyn packed her bag and sat in the window, waiting. When the streaking stars became still, and the image of a blue and green planet appeared in the window, her breakfast lurched into her throat. She forced it down with a hard swallow. It wasn't long before Kel came into the room.

"We have arrived," he told her casually, then walked into his private room.

Katlyn stood with her bag and waited for him by the main doors. When he returned, he placed a black hooded cloak over her shoulders. "It is still the cold season," he said, then took her bag. Her stomach was in knots, and it took every ounce of self-control she had not to look at him.

He activated the door control, gripped her arm, and led her down the corridor toward the hangar bay. Everything moved in slow motion, and she felt like a dead man walking.

The ship they boarded was a transport type ship. Small, but had seating on both sides for six passengers, and two seats for pilots. Two conscripts boarded with them and took their places at the controls. Kel didn't release Katlyn's arm until she was sitting down.

"Do you think I'm going to run off?" she asked with disdain. "Where would I go?"

He didn't answer. He stood in the middle of the short aisle as the door closed, standing with one arm holding onto a bar above his head. The other was underneath his coat and behind his back. He bore his weight on one leg, with the other bent slightly at the knee and lax. His holsters were filled with a weapon on each thigh. It almost seemed as though he were intentionally teasing her. She took a sharp breath and looked away.

"I am sorry it must be this way," he whispered.

"I just don't understand. You're treating me like I did something wrong," Katlyn said, trying not to let her voice crack.

"You did nothing wrong."

"Then what is it?"

"This is for your own protection," he said with a compassionate tone—a tone she had yet to hear.

"No," she retorted. "It's more than that because you said before that I could stay on the ship for a while. Then the Regent implied I could stay if I was useful," she reminded him. "I can be useful."

"Why do you wish to stay?"

Katlyn hesitated, not sure how to answer. She looked up at him briefly. He was gazing down at her with that look that he only gave her. His ruby eyes glistened in the ship light. Her breath caught in her throat, and she had to look away again.

"I guess I'm just not ready to be thrown into something else that's new and unfamiliar," she said.

"You cannot stay. I am sorry," he said, a hint of sadness in his tone.

"Why?" Katlyn asked, voice cracking.

"I do not—"

"Expect me to understand. Yeah, I know," she interrupted as she crossed her arms and leaned against the seat.

She looked to her left and noticed a small window at the back of the transport. She finally caught a glimpse of Kel's ship as they descended toward the planet. It almost blended into the darkness that surrounded it. The only reason she knew it was there was because the area was devoid of stars, and she could faintly see the outline of it. It was shaped like a teardrop; fatter at one end, and skinny at the other.

After a moment, Kel crossed her field of vision and sat down next to her.

"I have something for you," he said as he reached into a pocket.

She scoffed lightly. He was sitting right next to her with his thigh rubbing hers. She wasn't sure if it was intentional or accidental, but she turned away from him, withdrawing from his touch.

He held up a fisted hand. A red braided material intertwined around his finger. He opened his fist, and a coin looking pendant dropped down. It had engravings on it that she couldn't possibly recognize. Little symbols that could have been letters. A language she didn't understand. It appeared to be bronze and was about the size of a quarter.

He slipped it over her head. "It is the emblem of my house," he said. The pendant dropped just at the top of her breasts as he pulled her hair through. His cool fingers caressed her skin and made her shudder. "It will guarantee your safety."

"What?" She looked up at him with a scowl.

He took a deep breath as he looked at her. "It will inform others that you are under my protection."

"You really think a piece of jewelry is going to protect me?"

"Yes," he said as if he genuinely believed it, but Katlyn scowled at him anyway.

"Why? If your enemy wants to hurt you in some way, this isn't going to matter."

"I do not expect you to understand," he said... again.

She wanted to punch him in the face.

With clenched teeth, she murmured, "You say that a lot. Maybe you can try, for once, to help me understand. Give me a little credit."

He gazed down at her. "Even enemies have a code they live by, a mutual respect. This is recognized throughout, regardless of lineage or loyalties. I would never harm a human who possesses one, even a human who served my enemy. I am certain that none of my enemies would harm you. How do you think I will be able to protect Nia's family?"

"She doesn't have one."

"When she is released from my service, she will receive hers. Every enemy knows that humans on our ships are under their master's protection. If we are defeated in battle, and our ship boarded, the humans who serve us are not taken as prisoners," he said.

"I really wish you were consistently mean."

Kel tilted his head to the side. "Why?"

"This would be a lot easier." She turned away and began to cry. "I'm sorry that I can be difficult and obstinate sometimes."

"You have nothing to apologize for. Those traits have kept you alive."

They sat in silence for a moment. He finally got up and walked to the pilots, looking outside. Then he sat down on her right side.

"Do not be afraid."

"I'm not afraid," she said defiantly, voice faltering as she rested her head against the seat. Kel was leaning on his right elbow, left hand resting on his left thigh, watching her.

"May I touch you?" he asked.

Katlyn looked at him, confused. "What?"

"You said never to touch you again. I am asking for permission to touch you," he said with a tone that she interpreted as affection.

Her breath caught in her throat and she sobbed again. She felt like the weight of an anvil was crushing her, and she had to look away from him. He sat quietly, watching her, not putting a hand on her, waiting patiently for permission.

Through her sobbing and staggered breathing, she was finally able to tell him that he could touch her. To please touch her. He grasped her arm, lifting her from her seat as he stood and pulled her close to him. He wrapped one arm around her, reaching down her back to embrace her hip. The other hand slipped underneath her hair and grasped the back of her neck. Skin to skin. Cool alien skin on her burning neck. He pulled her as close to him as their bodies would allow. She wrapped her arms under his coat and around his waist, burying her face into his chest. Not knowing if this would be the last time she ever saw him. She didn't dare to ask that question. They held their embrace until the ship landed, and the door opened. Where Katlyn walked bravely into an uncertain future.

17. LEVERAGE

~James

The Amarok was leaving a few days early due to the recent data burst that the Vedans, Earth's supposed allies in the Cygnus galaxy, had abducted James' mother.

His mother always knew there was intelligent life besides Earth. Well, the Vedans were not highly intelligent, apparently, since they traveled to the Milky Way to kidnap his mother. He knew negotiations had gone badly with them, but he wasn't prepared for *this*. It was a bold move on their part, that much was certain. Director Nash was brave enough to pull it off, but why would he? What could he hope to gain? It would take seventeen days to find out—that's how long it would take to get to the edge of the Milky Way, FTL through the void, then punch through the wormhole in Andromeda to reach Cygnus.

During negotiations, Nash asked for help in the war against the dominant presence in that galaxy. A vampiric race, who needed humans for their survival. Nobody from Earth encountered them yet, but James heard plenty of stories about them from the locals. They were called everything from demons to apparitions, and even ghosts, but one thing was assured, they were a leech on the humans in that galaxy. James wanted to help but didn't have the means to do so. They only recently reached Cygnus. Intergalactic travel was still very new to Earth, and still very classified. They only had two ships capable of faster-than-light travel through the void between galaxies, and two were not enough to get involved in an interstellar war.

James settled into his quarters as he thought about his mother. He knew without a doubt that the Vedans' hands would be full. There was no chance that she would be the model prisoner. She would surely make their lives a living hell—a well-deserved living hell, that's for sure.

After unpacking his bag, James headed to the bridge to take his place in the pilot's seat. He was ready to get the show on the road.

~Kel

When Kel returned to the ship, one of the Regent's centurions notified him that the Regent wished to see him right away. He left the hangar bay and went straight to her chambers.

Upon entering her gathering hall, she was sitting in a chair at the table in the center of the room.

"Domina," Kel said, bowing deeply at the waist.

"Join me, Commander. Come sit next to me and touch me so I may share your mind."

"As you wish," he said, then he approached and sat next to her.

She placed her hand on the table between them, palm up. Kel took her hand, obligingly. Her mind was cold, like winter, and although the cool could be refreshing, she was a callous, bitter woman.

'I see you have sent your human away.' The Regent was young and had not mastered hiding her mind. She was very hostile when it came to Katlyn.

'Yes, Domina. She does not belong here.'

'Are you not going to look for her people?'

'Yes, I will, Domina. I gave her my word.'

'Do you think I do not know?'

'Domina?' Kel could feel her suspicion.

'That she comes from a distant star. Perhaps an intact world. That is the only explanation as to why she would help you,' the Regent said.

'I do not believe that to be the case, Domina.' At more than seven millennia in age, he had mastered the ability to deceive others, even when connected through the mind. He was confident Katlyn did come from another galaxy, but he did not wish for his Regent to know.

'Explain!'

'She knew what I was. She saw what I am capable of, but still aided me. Perhaps she had her reasons for doing so. One of them being passage from Veda, which I provided, and I agreed to provide if she freed me.'

'I can feel your passion for that human. Perhaps not at this moment, but when you spoke of her earlier, I felt it,' she said. Kel could feel her bitterness. *'Do not attempt to deny it. I am not a fool!'*

'Domina, please. I am grateful for what she has done for me. She returned me to my Regent,' he said passionately as he stood, maintaining contact with her, and bowed deeply.

'I do not doubt your sincerity. I believe that you are grateful to have returned safely. What I do doubt, Commander, are your intentions.' She was clearly annoyed.

Kel took a deep breath and sat down, still embracing her hand. *'Domina, I believe I have imprinted on her.'* He projected a feeling of uneasiness. *'I do not understand how such a thing could be possible, but I am certain that it has happened,'* he said, bowing his head.

'Ah!' the Regent said, then began to laugh. *'That does explain it. I cannot fault you for something that is beyond your control. However, I am disappointed that you did not tell me before now.'* She was clearly resentful at this discovery, but she was also amused and continued to chuckle as her thoughts

projected to him. *'I still wish for you to be consort, Commander. You cannot keep secrets from me!'*

He was surprised by her reaction to hearing that he imprinted on a human, but as she mentioned, it occurred beyond his control. If he had a choice at the time, he would not have allowed it—but now he refused to fight it.

'Domina, I would be honored—'

'I understand your station permits you the right to refuse my proposal, being Doyen—the Queen's nevos. So, if you were to accept, the honor would be mine. If I am to choose a consort, I would prefer you over any other.'

'You humble me'—he bowed his head—*'I cannot imagine a reason I would refuse your offer, and I know the Queen would bless our nexus. As for the unfortunate situation I find myself in regarding the human, I did not intend to keep that from you. I admit that I was abashed when I realized what occurred. I do not wish to cause you any offense,'* he projected with remorse and regret.

'We shall see. I would very much like to find her people. Perhaps these new humans who hail from a different galaxy are her people. We may be able to use that to our advantage,' she suggested.

'I would like to return to Veda. Perhaps I will be able to extract information from them. She is still unaware of how she arrived here. She does not remember anything before waking up in that cell,' Kel said truthfully.

'Is this going to be a problem for you, Commander? I am familiar with how imprinting works.'

Kel sighed heavily and continued to keep his mind closed to her. *'Domina, you know I cannot harm her. Even if I had not imprinted, I would still be inclined to protect her because of what she has done for me. I have no such loyalty to her people. I will make locating them my top priority if that is what you wish.'*

'Very well. Find her people, as well as the new humans I told you about. Even if they are not one and the same, we could still acquire their technology to travel between galaxies. We would be favored among many for such a discovery.'

They both stood to their feet. Kel bowed deeply as he brought her hands to his forehead. Once she walked away, he turned on his heel and left the gathering hall.

As he made his way to the bridge, he thought of Katlyn, and their embrace before she walked out of his life. He did not believe it would be forever, but he knew once he found her people, she would return home. He would find them, and not for his Regent, but for Katlyn. To get her home where she would be safe. He could not allow his Regent to acquire their technology, and he would do whatever he must to prevent it.

Upon entering the bridge, Kel informed the navigator to return to Veda.

"What is our mission, Commander?" Bry'aere asked.

"Our Regent requested I make finding Katlyn's people a top priority. She is aware that our new enemies from a distant galaxy could be Katlyn's people, and she is interested in acquiring their technology," Kel said to no one in particular.

"I see," Bry'aere said, glancing at Kel.

"She is also aware that I have imprinted on the human," Kel said forcefully, intending for the entire room to hear. Which provoked peculiar looks from everyone. "I will not be ashamed of something I am unable to control. I feel it is important for my men to know. Just as I felt that it was important for our Regent to know."

"Yes, Commander," the men said in unison.

As Kel stood with his hands clasped behind his back, Bry'aere brushed his elbow, signaling him for a private conversation. Kel dropped his arms to his sides so Bry'aere could make contact—skin to skin.

'Please tell me again why you sent her away?' Bry'aere asked. The image of Kel embracing Katlyn on the transport ship shot across his mind. Only with Bry'aere would he have allowed the memory to pass. He pulled it back, as well as the feeling behind it just as quickly as they appeared.

'Because she would not be safe here,' Kel said.

'Why is that? If you informed the Regent that you imprinted, what harm would there be in her staying?'

Kel gave a low growl. He was annoyed with the questions. *'I do not owe you an explanation!'* he snapped with fire.

'No, but you do owe it to yourself, as well as her,' Bry'aere snapped back. *'I saw the image you projected, and quickly withdrew.'*

Kel jerked his hand away. "I will be in my quarters!" he bellowed before walking out the door.

~Katlyn

She sat on a boulder by the river, twiddling the pendant between her fingers. The engravings were smooth, and great care had been taken in its creation. She still had no idea what it meant. Kel said it was the emblem of his house. She figured it was probably a family crest of some kind, but it was mostly symbols. It was probably lettering, his name maybe.

She was really trying to hate him for dumping her on a planet, but no matter how hard she tried, she couldn't get him out of her head. Dropping her somewhere wasn't part of their agreement. Leaving her wasn't part of the plan. He said he'd try to help find her people. He looked for maybe ten minutes before he gave up, and for that, she did hate him—or at least was angry with him for it.

"Jerk!"

She forced her breath out and tossed the pendant back into her dress. She dropped down off the boulder, picked up a couple of water buckets, then turned around to head back into the village—or whatever they called it. It wasn't big enough to be a town, but it was bigger than a village.

Her hostess, Taya, was super friendly—almost too friendly. Why someone would be so kind to a complete stranger was beyond her, especially a stranger dumped off by a Specter Commander. But then again, Katlyn helped a Specter escape a planet after only knowing him a week and having never seen his face. She wasn't one to talk about helping strangers.

"Katlyn, you don't have to walk to the river for water," Taya said as she collected firewood just outside her front door. She was a tad shorter than Katlyn. She had a fair complexion and jet-black hair that she kept twisted into a bun.

"Yes, I know. I don't mind the exercise, and I like to sit and think."

"Someone brought some mending for you."

Katlyn had taken up mending since she arrived. She always was good with a needle. She enjoyed sewing and cross-stitching at home, but on Earth she had a machine for sewing. She could pump out a dress in a matter of hours, but now, she only had her hands. A dress would take much longer, but it would keep her busy and pass the time quickly.

She usually sat outside when she sewed, enjoying the sun and fresh air. The outdoors was something she would have missed being cooped up on a ship. She always enjoyed the outdoors.

"What are the possibilities of me doing this full-time?" Katlyn asked Taya as she stepped into the tiny house they shared. Katlyn had only been there a few days but already felt like a burden. "Making clothes, not just mending, but creating things for people?"

"I think that's a great idea. Most people here do their own sewing, but you've been busy already. So, you can see that they'd rather someone else do it."

"How lucrative do you think dressmaking would be, though?"

"We trade with villages and space travelers, so I don't see why you couldn't make a decent living. At least enough to support yourself," she said, looking at Katlyn.

"I have no idea how long I'll be here. There's no reason I can't support myself in some way," Katlyn said.

"I understand," Taya said with a smile. "You seem very independent. I can understand why you would want to do this."

"I've already made a little money in the short time I've been here."

"Yes, you dove into keeping yourself busy as soon as the Commander left."

Katlyn cleared her throat and looked away when Taya mentioned the Commander. "I just need to get some fabric somehow. Either through buying it or trading. How often does the Commander... or Specter I mean, trade here? I know they have fabric."

"Your Commander is usually here every few weeks. His fleet is the only one that comes here usually. Since we are in their territory."

Taya's words excited Katlyn more than she cared to admit. The thought of seeing Kel again soon made her happy. Then she was overwhelmed with images of her children, and she suddenly grew despondent.

"You may stay with me as long as you need. I have enjoyed your company, but I know you're sad," Taya said with a sympathetic smile.

"I miss my family."

"I understand," Taya said. "Let's work on preparing our next meal together. You can tell me about your family and how you met the Commander. He has never placed anyone here before."

Katlyn chuckled. "Out of all the Specter for me to meet, I met him, a nice guy," she said, rolling her eyes. "Sometimes, I wish he would have just eaten me or whatever and gotten it over with, or finished me off, considering he actually *did* eat me."

Taya's face fell with shock. Her mouth opened, and she stuttered, "You have to explain what you mean!"

Both ladies spent the next couple hours preparing and cooking their meal as Katlyn unloaded. It took a few days, but she finally felt at ease telling Taya everything. Including where she came from.

"That explains why you were willing to help him," Taya said.

"I'd like to think I would have helped him anyway. Even if it were only to help myself," Katlyn said, chuckling. "I'd still be in that cell, or worse if I hadn't helped him. It was a calculated risk." She shrugged.

"I understand."

"We kinda saved each other," Katlyn said wistfully.

~Kel

"Director. Nash, I do not ask for much. Just tell me how to contact her people and why she is here," Kel demanded.

"Why are you so interested, Commander?" Nash garbled as blood filled his mouth.

"That is not your concern," Kel snapped. "I would prefer not to kill you, Director."

Nash scoffed. "I find that hard to believe."

"You appear to be the only one here with the information I require. Taking your life would be counterproductive. Perhaps I should take you to my ship, and merely wait for her people to come for you. Would you prefer to be a prisoner?"

"Not especially," Nash said, then he spat blood onto the floor. "If I'm on your ship, they'd be coming for you, too. I don't think they'd be pleased that you have her."

"I am not the one who abducted her from her home. I aided in her escape from your grasp. I am not concerned about her people. In fact, I would welcome their arrival," Kel said as he leveled his chin to the ground. "Perhaps I will hold you prisoner after all." He looked down at the bleeding man tied to the chair.

"Okay now. That's not necessary. I'll tell you what you want to know if you tell me why," Nash tried negotiating.

Kel bent down and put his hands on the armrest of the chair Nash was bound to. His arms were secured behind the chair, and his feet secured to each leg in the front. Conscripts stood on each side, prepared to knock him in the teeth again if he got out of line. Kel's face was so close they could share the same breath. Nash inhaled deep, holding it as he pulled his head back.

"Why do you wish to know?" Kel asked.

"Professional curiosity."

Kel stood up and squared his shoulders. He placed his hands behind his back as he paced in front of Nash. "Take him to the ship!" he commanded, then turned on his heel.

"Wait!" Nash shrieked.

Kel looked down at him over his shoulder. "Give me a reason not to take you prisoner. I have several reasons to keep you. I would love nothing more than for her people to come to *me*."

"She's from Earth."

Kel growled. "That much, I already know. Tell me something useful. I am losing patience!" He turned to face Nash.

"Her people are always here, but I think they alternate which ship is here at any given time," Nash said.

"How do I contact them?"

"They contact us. I have no idea where they are right now."

"Why did you abduct her?" Kel asked, scowling at Nash.

Nash hesitated, biting his lip.

"Do not make me ask again!"

"We took her to send a message to her son, Captain Wallace. He refused to help us."

"Help you with what?"

Nash took a slow deep breath. "We asked for their help fighting you. They didn't want to get involved."

Kel chuckled. "You abducted Captain Wallace's mother to use her as leverage because they did not wish to fight your war," Kel said. "This is a battle they would not win."

"We did what we thought we had to do."

"I was not aware that your people could travel beyond the void," Kel said with interest. "Why have you not relocated your people altogether? It is a well-known fact that we cannot travel beyond the void."

"I'm not answering any more of your questions. I told you what you wanted to know!" Nash barked at him, spitting more blood onto the floor.

"Humans are so fragile," Kel said with a hint of compassion, eliciting a peculiar look from Nash. "I have no doubt that her people are aware of her abduction. I look forward to them arriving soon to retrieve her." Kel turned toward the exit. "Leave him," he said to the conscripts, who turned to follow.

"You're just going to leave me tied up here?" Nash asked with a frantic tone.

"Your people are merely incapacitated and will free you soon. You will not be captive for long. The same cannot be said for what you did to us!" Kel barked before disappearing down the dark corridor and exiting the bunker.

When he arrived back on the ship, he ordered the navigator to move behind the planet's moon. He would wait for Katlyn's people to come—no matter how long it took.

18. WARNING

~Katlyn

Katlyn was settling in nicely to her new home. It had been a few weeks, and she managed to save up enough to rent a little space from one of the other villagers. It was a single room attached to the main cottage, but she had privacy. Her own space, a fireplace for cooking, and room to sew. She was getting better and faster at hand sewing. She started with making vests, wrap dresses, and even stockings for women. A simple wrap dress could be made easily, and they fit most people. She got the idea from the gowns Nia gave her, except Katlyn had more variety depending on the material. She was a lot busier than she thought she'd be. The locals really did not like sewing. They did it because they had to. So, when they found out she was a seamstress, or could pass for one, they were all incredibly supportive. She earned coin and fabric from mending and doing other menial tasks for people. Whatever it took to get herself established.

Since the weather was consistently warmer during the day, she did most of her work outside, usually by the river where she could be alone. Nobody bothered her there. She mostly kept to herself anyway; she didn't want to get attached to people. She was holding onto hope that Kel would come through for her. She still couldn't help but form attachments—no matter how hard she tried not to. Taya was becoming a dear friend, and she would hate to leave her, but no matter how homey Arlo felt, it wasn't home.

Her children occupied most of her thoughts while she sewed, and no matter how hard she tried not to, she couldn't help but think about Kel. Every time she got dressed, she saw his emblem caressing the cleavage of her breasts, taunting her. Several times she considered taking it off, but couldn't bring herself to do it. Not because she felt like it kept her safe. She still didn't believe that a piece of bronze had that much power. She couldn't take it off because he gave it to her, like a gift. That's how she saw it. As a gift from him, but his protection *was* a gift.

~Kel

"Commander! We have received a communique from one of our outposts," Bry'aere said with urgency. "An enemy has dispatched ships to encroach on several worlds in our territory."

Kel inhaled deep. "Which worlds?"

"It does not say, but they are in this system."

Kel walked to the center of the room, activating the large console. He looked over various star charts and the location of his fleet ships and allies throughout the system.

"Send ships to these worlds," he said, highlighting different planets on the screen. As Arlo appeared, he paused, gazing at the iridescent blue ball that shimmered before him.

"Are we to remain here?" Bry'aere asked as he approached the console. "We have been waiting for over a half-moon. They are bound to show soon."

184

"No, we will rendezvous with her people another time. Make a heading for Arlo," Kel commanded. "I will be in my quarters. Please join me when you are able," he said to Bry'aere, then turned to leave.

Kel was kneeling at the window in his private room watching the little flicks of light skitter by when Bry'aere arrived.

"You pine for her," Bry'aere said.

"I have gone mad!" Kel snapped as he stood to his feet.

"Not at all."

"I spent many cycles locked in a cell, hunger my only company, and a *woman* is how I lose my sanity." Kel sighed and shook his head.

Bry'aere stifled a chuckle. "Women are how most men lose their sanity. They either go mad because of a woman or because they have no woman."

"How could I have imprinted on, *and* have passion for a human?" he asked, turning to look at his friend. "How could this happen? She has consumed my thoughts since her departure."

"No one can control their feelings. How they react to them, that is different."

"Yes, and I am about to act foolishly," Kel retorted.

"What do you mean?"

"Our Regent knows I have imprinted. I have no doubt she suspects more, and I am about to confirm her suspicions by going back to Arlo to retrieve Katlyn. I must go—I cannot stop myself." Kel was flustered and confused. He knew Katlyn would not be safe around the Regent, but she was not secure on Arlo either. The safest place for her was with him until her people were found.

"That is your overwhelming desire to protect her. Our Regent knows this, you said so yourself," Bry'aere said. "If we were not going to Arlo, one of our other ships—"

"She sees me for *who* I am, Bry'aere, not *what* I am," Kel interrupted. "I never realized how stimulating that could be, and her bravery is...I cannot find the words."

"Does she even know what you are?" Bry'aere asked.

"What do you mean?"

"She knows you are a Specter Commander, but does she know you share lineage with the Queen?"

"There is no reason for her to know."

"Your men see you for who you are despite your station. They are loyal to you and will follow you anywhere. They respect you."

"I certainly hope so, because once she is back on this ship, loyalties will be tested."

~James

"Welcome back, Captain," Nash said with an amused smirk on his face.

"Don't give me that shit. Where is she?" James snapped.

Nash stepped back and put his hands up as if to defend himself.

"I'm not going to hit you, not yet. Where is my mother? Why did you abduct her?"

"I was trying to get your attention"

"Well, you have it. Take me to her right now!"

Nash took a couple more steps back. "She's no longer here."

"What do you mean?"

"Well, she escaped," Nash stammered.

James began to laugh, eliciting an unusual look from Director Nash. "Naturally!" James retorted and continued to laugh. "She's my mom. I knew she wouldn't put up with your shit. Where was she last?"

"Well," Nash stammered again, "that's the problem—"

"Get on with it before I punch you in the mouth!" James shouted.

"She escaped with another prisoner," Nash said, wiping the sweat off his brow.

James sighed. "Okay, and? We may be able to detect their life signs."

"She escaped with a Specter Commander. They're not on the planet," Nash said as he took several steps back.

"I'm going to kill you, Nash. I'm not just going to hit you in the mouth. I'm going to kill you!" James howled. "You're a dead man. You're telling me my mom escaped from you *and* escaped the planet... with a Specter of all things? A Commander?" James stifled an astonished laugh.

"Yes, Captain," Nash said, swallowing hard.

James scoffed and laughed wildly. "This honestly doesn't surprise me at all. She is *my* mom, after all. I knew you'd have your hands full."

"Your mom and that Specter killed several of my men when they escaped!"

"I wouldn't care if they killed every man on this planet. I'm just disappointed you weren't one of them!"

"Do you think she's still alive, Captain?" Lieutenant Marks asked.

"I'm sure she is. She has a certain way about her. I have no doubt she convinced that Specter not to kill her, but how do we find them?" James looked at Nash. "How did they leave?"

"He was able to contact his ship somehow."

"You're kidding me!" James barked, full of rage. "My mom is on a ship full of those animals? I should kill you, Nash!" James stepped toward the Director. Lieutenant Marks grabbed James' arm, pulling him back.

"That Commander came back here a few weeks ago asking questions about her. How to contact you and why she was here. He was a little too interested in the information. I'm sure he's close or will come back soon."

"So, this Specter Commander is looking for me?" James asked with apprehension. "That's just great. We've managed to avoid them altogether, and now because of *you,* we can't avoid them any longer." James grumbled in frustration as he walked away with his hands on his hips. "Well, you wanted us involved. It looks like we're involved, but we are *not* your allies in this war. I will meet this Commander *only* to get my mother. You're still on your own," James snapped with irritation, then motioned for his men to leave.

~Katlyn

Katlyn sat perched on a boulder in the sunlight, pushing needle and thread through material. Her stitches were getting quicker and tidier with each piece she created. The sound of the woods and the water were relaxing. It was easy for her to lose track of time, and before she knew it, her piece was finished. Another beautiful creation that she'd see don someone's body.

She felt eyes on her when she dropped the dress down into the basket on the ground. Someone was watching her. But she couldn't see anyone when she looked over her shoulder. She stood up on the boulder and slowly turned around.

"It's rude to stare!" she hollered into the emptiness. Then she sat back down with her knees to her chest facing the river. Not long after, she heard the faint crunching of leaves behind her. "How long were you going to watch me?"

"I was not there long."

The smooth, deep, regal sound caressed her ears, and the smell of honeysuckle tickled her nose. Her breath caught in her throat, and she turned her head in the opposite direction until she was able to breathe again.

"You... uh..." Katlyn stuttered. "I didn't think I'd ever see you again." She was afraid to see his face. She may not want him to leave. "What brings you back so soon?" she asked with hesitation, finally glancing over to him.

"We have just arrived and will stay as long as necessary."

"Why?" Katlyn asked with interest, but he clearly didn't want to tell her. He looked away and leveled his chin—none of that 'only for her' type of look. His was a stern look of seriousness. Even with his stoicism, she could tell something was wrong. "What's going on?" she asked. Still nothing. She dropped down off the boulder and slowly moved closer to him. "Why are you here?"

"I do not need a reason to visit a world in my territory!" he snapped as he looked at her.

Katlyn dragged her tongue across her top teeth and scoffed. "Okay, well, hello to you too!" she snapped back, then grabbed her basket and started to walk away.

"I wish for you to return to the ship with me," he said.

Katlyn spun around and looked at him in disbelief. And there it was, her look. He finally did it—the look he only gave her.

What a jerk! she said to herself. "Why? How do I know you won't get mad and throw me off your ship again?" she snapped at him without intending to.

His eyes darted away from her as he took a deep breath and squared his shoulders. "I was not cross with you."

"Kel," she scoffed. He looked at her again when she said his name. "You can't toss me back and forth. Either leave me here or keep me there. What's going on anyway?"

"This world is no longer safe."

"What do you mean?"

"We have received word that an enemy has decided to invade our territories. We are unsure which worlds they have chosen."

"What about everyone else here?"

"I will do what I can for them if someone arrives, but you are my concern at present."

"No!" she shouted as her basket fell to the ground. "You dumped me here, and I have made friends here. I have to warn them." She turned to run toward the village, but Kel grabbed her arm, pulling her close. "Let go of me!" she screamed as she struggled, attempting to pry his fingers off her arm. "You don't have permission to touch me!" she shouted at him, but his grip only tightened. "Let go!"

The muscles in his face and neck tensed as he gripped her arm. "No!" he said with more force than she ever heard in his voice. The intensity made her breath catch and her eyes widen with shock. "You are running into a battle you cannot win!" She could feel the fierceness of his words as he pulled her closer to him. "I cannot allow you to go. You must come with me now!"

Katlyn's face dropped into an angry scowl, and she continued struggling to free herself. "Allow me? I don't belong to you!" she screamed into his face. His head flinched back. "Let go!" she screamed again, then pulled her free hand back and slapped him across the cheek. He flinched again, and she fell to the ground when he released her arm. She jumped to her feet, and without looking back, she ran toward the village.

~Kel

He righted himself as he watched her run from him. He could easily catch her, but what would he do when he did? Throw her over his shoulder and take her against her will? She was correct; he put her there, and he was the reason she was in danger.

He cursed himself. He still did not know how to behave. Against his better judgment, and disregarding the overwhelming instinctual urge to follow her, he ran aggressively toward his flier. He must return to his ship. He had to believe his emblem would protect her, and if it did not, with the tracking device embedded inside, he would be able to find her.

19. TOGETHER

~Katlyn

At a steady walking pace, it usually took about ten minutes for Katlyn to reach the village from her favorite spot on the river. At a running speed, and in panic, it felt as if it took twice as long. She was a healthy woman, but no matter how hard she pushed herself, she couldn't run the entire distance. She had to stop periodically to catch her breath. Her legs were lead, and her lungs were on fire, despite the brisk air.

She expected Kel to pounce on her any minute, ripping her feet out from under her, forcing her to go with him, but he never came. It seemed as if he let her go, which was good because she'd never forgive him if he didn't allow her to warn the village.

Katlyn must have looked disheveled when she arrived in the village because she drew attention as soon as she stepped foot onto the dirt road at the tree line. She tried warning people when they saw her, but they didn't seem to take her seriously. Like she was some hysterical female. She even told them that the Commander who dropped her off there was the one who warned her, but his lack of presence was not convincing them.

"Taya!" Katlyn yelled, out of breath, as she burst through her door.

"What's going on?"

"Kel was just here..." Katlyn started. Taya gave a puzzled look. "The Commander. The one who dropped me off, he was here."

"What's going on?" she asked again.

"One of his enemies might come here. He tried to get me to leave with him," Katlyn sputtered, still trying to catch her breath.

Taya's expression fell. "If what you say is true, then you should have left with him," she said bluntly.

"I couldn't do that!" Katlyn snapped. "I had to warn you. He was trying to get me to leave with him without warning you." Katlyn inhaled deep, still out of breath from running. "I tried warning others, but they just looked at me like I was crazy."

"That's because nobody ever receives a warning such as this. They are unsure of whether to believe you or not. They may think you're crazy," Taya said. "I know you, and if I had never spoken to this Commander before, even I would be unsure of this information, if I'm completely honest."

"What can we do?"

"Honestly, nothing," Taya said, shrugging her shoulders. "It could be a false alarm. Not that I don't believe what you say is true, but even the Commander doesn't know if they're coming to Arlo or not. You said, 'might.' I'm assuming he didn't confirm it. Just warned you it might happen."

"This is so frustrating!" Katlyn snapped.

"You have done what you can. That is all you can do. I will gather some things, and you and I will go to the cave," she said with a smile.

Katlyn left Taya's home to pack her bag, but as soon as she walked into the village square, she heard screaming and saw people running, followed shortly by conscripts. They looked different than the ones on Kel's ship, but Katlyn knew what they were. She bolted back into Taya's home, grabbed her by the wrist, and jerked her outside. They headed in the direction of a cave she found not too long ago, but they didn't get far. Conscripts and what Katlyn assumed were soldiers or warriors blocked the dirt road.

The conscripts began rounding people up, binding their hands in front of them as they crowded everyone together on the road. Katlyn and Taya tried to run in a different direction, in between cottages to the forest, but their escape was cut off when a conscript appeared out of nowhere. He grabbed them both by the neck when they tried to run past him. He was squeezing so hard they were wheezing, trying desperately to pry his fingers loose. He dragged them to where the others were being held, and their hands were bound. The binding tore through Katlyn's skin, and she was already bleeding when she was forced to her knees with the others.

"Katlyn, you should tell them," Taya whispered into her ear. Her voice cracked as she spoke.

Katlyn looked at her, furrowing her brow. "Tell them what?" she whispered. Taya looked at her, eyes glazing over, then glanced down toward Katlyn's chest. Katlyn followed her gaze to the red cord around her neck. "No!" she said firmly.

"But you are safe," Taya reminded her.

"I'm not going to save myself while the rest of you suffer," Katlyn said. "No!"

"Katlyn—"

"Drop it! I'm not doing it."

Taya's breath shuddered as she and Katlyn looked at each other. Then suddenly, Taya jumped to her feet. "This woman is under another Commander's protection!" she managed to shout before being hit in the shoulder with a weapon, forcing her back to the ground. Katlyn caught her with her bound hands before she hit the dirt.

"Who?" one of the soldiers demanded. Katlyn remained silent, keeping her head down while the women around them were stood up and inspected. Then someone grabbed Katlyn's arm, yanking her to her feet. He saw the cord around her neck and pulled the pendant out of her dress. He drug her to another man who Katlyn assumed was in charge.

"Why did you not speak up?" he asked. Katlyn didn't answer him. She looked straight ahead, squaring her shoulders. He was dressed more like the soldiers, but she wasn't sure if he was one, or a Commander.

When she met his gaze, he struck her in the face, knocking her to the ground. The forceful blow knocked the wind out of her and made her nose bleed; pain shot through the side of her face. She was sure he had broken her cheekbone. She gasped for air as a conscript forced her to her feet.

"It doesn't matter why," the beast snapped as he held the emblem in his hand, inspecting it. "Doyen," he said, raising an eyebrow. "He doesn't bestow these on many. If you have acquired one, you are significant in some way. He may overlook this infraction—encroaching on his territory, but if I take you, he will not be so merciful." He released the pendant.

"I'm not more important than anyone else here!" Katlyn snarled at him despite the pain radiating through her face. Her eye was swelling, and she could barely hold it open. Her balance wavered and her head began to throb.

"He is here, in orbit above this world," the beast said, looking up toward the sky. "Our fliers are battling as we speak. He will come to you soon." He looked down at Katlyn. "Release her!" he barked. She tried to run back to Taya, only to be hit by a sudden bolt of electricity. Her vision tunneled, and she was unconscious before she hit the ground.

***

Katlyn woke up to the pitter-patter of rain stinging her face. She opened her eyes and looked for Taya, but everyone was gone. Her head was pounding when she sat up, and she saw what she assumed were fliers overhead. Several of them appeared to be battling each other.

With her hands bound and face stinging from the rain, she scurried to her feet and bolted into the forest to take shelter in the cave. It wasn't far, but the sun was setting quickly. Katlyn's eye was swollen shut, and her hands being bound made the trek challenging.

She fell several times climbing the short hill to the cave but reached it relatively unscathed. It wasn't big, maybe a few adults could fit in there snuggly, but couldn't stand up straight. She bent at the waist to walk in and dropped to her knees as she rounded a short corner where she'd be protected from the wind. She pulled her knees to her chest, her face ached, and her head throbbed. Her wrists burned as the binding cut into her skin. She couldn't find a comfortable position, but it didn't matter. The pain she was in was overwhelming. She quickly succumbed to the exhaustion, and her head fell back against the stone when she passed out.

***

"Katlyn, wake up." A hand caressed her cheek. She slowly opened her eyes, forgetting about the swelling until she saw a dim light radiating from a device in Kel's hand. She squinted, and the pain overwhelmed her, causing her to cry out. "Let me see," he whispered, caressing her chin. She flinched away and buried her face into the stone as she began to weep. He pulled out a knife to remove her restraints, which were stuck into the wounds they created. She stifled a whimper and tried to fight back the tears. Her face hurt too much to cry, but it hurt so much she couldn't stop it. "Are you able to walk?" he asked.

"Yes," she mumbled. "How did you find me?" She finally turned her head to look at his face.

When he saw her, his expression tightened, and his eyes flashed fire. He was clearly pissed. "I am a hunter," he said candidly. His mouth was agape, and he was hissing through his teeth. "Are you able to leave this cave on your own? I will carry you the rest of the way."

Katlyn accepted his outstretched hand, and he guided her out of the cave. He lifted her gracefully and cradled her in his arms as soon as they were able to stand upright. She wrapped her arms around his neck and buried her face as he began to walk.

"Where are we going?"

"I know where you have been living. We will go there so you may gather your things. We will leave at first light."

The nights were still chilly, and the morning was a full night away. So, upon entering the room, he laid her gently on her bed, then lit a fire. She wasn't there long before sitting up, breathing heavily. Her entire body ached.

"I fell in the mud earlier. I'd like to wash off," she muttered.

"I will step outside. When you are ready, I will heal your wounds."

"You don't have to leave. I have a divider," she said, pointing to the paneled divider at the end of the small room. "I may live here alone, but I'm still not used to washing and changing in the same place I eat." She laughed, but the pain stopped her, and she hissed sharply through her teeth.

"Very well," he said as he crouched down in front of the fire.

The room was small, and her bed was right next to the fireplace, but far enough away so stray embers weren't a problem. Kel was crouched right next to her bed, and the light of the fire danced on the side of his face as he looked at her. She could smell him, and she inhaled his scent deeply. Then she got up and stepped behind the divider.

The water was freezing, and she yelped and winced. She washed quickly and pulled a nightgown over her head.

"How did you know where I live?" she asked Kel when she sat back down on the bed.

"I know your scent," he said as if that were a totally normal thing to say to someone, but then she chuckled because *she* knew *his* scent. "What do you find amusing?"

"You know my scent. That would be totally pervy on Earth," she said, laughing gently, pain shooting through her face again.

Kel cocked his head to the side. "Pervy?"

Katlyn chuckled again. "Weird, creepy, but a totally normal thing coming from you," she said as she reached up to her face. He stopped her, placing her hand back into her lap.

"Lie down. I will heal your wounds if you wish," he said, then removed his coat and knelt back down beside the bed. "I will start here." He reached for her cheek as her head fell onto the pillow. His hand was cool on her hot swollen skin, and it covered the entire side of her face. "Please do not resist."

"What do you mean?" Katlyn asked warily.

"I am sure you remember when I healed your feet," he reminded her.

Her other cheek flushed. She remembered how it made her feel—it was arousing, and she had to kick him away.

"Yes," she whispered, looking away and swallowing hard. "I'm ready," she lied.

She couldn't look at him. She fisted her hands together and bit her lip as the energy moved through her body. She had to concentrate, so she didn't make a fool of herself again like last time, but she couldn't help it. She had no control over what was happening. She suppressed a moan when she became so aroused that she had to squeeze her thighs together to stifle the heat. Her heart was racing, pounding in her chest when he finished.

"The break is healed, and the swelling is gone. I could not heal the bruise. Where are any other injuries besides your wrists?"

She opened her eyes to look at him. She inhaled sharply, reaching up to her now healed face. "My knees from falling," she said as he rubbed his hands down the sides of her body. She winced in pain when he touched her left hip. "I have no idea where that came from," she said, startled. Kel averted his eyes while she lifted her gown enough to see the injury on her hip. "That must have happened when I fell after one of those bastards shot me," she growled. "I didn't realize it was there because my face was distracting me."

"I will heal your wrists now."

As he began to massage her wrists one at a time, he said, "If it is not my business, please say so." He looked at her. "When did your mate pass?"

Katlyn took a sharp breath, glancing away from him. "My husband. People don't usually call each other mates on Earth, although that is an accurate term. He died about two years ago." She bit her bottom lip as their gazes met. She welcomed the distraction. She noticed the sensation as he healed her wrists, but talking distracted her from it.

"How did he pass?" he asked when he moved to her knees.

What a way to distract someone, she thought to herself. "I'm not sure exactly. He was in the military and did a lot of things he couldn't tell me about. They never went into detail about his death."

When Kel finished healing her knees, he hesitated as he looked up at her. Was he waiting for permission to treat her hip? She moistened her lips and swallowed hard, then nodded her consent.

Her breathing shuddered, and her pulse quickened as Kel moved his hand underneath her gown to grip her naked hip. His touch was cool and firm, and his other hand gripped her waist. She stifled a quiet moan and grabbed his arms, but loosened her grip just as quickly and held her breath as the energy surged through her body. Her mouth fell open, and her head flew back when she became aroused. He was so close to her thighs that she lost all control of her faculties. She wouldn't have fought it even if she could.

She was filled with passion, and she knew that he knew it. She couldn't stop herself. She wanted nothing more at that moment than to be with him. She didn't care who or what he was. She hadn't felt that way ever in her life. It felt as if he responded to her every move. As her need increased, so did his attention. Her arousal spilled out of her, climaxing just from the energy between them. Waves of euphoria washed over her body. A fire was building inside of her, consuming her.

Her body had a mind of its own. Her legs parted as if to invite him in. His cool hands caressed her thighs, and she felt his chin on her knee. She couldn't control the moans of pleasure that escaped her. She shuddered when his lips touched the tender flesh of her inner thigh. His silken hair fell over his shoulder onto her leg. She clenched the bed sheet as her pleasure grew. A sudden cool breath tickled the crook of her thigh, causing her to cry out and grab his hands, holding them as he met her gaze.

~Kel

He felt the energy as it pulsed through both their bodies. Her scent was musky, sweet, carnal, and became stronger as he progressed. The leg closest to him bent up suddenly at the knee as her need increased. He opened his mouth as her aroma overwhelmed his senses, their desire growing together.

Both hands caressed the inside of her thighs, and his chin brushed her knee. She was no longer stifling her pleasure. Her head was back, baring her neck to him as her breath caught in her throat before escaping her lips as desire.

He exhaled slowly as his lips traded places with his hands, moving tenderly along her delicate skin. Her scent was overpowering, and he could almost taste her. Her gown still guarded her modesty while he explored, touched, pleased her. She was clenching the bed linen when he exhaled at the source of her arousal. Then she cried out and grabbed his hands, stopping him.

Their gazes met, and he saw confusion in her eyes. He pulled away and stood straight to his feet.

"I am sorry. I should not have done that. Please forgive me," he said, just as confused as she seemed to be. He then grabbed his coat and stepped outside.

Her scent lingered in his nose and mouth even as he inhaled the crisp nighttime air. He wanted nothing more than to take her in his arms, wrap her body around his, but he could not. Not like this. She was too vulnerable at that moment, the confusion showing on her face. He would not take advantage of her. He had never desired something or someone so badly. This was more than imprinting—his desire to bond with her was overpowering. Another thing that had never been done between Specter and human. His Regent would surely kill them both if he acted on such a desire. His deep-seated need to protect her was clouding his judgment, but at the same time, he knew bonding with her would forever protect her from any Specter who would steal her essence. Even if the bond only happened once, and he never touched her again. There was no greater protection than bonding.

~Katlyn

Katlyn got up from the bed and washed vigorously with icy cold water. She was confused. She should not want him touching her like that, or at all. But anytime he was around her, his presence consumed her. He could have taken her at that moment, and she would have let him. She would have allowed this man, this alien, a Specter who consumed humans, to have her. She was suddenly disgusted with herself; she should not want him—but she did. Even at that moment, all she could think about was him and his hands exploring every inch of her body. Him on top of her with her legs wrapped around him. And she felt ashamed for it.

She gathered her clothes and got dressed. She still had the shift that Nia gave her, but she also made one of her own. The same basic design, but even better support for her full breasts. There were no bras, but she couldn't just let the girls loose to fend for themselves, so she improvised.

She put one of her dark blue wrap dresses on and packed the others that she made. She wasn't about to leave her hard work behind. She began to question if she should leave at all. Would Kel get upset with her again after this incident and dump her on another planet? If he did it again, she would never forgive him. He couldn't just boot her off the ship every time *he* did something he shouldn't.

She put on a pair of underwear and stockings, then tossed the rest into her bag. There were no underwear either, so she made those, too. She put her cloak on before climbing back into bed, facing the door. She could see Kel's silhouette outside her window. She wished he'd come back in so she could see his beautiful physique, but at the same time, she hoped never to see him again. She hated herself at that moment.

Morning took forever to arrive. Katlyn couldn't sleep, and Kel never came back in. His silhouette eventually disappeared from her view. She had no idea where he was or what he was doing until the first rays of sun crept over the horizon, and he knocked on the door.

Just come in, you jerk, she thought as she rolled her eyes. She opened the door with her bag in hand and followed him out of the village—neither of them saying a word.

They trekked through the woods for at least a mile. Mostly uphill, with Kel leading the way. He didn't glance back once to make sure she was still there, but then again, he could probably hear her the entire time. She was struggling to keep up with his long aggressive strides.

She had to bite her lip several times to resist the urge to ask him where they were going. She refused to speak to him unless necessary. At least he was carrying her bag for her. He was being a ginormous dick, but being a gentleman was ingrained in him. He was even regal when he was being an asshole—a regal asshole.

They finally reached the top of what seemed like a mountain. It looked familiar, like the place the conscripts landed to dump her there. It was just a large clearing, almost intentional. A small ship was sitting in the clearing, but it wasn't a transport. It looked eerily similar to a fighter jet—only shinier, no landing gear, and more alienish.

When Kel approached the ship, a couple of steps popped out from the side, and the canopy opened. *I hope he doesn't expect both of us to ride together in a single passenger seat,* Katlyn said to herself, growling quietly.

Kel ascended the steps and put her bag in. She assumed behind the seat, but she was hoping that he put it in the *back* seat, where she would be sitting.

He dropped his right leg down to the bottom step and reached out to her. *Please no! I can't sit on his lap,* she prayed as panic set in. The way he was presenting himself to her, she could see the strength in his chest and legs. She started chewing on her lip and took a deep breath as she approached him.

"There is only one seat."

I hate you right now!

"I rushed to return. This is much faster than a transport." He must have seen her annoyance; she wasn't trying to hide it, though. "I am sorry," he said when she took his hand. "Step onto the second step and hold here." He pointed to a handhold above her head. "I will lift you in."

Of course, she thought, stifling an awkward chuckle, and refusing to look at him.

His massive body was against hers before he climbed into the cockpit. For a moment, he was in a delicate position, and she could have punched him right in between the legs, and not even felt bad about it. She would be sitting on his lap soon, and the urge to punch him in the junk out of spite was overwhelming—but for both their sakes, she resisted. She imagined he wouldn't even be a regal asshole at that point; instead, he might just rip her throat out.

"Are you ready?" He interrupted her thoughts as he reached for her. She looked up to him and he gripped underneath her arms, lifting her as if she were weightless. He placed her gingerly next to him—literally next to him, touching his thick body.

I really hate you right now. She was so glad he couldn't read her mind. He left her frustrated just hours before, and now she had to sit on his lap.

They were both standing where Katlyn imagined the pilot's legs and feet would go. Kel just stood there, staring down at her. She rolled her eyes dramatically and then burst into a fit of laughter. She couldn't stop herself. She couldn't even look up at him, but she was sure he was looking at her like she sprouted a second head.

"I'm sorry," she forced out, trying to stifle her laughter, but failing. She snorted loudly and continued laughing. Full belly laughs, struggling to stand upright, and nearly falling into him. Tears began streaming down her cheeks as she covered her face with her hands. She finally looked up to him, and to her surprise, he wasn't looking at her like she had gone insane. His face softened, and he gave her that look that was reserved for her, his mouth in a smirk. "Please sit down," she finally spat out.

Kel maintained the smirk, and his eye contact with her, as he scooted into the seat seductively. He squared his shoulders and opened his coat, baring his meaty lap to her.

Is he flirting?

One of her weaknesses was not being able to stay mad at people for long. She looked down at him, smiling, and trying not to laugh as a broad smile formed across his face.

Yep, he's definitely flirting, she thought to herself. "I'm trying to be mad at you, but you're making it very difficult," she said aloud.

He responded with a gentle tilt of his head and shrug of his shoulder.

With a huge smile across her own face, she slid into his lap rather aggressively—her back directly into his chest and her ass into his groin. He made a sound she interpreted as a moan or growl right into her ear—she wasn't quite sure. All she could think about at that moment was that she hadn't been that close to a man's groin in more than two years.

"I need to reposition you," he said.

I'm sure you do, cowboy, she thought and smirked as he moved her onto one side of his lap. She was now turned into him, and her legs were more in his lap than on the floor.

He fiddled with some buttons on the opposite side of her, then the canopy snapped shut, and the piloting gear moved right to where her legs had been.

Damn! She was hoping he moved her because she was sitting on his junk.

She didn't realize the engines started until they lifted off the ground. Kel must have felt her body tense up because he asked if there was any kind of flight on Earth. She told him that she flew all the time, but never did like takeoff.

She watched the trees get smaller as they went straight up. Kel motioned for her to look toward the front, then they bolted forward at an incredible speed. The sudden forward motion caused her to flinch right into Kel's chest—as if the inertia pushed her back. He began to laugh with a broad toothy smile on his face.

Katlyn turned her head to look in front of her, out the side of the ship. She watched the world below become smaller, and the sky get darker. Of course, she could also see Kel's formidable profile taunting her. The way his collar covered part of his neck as if hiding something that only a lover should see, stirred her for some reason. Or maybe it was the tattoo peeking out that teased her. For reasons she couldn't explain that moment felt even more intimate than her thighs being splayed open before him just hours before. Maybe it was because she was sitting in his lap, or maybe it was because she felt compelled to bite his neck. It was right in her face, calling for her. She had so much aggression toward him at that moment, she wanted to cause him physical pain, but at the same time, she wanted him.

She was suddenly aroused again. *Damn this body. I hate you too!* She was aggravated, and of course, he knew it. He had the nose of a bloodhound. His mouth opened slightly, and his nostrils flared. *I hope we crash or explode in space,* she thought to herself as she dropped her head in defeat.

It didn't take long for them to reach space. Kel positioned the flier so the big blue and green planet that was behind them was now on their port side so she could see it. Then they stopped moving.

She gasped in awe, barely able to catch her breath. She gawked at the beautiful orb in front of her as if she never saw anything majestic before.

"It looks like Earth," she said. Then she was overcome with emotion.

~Kel

From their previous conversations, Kel knew that Katlyn had only seen still images, photographs she called them, of her planet. Being in the flier was an opportunity to show her the beauty of space.

He put the planet to the port side of them, then shut off the engines. Katlyn gasped as her eyes widened. Then her mouth came open, and she said, "It looks like Earth."

Her body tensed as soon as the words came out. She was visibly overcome with emotion, but it was not sadness he sensed, it was indignation. He could feel her rage and fury. The muscles in her neck tightened with each heave of her chest. Her temperature rose, and her body trembled against him.

He wished to soothe her, but he knew touching her at that moment was not wise, especially in the confined space of the flier. If she shattered, she was liable to do anything. He would not harm her, but he would have to restrain her, so she did not harm herself.

Her breathing became more ragged as she inhaled, forcing the air through her nose. Her jaw clenched, but her lips were parted, and a sound escaped her that he never heard before. He could tell by her breathing the pressure was building. She was about to erupt. He attempted the only thing he could at that moment. "I have information about your people," he whispered, lowering his chin to look at her.

Katlyn's expression softened when she looked up to him. "What?" she asked, her rage dissipating.

"I returned to Veda." Her mouth fell open slightly, and her breathing steadied. "I spoke with Nash, the Director. After some convincing, he gave me the information I requested."

Katlyn's mouth began to form into a question, but he interrupted her. "I know you have questions, and you have my word that I will answer them once we are back on my ship," he said as he projected a feeling of calm over her. She seemed appeased; she made no further sounds.

20. LIFE

~Katlyn

Once they were back on the ship, Kel told her to unpack her things and take her time getting settled in, and he would wait in the sitting room. She was tempted to take a hot bath but chose to wait because she had questions. Instead, she took her shoes off, unpacked her bag, and put her things in the wardrobe. She was hesitant even to do that because she wasn't sure what was going to happen next. When she was finished and felt like she made Kel wait long enough, she went to meet him.

When she stepped into the sitting room, Kel was standing at the window—striking his usual stoic pose until he turned to face her. He invited her to sit on one of the cushioned bench seats. She sat down, and—out of everywhere to sit in that room—he sat down next to her, almost touching her with his massive thigh. Katlyn began playing with her feet out of nervousness. Her stocking covered toes peeked out from the hem of her dress.

"What are those?" Kel asked, looking curiously at her feet.

Katlyn drew her head back for a moment out of confusion. "Uh... back home, we call those feet," she said with a sarcastic tone.

Kel looked at her, raising one eyebrow. "What is *on* your feet?"

Katlyn began to snicker. "Those are stockings," she said, stifling an awkward laugh.

"I have never seen women wear anything on their feet, such as this."

"I made them myself. They keep my legs warm. I'm used to wearing pants." She caught him gazing down at her legs. His mouth came slightly open as he looked at her from foot to hip.

"Do they cover your legs as trousers do?" he asked as if he never saw a woman cover her legs before, but then again, maybe he hadn't. Katlyn had seen a lot of people, but all the women he interacted with every day wore dresses.

"Up to my thighs," she said, rubbing her thighs with her hands. Her face was stoic and emotionless as he looked at her, then looked at her thighs with a curious look on his face. She breathed in deep then pulled open the bottom front hem of her dress to expose the thigh closest to him. The stocking stopped just above the knee at the swell of her thigh and was laced with colored ribbon.

She was still aroused from earlier, and she couldn't help herself when she separated her legs gently, knowing he could sense her. Kel's head flinched back as if he were slapped in the face. He looked at her with glistening ruby eyes, then quickly looked away.

"Did I embarrass you?" she asked, trying not to laugh.

He sat back, squaring his shoulders. "No," he said firmly.

"You were looking at me like you wanted to see what I was talking about," she said straight-faced. He said nothing, just squared his shoulders more, and turned away from her. "I don't know why you're acting like that. You've already seen them," she huffed.

He snapped his head around to face her with the same intensity and speed she'd seen when he was fighting. As if he were an apparition. "I should not see you in this way." His tone was flat and dispassionate, but his eyes seemed to convey a different emotion. "I should not have done that."

Katlyn covered her leg and crossed her arms at her chest as she leaned back. "Are you going to get mad at me again and kick me off your ship?"

"I was not cross with you when I sent you to Arlo," he said as his shoulders softened and he looked at her. "You may stay here as long as you wish."

"How do I know you won't take me somewhere else again without discussing it with me first?"

"I will not."

"Please forgive me if I don't believe you. You were quick to get rid of me before."

"You have my word," he said, gently bowing his head toward her. "I will not relocate you without discussing it with you first. You may stay as long as you wish."

"I do have some questions."

"Please, go ahead," he said, waving his right hand between them, then placed it on his thigh as he leaned on his left knee.

Katlyn noticed that he only appeared to relax around her. Maybe that's because he knew she was no match for him. He could do whatever he wanted to her, and she'd never be able to fight him off. *I wish he would do things to me,* she thought to herself, but quickly pushed that to the side. She cleared her throat. "I have a lot of questions, actually. Not just about my people, but other things, too." He nodded. "Please tell me about my people," she asked as she dropped her hands into her lap.

Kel told her about his trip to Veda, and Nash revealing why she was there. "I knew my son did things that he couldn't tell me, but I never imagined anything like this," she said solemnly, then scoffed. "I cannot believe my son's work got me abducted by aliens!" she snapped, crossing her arms at her chest. "So, what do we do now?"

"We will return to Veda and wait for your son. I gave you my word that I would do what I can to return you home, but please keep in mind, they may have already arrived. We may have missed them. I will go back to speak with Nash."

"We're bound to run into one of their ships, I would imagine," she said. "How are they already your enemy if you haven't even met them yet?"

Kel took a deep breath. "My Regent declared them our enemy. That was not my decision." Katlyn scowled at him. "Because of their technology. Their ability to travel the void," he said candidly. "Humans are naturally our enemy. I am sure you can understand why."

"Why is another Specter Commander your enemy?"

"Do all humans on your world coexist peacefully?"

She shrugged. "I see your point."

"There are other factions who desire to dominate this galaxy. And some of them wish to overthrow the Queen on our homeworld. My Regent and my fleet defend her interests."

Katlyn sat quiet for a moment. "Okay, I have another question." He nodded for her to continue. "Why is Arlo in your territory? What does that mean?"

"You do not wish for me to answer that question," he said flatly.

Katlyn rolled her eyes. "Look, let's get one thing straight," she said as she leaned forward and dropped her hands to her lap. "I'm inquisitive. I'm also a grown-ass woman. If I *ask* a question, it's because I'd like an answer," she said abrasively. "I wouldn't ask if I didn't want to know."

"Very well," he said as he gently nodded. "We reap these worlds."

"Reap as in harvest, like cattle."

"Yes."

"Why are they so accommodating to their enemy?"

"They do not have a choice. Most of the worlds in this galaxy do not have the ability to resist. Some worlds are spacefarers, but most lack the ability to defend themselves against us."

"How do the populations on these planets sustain all of you? The village on Arlo wasn't big."

"We go into a state of quiescence or dormancy. Most of the men in my fleet are in that state now, but can be awakened at a moment's notice," he said. "We do not experience hunger while in such a state. Even if we were all vigilant at the same time, there are hundreds of thousands of populated worlds within our reach. Even without quiescence, there are enough humans to sustain us. The population of our homeworld is less than five-hundred-thousand, half are dormant at any given time—either on the planet or a ship like this one."

"Have you ever considered looking into other options?" she asked, raising an eyebrow.

"Such as?"

"I don't know." She shrugged. "You already said you eat regular food before you reach maturity. And can eat food now, it just doesn't digest like it does for humans."

"That is correct."

"Maybe figure out some way to use that in your favor," she suggested. "To be able to digest food, get nourishment from that. Since you desire peace and all."

Kel looked at her for a moment. "That would be worth exploring," he said. "I will speak with my analyst."

"Really? Just like that, you'll consider it?"

"Yes."

"Why?" she asked with disbelief. He mentioned wishing for peace, but she was skeptical that he'd agree so quickly to something so drastic.

"Many desire peaceful coexistence. Would this not please you?" he asked as he looked at her with that look that made her insides stir. She had to look away from him. "Do you have more questions?"

"I always have questions, but some may be too personal," she said, giving him a sideways glance.

"I will answer your questions, but first, we must go to Cora before returning to Veda. Please give me a moment," he said, then contacted the bridge. Only moments later, Katlyn could see tiny specks of light flashing by in the window. "We will return to Veda—I gave you my word. We have already missed our scheduled rendezvous on Cora, and we are running low on provisions." He looked at her. "Please, continue," he said as he took a relaxed sitting position with his elbow resting on one knee while gripping his thunderous thigh with the other.

Katlyn cleared her throat. "What does Doyen mean?"

Kel's neck tensed. "Where did you hear that?"

"The guy who hit me said it when he saw my pendant."

Kel took a slow deep breath as he looked at her. "That fleet is one of our greatest enemies," he said before looking away. "I am Doyen—leader. I command one of the Queen's fleets and represent her interests. I know her personally. I am a Commander, but I am in a higher position than most."

"Out of all Specter for me to meet."

"Moirai."

Katlyn stifled a chuckle and smiled. "I have another question." Kel waved his hand and lowered his chin slightly. "What does hunger feel like?"

He looked up briefly, then said, "Fire, as if a fiery stone is pressing on me. My chest smolders with every breath."

"How long can you go?"

"I was on Veda for more than seven of their cycles. That is the longest I have ever gone, but under normal circumstances, I can go three of our cycles before the discomfort begins."

"You could go with only hurting one human every few months?"

"Yes, as long as I am not injured."

Katlyn sat in silence for a moment, hands resting on her legs. "Do you enjoy it?" she asked.

He hesitated. "Yes, but not for the reasons you would imagine."

"What do you mean?" she asked, tilting her head to one side.

"It feels pleasurable, but you can feel pleasure without enjoying it. As for enjoying it, I would imagine it to be similar to quenching your thirst. You enjoy it because you are no longer thirsty," he explained.

"What does it feel like when you give it back?" she asked as she shifted her body toward him.

"It differs with who and why."

"If it's a friend?" She shrugged.

"It is enjoyable in a friendly or familiar way."

"A lover?" she asked hesitantly, tucking a thick curl behind her ear as she glanced away from him.

Kel inhaled deeply and appeared to hold his breath as he looked at her. His eyes twinkled like rubies. "It is similar to the apex of sexual intimacy," he said as he sat up, raising his chin but still locked in her gaze.

Katlyn moistened her lips and began to chew on them. She wanted to ask, but at the same time, she didn't. Her curiosity would be the death of her. "What about when you did it to me?" she asked, timidly. Kel continued to gaze at her, eyes twinkling. He looked at her in a way that made her womb ache. She had to shift her body to stifle the heat that crept up within her. "You don't want to tell me?"

He sighed as if trying to avoid the question. "It is difficult to explain. It was nothing like I have ever experienced. I never gave life to a human before, and you were injured. I suspect it would be different if you were uninjured," he said. "What was it like for you? Having it taken as well as receiving?" he asked as he shifted his body to face her.

Katlyn gave an awkward chuckle. "Well, having it taken felt like all my organs were going to combust. Like my nerves were burning and being pulled through my nose and mouth," she said as she looked away briefly. Recalling the memory made her uncomfortable. "It was the most painful thing I've ever experienced."

"I am sorry."

"I gave you permission. If I knew then what I know now, I still would have done it," she said truthfully.

"Why?" he asked, lowering his chin.

Katlyn rubbed her neck and tried to avert his gaze, but couldn't pull herself away. "I don't know, but I can honestly say that if you needed help again, I would help you if I could."

"Even knowing what I am?"

"You aren't a monster, despite what you might think about yourself. Everyone has parts of themselves they don't like or wish they could change."

"Thank you," Kel said softly as they looked at each other.

Katlyn cleared her throat. "As for receiving, I can't say. I was in and out of consciousness, so I don't remember." A sultry hunger was in his eyes. The look made her feverish, and her already aching womb was begging to be filled. She had to squeeze her thighs together to calm her arousal. He crossed his arms at his chest as he leaned against the wall. "Why are you looking at me like that?"

"I would very much like to know what the experience was like for you," he said. His red eyes seemed to bore through her. "I would be happy to do it again," he offered without hesitation. Almost in a needy way. As if he needed to do it again.

She shook her head. "I don't want you to hurt or kill anyone just to appease your curiosity."

"That would not be necessary. I am at full strength. I had to take a life because I was in a weakened state, but you should know that because you are in full health, doing so would add years to your life." She furrowed her brow. "It would make you younger."

"Like a fountain of youth?" she asked, then let out a boisterous laugh. He simply nodded as his lips parted gently, eyes still fixated on her with that hungry sultry look. Katlyn didn't know how to interpret his behavior toward her.

"You're very difficult to read," she said, still chuckling.

"The same could be said for you."

"One minute you're telling me that something is too personal, then you're sharing information with me. Then

213

dumping me on a planet for some reason, and now you want to do this," she said as she waved a hand between them.

"Consider this, scientific curiosity," he said with a faint smirk.

"Okay," she said, laughing and rolling her eyes. After several minutes of silence, he was still looking at her. "You're serious, aren't you?" she asked in disbelief.

"Why do you doubt my sincerity?" He almost sounded offended. His hands now clasped gently in his lap, and his head tilted slightly.

"I'm sorry. I didn't mean to offend you."

"I am not offended. It was merely a suggestion in the spirit of openness since we are having a friendly conversation. I am genuinely interested in what the experience is like for you," he said as he waved his hand toward her. "I realize you find my behavior puzzling. I have told you before that I have never had this type of association with a human. I find myself not knowing how to behave with you." His bluntness caught her off guard and made her cheeks warm.

"Well, that kinda explains a lot, to be honest. I'm assuming that receiving it won't be painful for me. If it's anything at all like..." she hesitated, "then I don't want to."

"I assure you; it is *nothing* at all like having it taken. I have experienced that myself."

"You can do that to each other?" Her brow furrowed, and her voice elevated.

"Yes. I allowed an enemy to get too close. It was a mistake I will never allow to be repeated," he said flatly. "Consider my offer. We can do it another time, or not at all, but if you agree, you must tell me what the experience is like," he said as he looked at her seductively.

Her cheeks flushed. "As long as it doesn't hurt, then I'm game, I guess." She began to chew on her bottom lip. "You know I'm trusting you because you could choose *not* to—"

"If I wished to harm you, I could easily overpower you," he interrupted. "I would not need to mislead you. I would hope by now you would trust that I will not harm you," he said with a hint of sadness in his tone that made Katlyn feel ashamed.

"I trust you," she said truthfully.

Kel stood to his feet and held his hand out to her. "I do not suspect anyone will enter my quarters, but I would prefer to go somewhere more private."

Oh no, she thought to herself when she took his outstretched hand. "Okay," she said as he led her to her bedroom.

"We do not normally share these experiences communally as humans do." He activated the door control, then locked it once they stepped into the room.

"That explains why you thought humans ate in private," she said, looking up at him.

He continued to hold her hand as they reached the middle of the room. His skin was cool, and she was sure his natural temperature was several degrees lower than hers. Even two or three degrees would be enough to notice, especially since she was usually fevered around him.

Why did I agree to do this? she said to herself when he removed his coat and laid it on the window seat. She started chewing on her bottom lip and fidgeting with her hands.

"You are free to change your mind." He must have noticed how nervous she was acting.

"Nope," she squeaked out without looking at him. "I'm a little curious, to be honest," she admitted. She *was* curious, but not for scientific reasons. Him healing her did things to her body, and she was dying to know what giving life would do, but something told her that it had nothing to do with scientific curiosity for him either.

"Very well," he said, then moved closer to the bed.

You have got to be kidding me, she said to herself. *If he gets on my bed, it's over.* But he didn't. He just stood next to her bed. *Maybe he's standing there in case I collapse, which could happen as soon as he puts his hands on me. Shut up Katlyn and walk over there!* She tried to coax herself when she realized her feet were already moving, and before she knew it, she was standing in front of him. His robust body was inches away. *Oh my gosh, I think I might faint*. Katlyn exhaled shakily.

"May I touch you?" he whispered. His deep voice had a hint of seductiveness.

"Mm-hmm," she mumbled, nodding her head.

Kel put one hand at the small of her back and the other on the back of her bare neck. The sudden coolness made her breath catch.

"Do not be afraid," he said as he lowered his chin toward her.

"I'm not afraid. I'm nervous." She stifled nervous laughter.

Kel removed his hands from her, and took her hands into his, placing them on his chest. Katlyn could smell his earthy woody musk. It was intoxicating, and to her surprise, calming. She could feel his hard body underneath the shirt. His scent may have been soothing, but touching him wasn't.

He placed his hands on her again, pulling her body as close as they could be without being intimately entwined. "Look at me," he commanded. Every word that escaped his lips was dripping with passion. Katlyn was sure she was going to faint, and she was definitely aroused. His touch did things to her body that she couldn't explain.

She looked at him as he commanded, their faces only inches apart. He gripped behind her neck tightly, but not painfully and leaned toward her as if to kiss her. She pulled back, meeting his gaze. His eyes were always red, but every so often, when he looked at her, they reminded her of polished ruby gemstones glistening in the light.

"You must trust me," he whispered.

She wasn't sure how it started. All she knew was that Kel was standing over her, mouth agape. The more he exhaled over her face, the more she opened herself up, accepting the gift he gave—the heat. Instead of his breath being cool, it was like he was breathing fire into her, but not burning—exciting and passionate. Her entire body flushed as he exhaled. The heat of an impending orgasm engulfed her body. The pleasure building, but instead of starting at her sex, it started at her head and radiated down to her core, bursting into all her limbs. His healing touch paled in comparison to what he was doing to her at that moment.

She was vaguely aware of what she was doing, but she knew she had wrapped one of her legs around his thigh, had clenched onto his chest and was moaning. An actual orgasm was imminent, and she didn't have the wherewithal to clench her thighs together to stifle it. She wouldn't have anyway. She welcomed it; she needed it. This beautiful man standing over her had the ability to send waves of pleasure into her intimate flesh without being anywhere near it.

At that moment, she wanted him and didn't have the willpower or the want, to stop it.

~Kel

He parted his lips, inhaling her sweet, musky aroma as she relaxed in his grip. Her scent was more potent than before, and her eyes were a brighter blue than he remembered. Looking into them made him feel at peace. Her skin was warm and tantalizing. The more he touched her, the more he desired her. He could not tell her before that giving life felt like making love, and he wanted to do it again. He wanted this, and from her scent, she did, too.

He gave her the gift slowly, relishing in it as she did. He did not wish to rush it. He quickly knew how it was affecting her. She was clutching onto him, and he could feel her body tremble. Her temperature was rising, and heat radiated between them.

She wrapped her leg around his, and without realizing it, he put his hand into her gown, gripping her thigh and pulling her closer. She began to pant and suddenly grew still. Her eyes closed as a gentle moan escaped her lips, and her head fell back against his hand. Her entire body clenched against him, then went limp. She lost the ability to carry her own weight.

Kel raised his head and inhaled her scent as he watched her lying in his arms. Her hands still clenched his chest. The smell of her arousal engulfed his senses and sent his own organ ablaze. She finally raised her head to look at him. He no longer saw her as he knew her before. He saw desire. And for the first time in his life, he was afraid. Afraid for her because he wanted her, but she was forbidden fruit.

Katlyn pulled at him with her leg as she grasped his hand with hers, squeezing his fingers into her flesh. She let out a soft moan when he rubbed her cheek with his, then began nipping at the tender flesh of her neck, careful not to break the skin. Her skin was fevered next to his, and little bumps sprang up when his lips caressed her neck.

In one fluid motion, he whipped her around, laying her on the bed. He gripped both her thighs, and she winced when he slid his wide hips between them. He pressed his firm body against hers, and they both moaned when he buried his face in the crook of her warm neck. His hips were so much broader than hers. He was not sure if he would fit, but she did not seem to mind as she pulled at him wantonly.

As he pushed against her, it took every ounce of self-control he had not to bite her. He gripped her thigh in silent protest. He never felt compelled to bite before. The urge to do so was an indication of his desire to bond with her.

He lifted his head to look at her. She was baring her neck to him and untying her gown. Her chest was heaving with desire. When the ties came loose, she looked at him and began to open her shift, but he stopped her.

Pleasure escaped her lips as he kneaded his massive hips into her. He snaked his hand into her shift and cupped her breast. His thumb brushed against the fleshy tip. She inhaled sharply and grew still as he continued rubbing his pelvis against hers. Then she clenched her legs around him, put her head back again, and moaned as pleasure skyrocketed through her, making her thighs quiver at his sides.

He wanted nothing more than to please her, to make love to her, but he knew he could not. He did not wish to hurt her, but he would have done anything else she asked of him.

He shifted his weight onto his right side so he could see her. As her breathing leveled out, he cradled her head on his right arm and seized her right hand in his, grasping her wrist above her head. He caressed her neck, wrapping his left hand around the base, then exploring the valley between her breasts with his fingertips.

He caressed the visible skin of her stomach, and her foot hooked behind his knee, pulling at him. He moved gingerly along her hip to the inside of her warm thigh. He could feel her heat as he inched his way toward the source of her arousal. He tucked his fingertips into her undergarment's waistband and watched her as he explored, learning how to please her. His mouth opened more with every moan that escaped her lips. As she continued to pull at him, he progressed his hand farther down. He wanted to touch her to find the source of her pleasure. Her breathing picked up, and she let out a gentle moan when he grazed a tuft of hair.

Then the door control panel buzzed.

Someone was standing on the other side of the door. Katlyn's head shot up, and the brilliant shine in her eyes was replaced with fear. She was suddenly terrified. "It is locked," Kel whispered when she started to tremble. The door buzzed again, and Katlyn whimpered. Then a voice called for her.

"Mistress Katlyn," Nia said. "I'm sorry to bother you, but we'd love for you to join us for a late snack if you're up for it."

Katlyn inhaled sharply. Her body shuddered as she exhaled. The muscles in her neck were rigid. "I..." She swallowed and cleared her throat. "Yes, I'll be right there. Don't wait for me. I'm coming." Her voice was raspy and shook with each word.

"Wonderful! See you in the kitchen then." And the panel clicked off.

Katlyn trembled underneath him, refusing to look at him. She unhooked her foot and pushed against his hand. She had already pulled her dress closed, pinching it at her breast. Kel slowly moved off her, sitting back on his knees, holding his hands up so she could see them. As soon as Katlyn was free of him, she snapped her legs together and bolted off the bed.

When she reached her lavatory, she turned around to face him. He was still kneeling on her bed with his hands up and his chin down, watching her. She glanced at the door panel, then back at him.

"It is off. Even if someone is there, they cannot hear us," he whispered, unmoving.

"Did you know it was going to do that to me?" Katlyn snapped.

Kel lowered his hands and straightened his back. He knew how it would affect him, but he did not know how it would affect her. Her reaction was a complete surprise to him.

"On my honor, Katlyn, I did not," he said, gently bowing his head. "I understand if you are angry with me. I lost control. Please forgive me."

"Both of us lost control. That should never have happened. It had to be what you did. It's like a drug. Please never do that again, and please don't ask me to explain what it was like. I am positive that you're smart enough to figure that out on your own."

He sighed heavily. Her words stung. She was clearly unhappy with what transpired between them. "I have brought shame upon myself. Please forgive me."

Katlyn walked back over next to the bed. "Look, we were both out of our minds, I guess. I knew what I was doing, but I didn't want to stop. I haven't had a man's hands on me in more than two years. I know that isn't an excuse, but I'm just as much to blame as you are."

"No," he said firmly as he placed his foot on the floor and stood up. "I should be able to control myself. There is no excuse for my behavior," he growled, then snatched his coat off the window seat. "I have brought dishonor upon myself!"

"Kel, look," Katlyn said as she rubbed her face, "dishonor would be if I told you no or asked you to stop, but that's not what happened. I gave you permission. I'm not mad at you, or afraid of you."

"Your expression said otherwise."

"I was... I'm not afraid of you. I was at that moment because of the situation. And honestly, I mean..." her voice trailed off and she started chewing on her top lip. "I'm not sure what else to say. You should probably wait here in case Nia didn't take my advice and is out there waiting for me."

Kel squared his shoulders and leveled his chin to the ground, not making eye contact with her. "Very well."

Katlyn disappeared into the lavatory for a moment. Before leaving, she turned to him and said, "For what it's worth, I did enjoy myself, and I hope you did, too, but that..." she paused, shaking her head, "you know that can't happen again, right?" Kel only nodded in response. "We just have to be responsible and not put ourselves in that position again. If that means me moving to a different room, then I will."

Kel turned to look at her. "That will not be necessary," he said. She would be safest in his quarters, and he preferred to keep her close. He was not concerned about his men, but his Regent knew about the imprinting, and she made her feelings about Katlyn abundantly clear.

"You can't avoid me either, or treat me like I did something wrong. I know you aren't used to having a friendly rapport with humans, and I can respect that, but this isn't exactly an everyday thing for me either." Katlyn chuckled lightly. "I'll be out of your hair soon." She turned toward the door and looked at him over her shoulder. "Maybe if both of our situations were different," she said pensively. He looked at her, desiring for things to be different. Perhaps someday they could be. "You should stand out of sight of the door. If Nia is in there, I'll grab her and leave quickly. You shouldn't have to wait long."

After Katlyn left, Kel put his coat on, straightening himself to give her time to leave the sitting room. Her scent was stronger than ever, and she was all over his body. It only made his need for her grow.

He left her room and quickly went to his. He removed all his clothes, leaving them out so Rory would know they needed to be washed. He had to remove her scent from his body and clothes, not only for his sanity but for her protection. If she lingered on him, his Regent might get suspicious.

As he washed and dressed, his mind lingered to parts of their conversation and interaction. Hearing her say she trusted him and his sudden desire to bite her. If he was not sure about his feelings for her before, he was convinced at that moment. He desired to bond with her. Even if she only allowed it to increase her protection.

Kel headed to his primary analyst's lab upon leaving his quarters. On the way, he thought about Katlyn's suggestion. Some means of stimulating their systems to gain nutrients from food. He was more than willing to investigate the possibility. He could not help what he was, but if there were a way for his kind to not rely on humans for their alimentary needs, that would be an incredible feat.

Bry'aere may be correct; Katlyn could be the catalyst to peace, and perhaps their situations could be different.

~Katlyn

There were several people in the kitchen when Katlyn arrived. They had light snacks and were already drinking wine. As she joined them, her mind reeled back to what just happened—Kel on top of her. The pressure of his weight on her hips was uncomfortable, but not enough for her to stop him. She was painfully aware of how large he was. She recalled feeling him as he pushed against her. The thought made her shiver.

"Are you all right?" Nia asked. Katlyn nodded her head and smiled, then took a drink of her wine.

She was thankful for the distraction and Nia's interference. If she hadn't, there's no telling how far they would have gone. And as much as she wanted him, their being together was wrong. *Why is he acting this way?* she thought angrily as she downed her glass of wine and tried to push the day's events to the back of her mind.

21. COURTING

"She has been here less than a day, and you are already in anguish!" Bry'aere snapped while Kel paced and huffed in the small sitting room. "Did you bed her?"

Kel stopped abruptly in the middle of the room, turning to his friend with fury. "No!" he barked, then continued to pace. "Not exactly."

"What was that?"

"Almost!" he bellowed.

"Do not be cryptic. Answer the damn question!" Bry'aere retorted.

"Almost! I would have, but I knew I could not," he said, stopping at the door to Bry'aere's quarters.

"Why? I see no reason you could not."

"I do not wish to hurt her, but I would have bent to her will, and done whatever she asked of me." Kel's eyes closed as he thought of Katlyn beneath him. Then he began to pace again. "Besides, we were interrupted."

"What happened?"

"Nia buzzed the door, and Katlyn was suddenly terrified." He sighed heavily, remembering the fear in Katlyn's eyes as she looked up at him, realizing their delicate situation. "She then made it clear that what happened between us was a mistake. Perhaps I misread her. I have never been so stymied in all the millennia of my existence. She has beguiled me!"

"Perhaps you should court her," Bry'aere suggested.

"I should not be entertaining this, Bry'aere, and you should not be encouraging it. If our Regent finds out, she will be displeased. How am I to court someone I should not be courting?"

"Perhaps you can tell our Regent that your extra attention is for the purpose of her plan; to use Katlyn as leverage against her people."

"I cannot use her as leverage, Bry'aere. It may cost me dearly, but I will not do it!"

"I did not expect you to, but our Regent need not know that. She does not have as much power as she likes to believe."

"She is our Regent!" Kel snapped.

"You have more influence than you like to admit," Bry'aere said. "You need to consider your station, your lineage. You are the Queen's nevos. Our Regent is merely a face, continuity. The power lies with you."

"Perhaps, but I am also Commander. That is where my focus is currently."

Bry'aere laughed. "No, your focus is on the human sharing your quarters."

Kel snapped his head toward him. "I am pleased that you find this amusing," he said through clenched teeth.

"It is no matter. She will be leaving soon. You should enjoy her company while you are able. Spar with me tomorrow morning and release some of this aggression."

"Fine," Kel hissed.

~Katlyn

Katlyn woke up with a splitting headache. Even the ship's dim lights were torturous. The wine she drank the night before didn't hit her until she got up to walk to her room. Then her world started spinning, and she nearly fell into the conscript at the door.

"Good morning!" Nia said with more enthusiasm than was necessary. Almost as if she were mocking Katlyn.

"Dear God in heaven, Nia. Please don't yell at me! Are you guys trying to kill me?"

"Why would you ask such a silly question?"

"Because you kept feeding me glass after glass. I think there's a vice on my head. Please stop talking and turn the lights down," Katlyn stammered.

"They are on the lowest setting. If I turn them down more, they'll be off. I will get the Commander."

"No!" Katlyn shrieked, but Nia was already out the door.

Katlyn didn't take a bath before she stumbled into bed. She knew she still smelled like the night before. The last thing she wanted was Kel putting his glorious hands on her. Even if it was just her head, and even if she felt like death warmed over.

"You overindulged," said a sultry voice from above. She didn't hear him come into her room. "I can help with the headache, but you will need water."

"Can you kill me instead?"

"I think not. Nia will run you a bath. Will you allow me to help you?"

Katlyn groaned and mumbled her approval. Before she realized he had touched her, it was over. She barely felt it, but that may have been because she was too ill. Her stomach churned from hunger and dehydration, but at least people weren't yelling at her anymore.

"Thank you," she said.

"Your breakfast is waiting. Do you mind if I join you?"

"Uh, sure," Katlyn said, giving him an odd look. "I'll be out there soon."

Kel and Nia both left her to get ready on her own. She wanted to sink in the tub and drown, but she quickly washed her body, got dressed, and stepped into the sitting room. Kel was sitting down at a table looking at a handheld device. On the table sat two place settings.

"Good morning," he said as if the day before didn't happen. Then he stood and pulled her chair out for her. She slowly took the seat and gave him a curious look as he sat down on the opposite side of the table.

She raised an eyebrow and darted her eyes around the room. "Good morning," she said slowly as she looked at him, tilting her head in confusion. "This is an unexpected surprise."

He placed a napkin on his lap before picking up a two-pronged fork with his left hand. Katlyn watched him with unabashed curiosity. For someone who didn't eat food, he was very aware of table manners.

Without taking her eyes off him, Katlyn took her napkin and fork, but she couldn't eat. That would mean looking at her plate, and the view before her was too peculiar not to watch.

"Are you going to eat?" he asked.

"I should, but I can't help but wonder why you're sitting in front of me eating," she said with more attitude than intended.

"I enjoy your company," he said in between bites. He even ate sensually: placing the fork in his mouth, pulling the food off with his top teeth and tongue. His sharp eyeteeth peeked out with every bite. He was looking at her, taunting her. Almost as if his actions were intentional.

I can't even get through breakfast, Katlyn said to herself as she clenched her thighs together aggressively and whimpered. He either didn't notice or pretended not to.

"We will arrive at Cora later today. Normally, I would know our schedule, but since we are late, I do not know what they will be doing. We typically stay for a few days," he said before seductively pulling a bite of potato off his fork. "The humans in our service have family there."

"People," she blurted out. He paused mid-bite. Looking at her with his tongue gently caressing the bottom of the fork. She had to bite her top lip to stop herself from whimpering. He then cast her a curious look as he pulled the food off the prongs. "Humans are people," Katlyn said as she stabbed a potato.

Kel took a deep breath. "I spoke with my primary analyst about your suggestion." Katlyn's eyebrows shot up, and now she was the one with a fork hanging out of her mouth. "He informed me that it is not impossible. It is something that most would never consider, but it has never before been mentioned."

"Wow! Thank you for telling me," Katlyn said as she picked up her water glass. She didn't realize how thirsty she was until she took a drink. She couldn't help but down the entire thing in one fell swoop, slurping greedily as the heavenly liquid coated her throat. Kel stood over her with a pitcher of water before she had a chance to put her glass down. "I promise I have table manners. I'm just so thirsty," she chuckled as he filled her glass, then placed the pitcher on the table between them.

"Change takes time," he said when he sat back down across from her. "This kind of change could take generations."

"I think it's important for people to see that you can get along with humans. As friends, not just in an intimidating way. I'm sure most people are nice to you because they don't want you to eat them. People need to understand that you don't treat them that way out of malice or hatred."

"Would you be willing to allow others to see that we are friends?"

"I'm not ashamed to be seen with you if that's what you're wondering," she said. "Once we find my son, I can talk to him about helping your analyst. I already know my government will try to keep me quiet—"

Kel snickered.

"Oh, is that funny?"

A broad smile formed on his face.

"Yeah, I'm not meek and obedient—I think you've realized that by now. My son knows I'm a handful, and his job got me abducted by aliens, so they owe me. There is no way in hell my government will keep me quiet unless I choose to be."

"I am sure you underestimate your government," he said when he finished eating.

"If they want to mess with me, I'll just stay here."

Kel looked at her. "You would do that?"

"If what you say is true, that you're looking into another option, then yes. You'll need humans who trust you. The fact that you're even considering it means a lot, and people need to know that. My son's people may be able to help you. He has no reason not to trust you."

"Your son has every reason not to trust me, unfortunately."

"I trust you," Katlyn said. "That will be enough for him."

"What if it is not?"

"Well, then I'll just rub it in his face that his job got me abducted by aliens, and you're the one who came to my rescue." Katlyn shrugged and began laughing.

Kel leaned back in his chair. "After you are finished, I would like to show you something."

Katlyn finished her breakfast and drank a couple more glasses of water. Then they left the room together. When they walked past the conscripts, Katlyn reminded him that he never told her about them. While they walked around the ship, he told her that conscripts were clones. DNA from a female— usually the fleet's Regent, and her drone was used to create them, which explained why the conscripts on Arlo looked different. Conscripts were basically cannon fodder, not sentient, and only responded to a Specter's commands. During their discussion, she also found out that each fleet had a Regent, but their homeworld had a primary Queen who ruled over all of them.

Kel showed Katlyn the hangar bay, which was a vast open space with multi-levels and gangways between landing platforms. The upper and lower levels had fliers, and the main level had transport ships and reapers.

Two levels up from the ship's main level, they walked down a corridor leading to the recreation room. It was just past the lift, then the primary analyst's lab was just past that. Farther down the corridor, they came to a 3-way intersection. Straight ahead, there didn't appear to be much but the same as what was behind them. To the right of the crossing was a short corridor that opened into a large room. Kel held his hand out at the door.

When she walked through the door, the room was empty except for racks of various weapons. He told her they used the room for training, but what he wanted her to see was up.

He took her to the middle of the room and had her close her eyes. When she opened them a moment later, she looked straight up at the ceiling. It was a giant domed window, and because they were traveling, billions of stars were darting by. The experience gave her vertigo, and she nearly fell over.

"When we reach Cora, the navigator will put us in orbit on the northern pole of the planet. From there, you can see a nebula. You may not be able to see it from your room, but you can see it from here," he said as he looked up. Katlyn had to keep her chin level to the ground while her eyes shifted up. Otherwise, she'd get dizzy again.

"I never imagined I'd be flying in space talking about seeing nebulas from an alien ship's observatory."

"We will arrive soon. Perhaps you would be willing to help Nia prepare for the visit?"

"Oh, I'm allowed to help now?" Katlyn asked sarcastically.

"I suspect you would even if I had not suggested it."

"You're right. I would have done it anyway. And all the women would be gawking at how openly disobedient I am." Katlyn was really proud of herself as she stood there with a broad smile on her face. Kel gazed down to her for a moment, and his eyes twinkled.

"I have agreed to train with someone today. I will not be accompanying you from here," he said.

"I can find my way back. Thanks for having breakfast with me."

She glanced over her shoulder as she was leaving the room and saw him watching her. She flashed a coy smile before he turned and removed his coat.

She rounded the corner and got about halfway down the corridor when she had an overwhelming urge to go back. She stopped briefly before turning around and heading back, stopping at the corner, just out of view. She could hear feet shuffling on the floor. Some steps were faster than others, some were slower, but overall, the movements sounded intentional, fluid, almost like a dance.

Katlyn hugged her body against the corner and peeked her head around so she could see inside the room. Kel was moving in a way that she could only interpret as sparring, but he was alone. She was mesmerized by the way he moved. Her mind flooded with the memory of him on top of her and how his body pushed into hers. The way he fought was similar to the way she imagined he'd make love—passionate and fierce. She couldn't look away from him. He was intoxicating. His clothes hugged his form, and every motion of his body excited different muscles, and she could see them straining against the fabric. She was suddenly angry at Nia for interrupting their encounter the day before. All that occupied Katlyn's mind as she watched him was imagining his massive body towering over her and feeling him fill every crevice of her. Watching him move was exciting her in all the ways she wanted to be excited. But it wasn't just about feeling his body next to hers. She genuinely cared for him. She might even say she was falling in love with him.

Katlyn's pulse raced, and her breathing got heavier. If she had touched herself, she'd probably climax instantly. As she watched the beautiful, elegant, regal man before her, she suddenly felt a cold hand clasp her mouth and flip her around, pushing her back against the wall. She had forgotten entirely that Kel said he was training with someone. She had been caught watching the Commander. Katlyn couldn't move or even whimper, she was frozen. The man clasping her mouth looked familiar, but she couldn't place his face.

As she stood with her back against the wall, the man put the forefinger of his other hand against his lips, as if to motion for her to be quiet. She relaxed a hair. She knew all she had to do was scream, and Kel would come running. She gave a quick nod of her head, and he removed the hand that covered her mouth and brought both his hands up so she could see them. When her shoulders relaxed, the man gently pushed on her arm to direct her to walk with him. They walked in silence until they were about halfway down the corridor.

"You should not be here," he whispered when he turned around to face her. At that moment, she remembered who he was. He was second in command. The one she chewed out in Kel's sitting room, and he told her she'd make a great Regent if she were a Specter.

She squared her shoulders and looked at him. "He had just shown me the observatory moments ago, and we've been walking around the ship for a while. I think I'm allowed to be here."

"It is not about that. Everyone knows you are allowed. If someone else caught you watching him." Katlyn blinked in surprise. She could feel her face flush, and she knew that he knew it. "I will not speak of it, mistress," he said, bowing his head gently. "You have my word."

Katlyn gave an awkward chuckle. "Uh... I'm gonna go," she said as she pointed both hands in the direction of the stairs and flashed an uncomfortable smile. Then she turned and ran the rest of the way down the corridor.

~Bry'aere

He watched as Katlyn ran down the corridor and couldn't help but chuckle at her and Kel'ardent. He was positive that his friend had not misread Katlyn. Both had an obvious affection for one another, but their situation was not ideal.

Thankfully, Kel'ardent took his advice about courting her and convinced their Regent that publicly befriending Katlyn would garner her trust, and aid in their plan to use her as leverage. Of course, Kel'ardent would never use her in such a way, but he could not court her without their Regent finding out. With her blessing, even under false pretenses, Kel'ardent was free to escort Katlyn around the ship. As well as any world they were to visit. Hopefully, that would smooth things over between them, and one, or both, would finally admit their feelings, and Kel'ardent would stop brooding about like a lovesick youngling.

22. WALK WITH ME

~Katlyn

When Katlyn arrived in the kitchen, all the servants were there, men and women getting ready to go to the planet's surface. They were preparing to move empty food baskets and crates to a ship in the hangar bay, as well as personal belongings for their stay.

After a couple of hours, it was almost time to leave, so they began loading their things onto the ship. Nia told her it was a reaper. It was bigger than the transport that took Katlyn to Arlo. It had the same configuration; it just carried more people.

Even with all the crates, baskets, and personal belongings, everyone fit comfortably and took a seat, waiting for anyone who was going to join them from the crew.

As Katlyn and Nia sat down, Katlyn asked her who all from the crew goes down to the planet, and what does everyone do. Nia told her that the Commander only goes down to hunt, and he's usually gone for a couple of days. The Lodestar and a few of his other men go down for trading or assisting with supplies, but none of them stay long. They drop the people off, then pick them back up a few days later.

"I have no idea what I'm going to do while I'm there," Katlyn said.

"I'm not sure what the village will be doing since we're behind. I know it's the end of the hot season. They should be harvesting soon. The wine we have on the ship, we get from Cora. It's one of the things we trade for."

"Oh, the delicious evilness that knocked me on my ass. You get that from *this* planet?" They both laughed.

"If my memory serves me, they should be harvesting any day. It would be a lot of fun if we were able to help make it. We usually miss the opportunity because of scheduling."

"Do they stomp around in a big bucket?" Katlyn teased.

"Yes."

"I was totally teasing."

"Well, that's how it's done. All the village maidens participate. It's a lot of fun."

"Why the maidens?"

Nia laughed. "Well, if they're doing it, you'll see. You should be able to join in."

"Honey!" Katlyn gave a boisterous laugh that made everyone look at her funny. "I am not a maiden. I was married for almost thirty years."

Nia gave a light chuckle. "I hope this doesn't offend you, but you're not married anymore," she said with a wink.

Thanks for reminding me that I'm free to sleep with anyone I choose. That definitely doesn't help my current situation, Katlyn thought to herself just as several Specter boarded the ship. Two of them going straight to the pilot's cabin. The Lodestar boarded, accompanied by another man Katlyn didn't recognize. They both stood in the aisle. Katlyn glanced at the Lodestar, who acknowledged her with a simple nod of his head. After several minutes, Kel strode onto the ship in all his masculine glory. Just a few hours before, she had been caught spying on him, and even though the man who found her gave his word not to say anything, she still couldn't look at Kel. She was glad when he stopped in the aisle to speak to his men.

That didn't last long.

In two broad steps, he was standing next to her. She sank into her seat when he sat down. Right next to her. His massive thigh brushing against hers as he leaned back into the seat. Katlyn couldn't help but notice how he sat with his legs so wide apart. *Could that be to accommodate... damnit, Katlyn, knock it off!* The last thing she needed was her scent wafting through the small ship.

"We do not have a schedule," Kel said to nobody in particular. Everyone looked at him as he spoke. Katlyn crossed her legs and started chewing on her lip and finger as if she were a teenager in heat. "I will still hunt as usual," he continued, "but I am not sure when, or how long we will be here. You will have at least three days, possibly longer. I apologize for the delay in seeing your families. It could not be helped."

Everyone began chatting amongst themselves, then Kel turned to Katlyn and asked, "Do you expect to stay on the planet while we are here?"

His question caught her off guard. Where would she stay? "I hadn't thought about it," she said.

"You could stay with my family," Nia said.

"I don't know. I'll play it by ear. I didn't pack anything."

"Well, if you help with what we discussed, you'll need to change anyway."

"Change into what?" Katlyn raised an eyebrow.

"You'll see," Nia said with a broad smile that scared Katlyn a little. Nia was almost mischievous. As if she were up to something.

Katlyn laughed and held a hand up as if to stop someone, and she said, "Please don't tell me you dance on grapes naked? Cause that is not happening." Katlyn heard a low grumble from Kel, and then he exhaled sharply. She looked at him, and he was staring at her. "I am not dancing naked, okay!" She turned back to Nia and laughed again.

"No! Not naked," Nia laughed. "Not exactly anyway."

"What the hell do you mean?"

"Well, it's maidens who do it to attract the men."

"You have *got* to be kidding me?" Katlyn snapped with nervous laughter. "I am not going to dance naked on some grapes to attract a man from this planet. You're out of your mind." Everyone started laughing and telling her how fun it was, and if they're doing it, she should participate.

"They're not naked," Nia said. "I assure you." She leaned over to whisper in Katlyn's ear. "And you wouldn't be trying to attract a man from the planet anyway..." Her voice trailed off as she pulled her head back. Katlyn scowled at her and shook her head, chuckling awkwardly.

After an uncomfortable silence, Kel finally said, "I do not know how long it will take to find your people. You may need a few things before then. If you see anything, please let me know. I plan to do some trading myself."

Katlyn sat quietly, not realizing she was fiddling with the pendant around her neck, and Kel was watching her despite everyone else noticing. She did everything in her power to avoid eye contact, but she couldn't help it. No matter how hard she tried, if he was around, she had to look at him. He was intoxicating, like a drug. He was sitting so close, his scent violated her nose, which violated every other part of her body. She wanted him but didn't. When he stared at her with those bright ruby eyes, like a man at a buffet, it didn't help.

We were both out of our minds at the time, right? Katlyn asked herself. *There's no way he could actually want to be with a human. Maybe he's curious about human interactions? Yeah, that's it. That's the only reason we ended up on the bed, his curiosity. But why in the hell is he looking at me like that? And in front of all these people!*

He was driving her mad. Before she realized it, she had her head resting on her hand and was staring at him, too. Both just staring at each other, like lovers. As if there was nobody else around to see them. Katlyn was vaguely aware of the Lodestar shifting positions, attempting to block prying eyes from seeing them. What are friends for anyway, right?

On the planet, everyone poured out of the ship carrying baskets and bags and greeting loved ones. Kel apologized to the families for the delay. Katlyn noticed the different emblems people wore, which made sense because most of them were families of servants who bound themselves for protection. Nia introduced Katlyn to her parents, who were wearing the same emblem Katlyn wore.

After the greetings, Nia's father, Robert, who was the leader of the village, told Nia that others were in the fields picking grapes for harvest and would be doing the celebration the following day.

"We got here just in time, Katlyn!"

"Oh, yay!" Katlyn feigned excitement as she twisted her fingers in the air.

"Are you unmarried?" Nia's father asked.

"I'm actually a widow."

"You can participate," he said. "You're still young."

"I'm not here looking for a husband, sir."

"Katlyn, please!" Nia begged. Her behavior was out of the ordinary. She was very laid back. Katlyn felt that if they had met on Earth, they'd be fast friends. Of course, she already considered them friends, but Nia's personality seemed completely different on the planet. She appeared to be a lot like herself. And the face she made, begging Katlyn to join, was almost irresistible. She reminded Katlyn of Natalie, and a pang of sadness hit her suddenly.

"I'll think about it," she said just as Kel walked up beside her. "But if you guys are naked, it's a hard pass. Sorry," she laughed. Nia's father wrapped his arm around his daughter, and they walked down the dirt path leading from the meadow to the village.

"Walk with me?" Kel held out his elbow, inviting her to wrap her arm around it. "We are to be seen as friends, are we not?"

Katlyn chuckled. "Yes, that's right," she said as she accepted his arm, but she was not having platonic thoughts about him.

The ship landed in a meadow not far from the village. They walked along a dirt path leading to a tall brick wall that surrounded the village. A thick wooden gate guarded the only entrance.

Inside the gate, the houses seemed to be on a grid, with cobblestone roads in between. In the center of the village was a large fountain, and people had carts and tables set up for trading. The entire experience had a Renaissance vibe to it, so Katlyn figured they were in the Renaissance age. Their clothing was very Renaissance era. Which made Katlyn chuckle because that happened to be her favorite period of Earth history.

"What do you find amusing?" Kel asked.

"Everyone is so pretty. Earth is a lot more advanced than this. This period of Earth history is called the Renaissance, and it happens to be one of my favorite periods."

"Oh? Why is that?"

"Look at all these women, they're beautiful," Katlyn said as she waved her hand around. "I love the dresses they wear."

"Perhaps you should look into acquiring some of your own."

"I don't need dresses. I have enough that I made myself. We'll just walk around the carts and stuff to see what everyone has."

A Specter Commander escorting a human drew quite the crowd. Everyone knew who he was, but they had no idea who she was. They also knew he was breaking from his regular routine of hunting. People gawked and stared, trying not to make it too obvious. Katlyn noticed but didn't care. If Kel saw, he kept it to himself. She also noticed the Lodestar watching them from a distance. He seemed to be on guard more than anything.

Just about when they were ready to call it quits on trading, something caught Katlyn's eye from a few tables away. She made a beeline for it, and sure enough, it was exactly what she thought it was. It was a wooden box that was several inches deep, and on the top was a checkerboard pattern. The lid opened to store pieces inside—it was a chess set. Katlyn could not contain her excitement. She was jumping up and down like a kid on Christmas morning. She pulled out the pieces to make sure they were all there. The pieces were different than what she was used to, but they weren't so different that she couldn't figure out what they were supposed to be. And even if it wasn't technically a chess set, that didn't matter.

"Would you like to have this?" Kel asked.

"I don't have anything to trade for it."

Kel shook his head. "That is not necessary. If you would like to have this, I will get it for you."

"I can't ask you to do that. I can always come back with some of my dresses to trade for it. I have things to trade, just not with me."

Kel lowered his chin slightly to give her that distinctive look that he only gave her. Now when he did it, it made her blush because she knew it was special for her. And she didn't even care that people were staring at them.

"If you would like to have this, I will get it for you now," he insisted as he reached to the side of his belt and untied a small leather bag. It looked like a little coin purse that could fit in the palm of his hand. He untied the strings keeping it closed, then reached inside for what sounded like coins, but pulled out a sizeable nugget that she assumed was a precious metal of some kind.

Katlyn stood there, shaking her head with a huge grin on her face. "That's really not necessary, Commander." It took every ounce of self-control she had not to call him Kel in front of everyone.

"I insist."

"Okay, fine, but you have to play a game with me. There's no point in me having it if I can't play."

"You will have to teach me."

"I can do that!" Her excitement was contagious. Kel even smiled at her, and she had never seen him be anything but serious in front of other people.

"You may use my name in public. You do not have to address me as Commander. I am not your Commander," he said as he paid the merchant.

"I didn't think you'd want people knowing your name."

"I do not mind if they know my name. They are not friendly enough to use it."

"Okay, Kel," she said with a huge grin on her face, which only made him smile again. Katlyn preferred saying his name.

~Kel

The merchant stared at him wide-eyed when she heard Katlyn say his name. He relished the way it sounded rolling off her tongue. He knew their interactions would cause a sensation, and he was aware of the looks he and Katlyn received from the villagers as he escorted her around the square. Katlyn also noticed but did not seem to mind. A couple of times, she drew closer to him while they walked.

After their purchase, Katlyn walked around holding her new game as she would carry a youngling. She was obviously incredibly happy with what she had discovered, and he looked forward to playing with her.

As they neared the final merchants, Nia and Robert approached them.

"Katlyn, come with me. We need to get measured," Nia said.

"For what?" Katlyn said with a slight scowl on her face.

"I will take your game," Kel offered as Nia tugged on Katlyn's elbow.

Katlyn released the box reluctantly. Bry'aere joined them just as Katlyn and Nia walked away. Kel desired to watch her, but he squared his shoulders and looked down at Robert instead.

"Commander," Robert said with a respectful bow of his head. "The festival is tomorrow. I'd be honored if you would join us. You have never been here during our wine festival. I know you normally go hunting—"

"We will be here for a few days. I will leave to hunt overmorrow," Kel said.

"Wonderful! You may all stay if you wish," Robert said, looking at Bry'aere.

Bry'aere responded with a gentle bow, then Robert walked away.

'You plan on staying?' Bry'aere asked, touching Kel lightly on the wrist.

'Katlyn is participating. I am curious,' Kel said as he looked in the direction she walked, but she was nowhere in sight.

"Please take this to the ship. I need to make some purchases," he said aloud, handing the game to Bry'aere.

As Bry'aere walked away with Katlyn's game, Kel turned on his heel and stopped the first villager who crossed his path, asking where the dressmaker was. Earlier that morning, he asked Nia how to make Katlyn's stay more pleasant. She suggested watching Katlyn as she perused the square, keeping a watchful eye on things that drew her attention. While Katlyn was busy with Nia, he planned on making a few purchases, gifts for her. What woman does not enjoy gifts?

~Katlyn

Nia tugged at Katlyn hurriedly as they made their way across the village. The woman in charge of the grape smashing needed to get Katlyn's measurements for whatever ridiculous outfit she'd be wearing.

"I can't believe I'm considering this," Katlyn mumbled as she rubbed her face in frustration.

"You said you wouldn't do it if we were all naked. Well, we're not! So, I guess you're doing it, right?" Nia asked with a smile.

"It still depends on *what* I'm going to be wearing. I've always been modest. I'm still not sold on this idea. I know you're up to something, Nia. I'm not looking for a husband, so this is a huge waste of time."

"Having fun is never a waste of time. I'm not looking for a husband either, but I'm still participating."

"Okay, whatever you say," Katlyn laughed.

"If a man approaches you just turn him down," Nia said. "Unless it's someone you're interested in. Not that I'm saying you're interested in anyone."

"I knew you were up to something." They both laughed.

The outfit wasn't as bad as Katlyn thought it would be. It was more than a lot of women wore at the beach back home. The top was a long piece of fabric. The middle was worn at the back of the neck; then, it crisscrossed in the front to cover her breasts before it wrapped around the waist in an intricate pattern. It tied neatly at the back. Fortunately, it offered decent support considering they'd be jumping around in a vat of grapes covered in juice. The bottom was a skirt that went to about mid-thigh. It wasn't terribly short, but it was still short enough that Katlyn couldn't bend over confidently. Her voluptuous rear might fall right out of it, but that didn't mean she couldn't bounce around like a hussy. The last added touch was more long pieces of sheer fabric worn about the waist that hung loose around the hips and draped down the legs. The more she thought about it, the more excited she got about participating.

"Are you staying the night here?" Nia asked as they walked through the village toward the meadow.

"I'm still not sure. It depends on if Kel will bring me back tomorrow."

"I still can't believe you use his real name. I've never heard anyone call him anything but Commander. Not even the Lodestar, and they grew up together."

"I didn't know they were close friends," Katlyn said. *That explains a few things*, she thought to herself. "I'm sure Kel will bring me back if I ask. He still needs to go hunting anyway."

***

Katlyn tried to see the nebula when they returned to the ship, but the room was occupied, and everyone in there didn't seem too friendly at her presence. So, she decided to try another time. Kel said they'd be there for a few days, at least. She knew she'd have another opportunity to see it.

In Kel's quarters, Katlyn got the chess board set up. She loved playing chess, and finding a set was exciting. The box was made from beautiful dark wood. The squares on the board were black and white stone inlaid into the wooden lid, the pieces were made from stone, and all of them were carved into intricate designs. They were so beautiful, and Katlyn was nervous to even touch them. The pawns were fatter than regular pawns, and the tops were flat rather than rounded. The rooks were also fatter, but taller, and the tops were more rounded rather than the squared castle tops. The knights were a different type of beast. One she'd never seen before and didn't have a rider. The bishops were twisted like an old tree that had been twisted upwards by the wind. The queen was a woman, and she appeared to be coming out of the water holding an orb. The king was similar, except it was a man, and the piece was shorter, but both pieces towered over all the others.

Kel picked the game up very quickly. Apparently, the Specter were good at strategy games. Katlyn was hoping to beat him at least once. She wasn't entirely convinced that he didn't already know how to play. She only had to tell him one time how each piece moved, and the object of the game, and he was winning every match.

They played several games before Katlyn was yawning and fighting to keep her eyes open. "You should rest. You have a busy day tomorrow," Kel said.

"Yeah, I guess. Thank you for playing with me. I had a lot of fun. And thanks again for the set. I love it!"

"You are most welcome," he said as they both stood. "I have something else for you." He turned toward his room, disappearing momentarily, then returning with a burlap bag. "I purchased these while you were with Nia trying on that clothing you do not wish to discuss."

He was right about that; Katlyn did not want to talk about that outfit. He asked about it a couple of times, but she refused to discuss it and even changed the subject.

"Seriously? You'll just have to go then if you want to know so badly," she laughed. *Please don't go. I was teasing,* she thought to herself.

"I plan on it," he said with a smile that showed a hint of eyeteeth.

"Oh, that's fantastic!" Katlyn yelped sarcastically. "Don't you need to go hunting? I wouldn't want to keep you from your normal routine," she said, trying to change his mind.

"Robert invited us. It would be impolite not to attend," he said as he lowered his chin and gave her the bag.

"Us? As in more than one? There are several of you going?"

"Bry'aere will join me, as well as a few others."

"Who is Bry'aere?"

"He is my second in command. We have been friends since we were younglings. You have met him, but I can reintroduce you."

"I know who he is. I just didn't know his name," she said. She was very familiar with him, unfortunately. He caught her spying, after all.

Katlyn sat the bag on a table and started pulling the items out. The first one was something she had shown interest in while at the market. A blue and purple infinity type scarf that was big enough to be worn around her entire upper body like a wrap or shawl, but could also be used as a scarf. It was one continuous solid piece—a stretchy woven material. The next item was wrapped in paper and tied with twine. Katlyn squeezed it and looked at Kel, who was standing in the middle of the room, seeming to be mighty proud of himself. She chuckled lightly with a broad smile on her face as she untied the twine. There were two pieces. She presumed they went together. The first piece was a white gown with a stretchy, but snug fitting bodice. It was noticeably light and airy. The second piece was a bit heavier and red, and it was a soft velvety type material. The sleeves billowed out from the elbows, and the bodice cinched together snugly just below the breast. Both pieces were floor-length. It was definitely a Renaissance style dress. Kel had been very observant while they were at the market.

"Thank you so much," Katlyn said with a huge smile on her face. "I love it!"

"Will you try it on?"

She beamed from ear to ear and nodded. Then she went to her room to change.

~Kel

He waited patiently for Katlyn to return. He was pleased that she seemed to enjoy the things he purchased for her. When she finally entered the sitting room, she was giddy with excitement. She held the sides of the dress and twirled around, giggling.

"I've never had a dress like this. Thank you so much!"

"You are welcome," he said with a gentle bow. "You should get some rest now."

She began to pick up the waste left behind. "You're probably right."

She started to walk back to her room, but turned around and looked at him. He was standing in the middle of the sitting room with his hands clasped behind his back, watching her. She approached him and cleared her throat. "Thank you for being so kind to me. I really appreciate everything you've done." He lowered his chin gently to her. "May I give you a hug?" she asked.

After their encounter the previous evening, and her obvious discomfort with the situation, he was noticeably surprised when she requested such an intimate gesture. With so many people around, escorting her around the village was hardly intimate.

Kel unclasped his hands and brought them out to his sides, inviting her into his embrace. Katlyn hesitated for a moment, then reached up toward his neck. He bent down toward her, but she still had to get on her tiptoes to reach. As she wrapped her arms around his neck, he embraced her, wrapping one arm around her waist and the other around her shoulders. He buried his face into the crook of her neck and inhaled deep, taking in her scent. She squealed softly when he righted himself, lifting her feet off the floor, but she quickly relaxed as he held her.

She requested to be there. They both desired it. He could have stayed in that moment forever.

23. GRAPES &
MISUNDERSTANDINGS

~Katlyn

It was late afternoon when the transport landed in the meadow. Katlyn barely made it off the ramp before Nia was jerking her by the arm to get ready for the festival.

"I know we're not late," Katlyn said.

"No, I'm just very excited," Nia said as she pulled her toward the village.

"So excited," Katlyn feigned enthusiasm.

"Come on! You seemed more open to the idea last night."

Katlyn looked behind her to see where Kel was. He and his men were still standing on the ramp. "That was before I knew Kel planned on staying." Nia's eyes were as big as saucers when she heard the Commander and a few of his men would be there. "Apparently, your father invited them."

"We didn't think they'd actually take him up on his offer. The Commander usually goes hunting."

"Yeah, I tried to convince him that hunting was a better idea. He seemed hellbent on attending this festival." Katlyn rolled her eyes and Nia snickered.

Nia told Katlyn that the men were setting up on the beach, the festival was always held there. Everyone would usually swim in the ocean after the grapes were smashed, so they didn't walk around sticky from the juice. Katlyn was excited about going to the beach. She loved the ocean and used to go as often as she could.

As women helped each other get dressed and do their hair, many of them talked about the men in their lives. Most of the women were in their late teens and early twenties. Young enough to be Katlyn's daughter. There were a few older women and even another widow, but Katlyn still felt like she was the oldest one in the bunch.

While Nia fixed Katlyn's hair, a few of the older women asked her about her late husband and children. One was even bold enough to ask about the Commander and how Katlyn ended up on his ship if she didn't serve them.

"You are under his protection," one lady said.

"Yes, but that's because I saved his life," Katlyn told her.

"Slavery is illegal where she comes from," Nia told them as she pinned Katlyn's hair up and added wildflowers. Which only brought on more questions from the curious women.

"I have known him for many years," one woman said. "He has never behaved so strangely."

"What do you mean?" Katlyn asked.

"He's escorting you around the village, and now he's attending this festival," Nia said. "I have served him for many years. My grandmother served him before she was married, and although he has always treated us well, he has never behaved this way."

"Your grandmother served him?" Katlyn asked.

"He released her when she was ready to have a family of her own. I suspect he'll do the same for me. My husband and children will be under his protection just as my grandmother's children are—my father, his siblings, and their spouses."

Katlyn listened as the women continued talking about the men, including Kel. She let them draw their own conclusions. She wasn't ashamed to be seen with him, and even though most of the women thought it was more interesting than anything, there was the occasional woman who was put off by it.

"They consume people. I don't understand how anyone could be their friend," one woman mumbled under her breath.

"Did you ever stop to consider that they don't have a choice?" Katlyn snapped, not meaning to defend them so openly.

"You're defending a Specter," the same woman said. "And a Commander, no less. They're usually the worst."

"Yes, I am, because I've had the opportunity to sit down with one and talk to him. He happens to be genuinely nice and polite. Which can't be said for most human men I've encountered throughout my life."

Katlyn was getting so angry, but for a moment, she forgot that none of these people, not even Nia, saw Kel as she did.

"You'd feel differently if you'd lost family or friends in a reaping," an unknown woman said.

"I have actually. I was living on Arlo when an enemy reaped our village, and upon seeing Kel's pendant, he struck me so hard that he broke my cheekbone!" Katlyn snapped, then pointed to the bruise on her face and fought back tears. For a moment, she almost told them about helping Kel on Veda, but thought better of it. Them knowing such a thing would not help her argument. They knew she saved his life, but they didn't need details.

"I think we should change the subject," Nia interjected. "This is supposed to be a fun day. Let's stop talking about the Commander. Katlyn is right about him. He is different and always has been. That's why I agreed to serve him."

"He saved my life," Katlyn said. "More than once. I'm grateful."

"I'm sure he has an ulterior motive. They always do," the unknown woman said.

"I don't think so," Nia said. "And I still think we should drop it."

"It's about time to go anyway, ladies. Take a cover," the older woman in charge said as she began handing out linens for them to cover up with.

As they left the village and walked to the beach, Katlyn couldn't help but think about how she openly defended Kel. She was realizing more and more that she did care about him very much and would do whatever she could to make other people see him as she did.

After a brief trek in the forest, Katlyn could hear and smell the ocean. She picked up her pace, trying to reach the clearing quickly. When she stepped through the trees, the ocean was a teal blue color, and the sand was white. It reminded her of the Bahamas. On the beach were several large wooden tubs. Katlyn's eyes were immediately drawn to Kel, who was standing off to the side with Bry'aere and the others. His image took her breath away. If it weren't for his men being around, she would have run to him and wrapped her arms around his neck. When he saw her, he raised his chin, then lowered it—gazing at her in the way he always did. Katlyn smiled at him before Nia grabbed her arm and whisked her away.

As the women stood around the tubs, they started taking their linen covers off. Katlyn froze. *Oh no, I can't do this,* she thought to herself. She tried glancing over her shoulder to see Kel, but before she could, Nia was tugging at her linen. "I can't do this!"

"You never came across as being shy," Nia laughed.

"Just because I have a sassy mouth doesn't mean I'm not shy," Katlyn said just as the woman in charge snatched the linen off her shoulders against her will. Katlyn fisted her hands beside her body and yelped loud enough to draw everyone's attention. *Just what I didn't want, everyone looking at me,* she thought as she squared her shoulders and raised her chin trying to act as if she wasn't embarrassed.

The tub was about breast-high, and there was a step stool to help them get in. Before getting in, someone doused their legs and feet with water to reduce the amount of dirt and sand in the tub. As Katlyn started climbing over the edge, she glanced up to see Kel. He had a broad smile on his face watching her from the other side of the beach. Before she had a chance to smile back, Nia pushed her into the tub. Another yelp screeched past her lips, and her arms and legs flailed about as she flew, landing on all fours amongst the other women. She got to her feet clumsily and moved to the edge of the tub.

The others had begun smashing grapes, and Katlyn was already covered in grape juice. "I'm pretty sure I have an entire glass of wine on my skirt alone," Katlyn teased.

Nia took a spot next to her, pushing Katlyn gently to get her moving around the tub. Once she got her legs moving, she loosened up and rather enjoyed herself. They danced and had a grape fight, pushing each other around the tub and getting as saturated with grape juice as they possibly could. By the time they were finished, there wasn't a clean spot on any of their bodies.

After they were finished, the women helped each other out and immediately ran into the ocean to wash off. The water was warm and refreshing. Katlyn sat down and looked out toward the horizon, and for a fleeting moment she forgot where she was. It almost felt like she was in the Bahamas again.

Nia sat down beside her, then Katlyn closed her eyes and let the waves lap over her body. After a few minutes, Nia tapped her shoulder, and Katlyn followed her back onto the beach where various men were wrapping the ladies back into their linens. Katlyn watched with amusement, then a pair of hands placed a piece of linen over her shoulders.

~Kel

Kel and his men waited on the beach, putting some distance between them and the villagers. He offered to help them prepare, but they declined. They told him and his men that they were guests and to enjoy themselves. It didn't take long before all the women appeared from the village. Many of them wrapped in linens taking their places around the tubs. Kel kept his eyes on the tree line waiting for Katlyn to appear. When she did, she scanned the beach, her gaze falling on him. Then she gave him a broad smile before Nia stole her attention.

The other three men who accompanied him and Bry'aere decided to leave the beach. Kel barely noticed their departure. His eyes were fixated on Katlyn, who was fighting with Nia, clutching at her cover. Then, another woman took it from her shoulders, eliciting a loud screech from her. In her usual prideful way, she squared her shoulders and stood as if her face wasn't suddenly flush from embarrassment.

Kel watched Katlyn with yearning as she climbed over the edge of the tub, then suddenly flew in when Nia pushed her aside. When she stood, she was covered in juice. Kel could not stifle his amusement.

"You should tell her how you feel," Bry'aere said, interrupting Kel's thoughts.

Kel grumbled. "Why do you persist? She vexes me. Her scent says one thing, but when I act on it, she tells me it was a mistake, and it would never happen again."

"Do not go by her scent, Kel'ardent. You must go by her words, her actions. Just because she smells a particular way does not mean she wishes to be intimate. Human females are different."

"For someone who has never bed a human, you know a lot about them."

"I am a scientist, remember?"

"I do not think now is the right time."

"If you do not, I will court her and bed her myself!" Bry'aere snapped.

"And I will gladly take your life if you should attempt it," Kel hissed.

"You must trust me, friend, tell her. You do not know how long she will be here. If she leaves tomorrow, you will regret not speaking your mind."

Kel grumbled as he continued to watch Katlyn. She was dancing with the other women, laughing and seeming to enjoy herself. Her body was soaked, and the sheer fabric clung to her, accentuating every curve. The fleshy tips of her full breasts poked out tauntingly. His mind wandered, recalling the image of her beneath him. When his hand caressed her warm skin.

When Katlyn jumped out of the tub, he watched her as she moved across the beach. He crouched down, focusing his attention on the only woman he would ever want in his life from that moment on.

Watching her distracted him, and he did not notice Robert's approach until he was standing next to him. Bry'aere stepped away to allow them a private conversation.

"Begging your pardon Commander, and please don't take offense..." his voice trailed off.

"What is it?" Kel asked as he continued to watch Katlyn.

Through his peripheral vision, he could see Robert inhale and appear to hold his breath as if nervous about continuing. "We may be different men, sir, but I know the look of a man who's in love," he finally said. He carried linen in his hand and grasped it tighter.

Kel turned his head toward him sharply. "You are brave to say such words to me," he grumbled as he stood to his feet.

"Perhaps. My family knows you are decent and fair. Everyone deserves to be happy," he said as he handed the linen to him and glanced in Katlyn's direction before walking away.

Kel stood frozen, dumbfounded. He was not sure whether to be offended or thankful that a human would approach him in that way. If it were any other man besides Nia's sire, he would have been angry and made his irritation known.

As Bry'aere approached him, Kel darted his eyes back to Katlyn, who was coming out of the water. He squared his shoulders, lifted his chin, and walked brazenly across the beach, not noticing or caring whether anyone saw him as he approached her, placing the linen over her shoulders. She froze, then brought her hands up to his and turned her head. She gave a broad smile when she saw Kel's face.

~Katlyn

Despite Nia's persistence, Katlyn wished to forego the evening's festivities. She was anxious to get back to the ship. She retrieved her belongings from the village and headed straight to the transport. She took a seat, and Kel sat next to her. It took every ounce of self-control she had not to stare at him. Bry'aere stood in the aisle, and another man Katlyn only saw recently sat across from her.

"Thank you for bringing me back here today," she said, then she smiled at Kel and Bry'aere, trying not to draw attention from the other man. She accidentally cast a side-eye glance at Kel, and her face flushed.

"Did you enjoy your day, pet?" the man across from her asked.

"What did you call me?" Katlyn noticed that Kel's body shifted immediately.

"You are the Commander's pet. Nothing more," the man hissed.

Katlyn bolted up from her seat, and before she realized it, she was standing over him. He stood up slowly, and she didn't miss a single inch of his menacing form as he rose from his seat.

"You are becoming too comfortable," he snarled down at her, his cool breath wafting over her face. His long hair slipped over his shoulders as he lowered his face to peer down at her.

"I'm not afraid of you," she said, craning her neck to look him directly in the eyes.

"You should be." His face hovered over hers, their noses almost touching.

"That is enough!" Bry'aere snapped, then grabbed Katlyn's arm, pulling her away.

Katlyn turned to take her seat and saw Kel unmoved and dispassionate. His back straight, chin level, and hands fisted on his thighs. She sat down next to him, but as far away as she could. She was seething, and her chest heaved with every breath. She wasn't mad at what the other man called her. She was mad that Kel sat there speechless as if the incident didn't occur.

She stared at the floor and saw the man's feet shift when he sat back down. She looked up at him, and he was staring at her. Both scowled at each other from across the aisle. The tension in the air was growing. Kel finally stood up and moved to the middle of the aisle to block their view of each other. Katlyn flinched, and her breath shuddered as soon as she saw his form standing in front of her. She slowly looked up at him, but he was looking at Bry'aere, who was looking at her. She suddenly felt uncomfortable and attempted to cover herself with the flimsy linen wrapped around her shoulders.

I should have stayed on the planet, she said to herself. *This is total bullshit!*

As soon as the transport landed and the door opened, Katlyn pushed past Kel and bolted through the hangar bay. She darted around the corner and into the kitchen, closing the door behind her.

She was so confused. Kel had been escorting her around the ship and planet with the intent of others seeing them as friends. She didn't expect him to jump up and defend her honor. She was perfectly capable of defending her own honor, but for him to sit there stoic as he did, hurt her feelings.

She sat down at the opposite side of the table with her back to the door in case Kel followed her. If she saw his face, she didn't trust herself not to lose it or melt. She wanted neither at that moment. She hoped he didn't have the balls to follow her, but she was quickly disappointed when the door opened.

"Katlyn." Her name rolled off his tongue as if he were born to say it.

"Please, go away."

"Very well." Followed by the whoosh of the door, then silence.

24. ENOUGH

~Kel

"Will you please sit with me?" he asked Katlyn when she walked through the main doors to his quarters. He took a deep breath, lowering his chin slightly. She seemed to be terribly angry as soon as she looked at him.

"Don't look at me like that!"

"You are angry with me. I understand," he said softly as he moved toward her. "Will you please sit with me?"

"I don't know. I'm trying to be mad at you," she said as she rolled her eyes and crossed her arms. "You're making that difficult standing there half-dressed."

He chuckled and continued to approach her. "I would like to speak with you."

"Fine," she said, shrugging her shoulders. Kel turned around to walk toward his room, but stopped at the door. "Oh, you want me to sit with you in there?" Katlyn asked, stuttering. "No, I don't think so. I kinda just want to stay mad at you."

"Very well," he said. "Stand with me, then?" He waved his hand toward his room. "You did not get to see the nebula. I have moved the ship so you will have a view from my window."

"Fine," she said flatly, then walked toward him.

Once in his room, he guided her to the window where she could see part of the nebula. "I thought we could enjoy the view for a moment," he whispered as he looked at her, but her eyes were fixated on the nebula.

"It's beautiful."

"Yes," he agreed, but he was not looking at the nebula. He was looking at her and soaking her in, the look of her. Her black coiled hair, sun-kissed skin, full pink lips begging to be embraced. Her scent and the way he could see her pulse quicken in her neck, and how his emblem caressed the valley between her breasts. His yearning for her was fierce and passionate. As if his sole purpose in life was to please her. Every fiber of his being called to her. "Are you happy here?" he asked.

"Am I your pet?"

Kel sighed heavily. He felt terrible for allowing someone to be so disrespectful to her, but his hands were tied in that situation.

"You are not."

"Why would someone call me that? You didn't disagree with him."

"That man is one of my Regent's personal centurions. I could not openly disagree with him," he said. "I have something I must tell you. You are going to be upset, but please allow me to speak before you ask questions." She hesitated, then nodded her head. "My Regent wishes to use you as leverage to gain an advantage over your people. She is under the false belief that my attention toward you is for that sole purpose. My men, except for Bry'aere, are all under the same falsehood."

He could tell by the expression on her face that she was angry. Her chest heaved as she drew breath. "I have no intention of following through with her expectations. I wish to look further into your suggestion, and when we finally contact your people, you are free to go at your leisure. You may not believe my words, but Bry'aere will confirm what I have told you if you wish to speak with him."

"I believe you. If what you say is true, then I do understand why you couldn't speak up, but you'd just disobey your Regent like that? What will she do?"

"She will be angry, but you will be gone and safe. What happens to me should not concern you."

"Why are you telling me this?"

"I do not wish for you to believe that you are a commodity, a trifle. I do not see you that way. It took every fiber of my being not to rip his throat out when he spoke to you with such disrespect, and I will make it right." Katlyn chuckled, and her stiff body loosened. "This evening is not going how I planned," Kel said, shaking his head. "Besides this incident, are you happy here?"

"Why are you so concerned with me?"

"You saved my—"

"If you say that shit to me one more time, I might scream!" she snapped. "I'm sorry. You are just so difficult to read sometimes. But yes, I am happy here, considering the circumstances."

"Are you where you wish to be?"

"I wouldn't be here if I didn't want to be. I'm sure there are other worlds I could go to."

"You might be safer on a world rather than here."

"Maybe, but if I have to be here, in this galaxy, I'd like to be happy where I'm at, at least. What about you?"

"My happiness is irrelevant," he said stoically as he squared his shoulders and raised his chin.

"That's not what I asked you."

"I am." He nodded.

"But are you where *you* want to be?" she asked, raising an eyebrow.

"At this moment, yes," he said, looking at her.

She pulled her head back slightly as if she did not understand. "Okay, what about the future? Does your current situation lead you to where you'd like to be in the future?" she asked as she tilted her head.

"I am not sure."

"What do you mean? Either you're on the path to where you'd like to be, or you're not. Surely even you, a Specter, and Commander wants something for yourself. Something personal."

"Yes, I desire something." She looked up at him, tilting her head again. "I desire something I should not."

"Why should you not want it? Are you not allowed to want for yourself?"

"It may be considered unnatural or deviant. It has never been done before."

"Are you worried about what your men might think?" she asked.

He pondered for a moment. "No, my men are loyal to me. Their opinion of my personal affairs is not their concern. Nor would they make it such."

"What is stopping you from going after what you want then?"

"I do not know if I am allowed," he said longingly as he looked at her. "I do not know if I have permission, consent to take what I desire."

"Have you considered asking?" she said with a short chuckle, slightly tilting her head to the side.

"I do not know how to ask. I am unsure of how to behave," he said candidly. "I do not know if they desire the same," he said as he looked at her again.

"So, you desire someone?"

"Yes," he said firmly.

"Maybe she's afraid for some of the same reasons you are," Katlyn said as he took a step closer to her. "Maybe she feels like she shouldn't want you, as if being with you could be dangerous in some way, and she may not know if you want what she wants. Maybe you both want the same thing; you just don't know it." She took a deep breath and looked away from him.

"Perhaps."

"So, what is it that you want?" she asked, looking at him again.

"You," he said bluntly as he stepped closer to her. "I desire you. I desire to be with you. I desire to be intimately entwined with you. I desire to bind myself to you until my death," he confessed passionately.

"You shouldn't say such things to me." Her voice trembled when she spoke.

"Perhaps. If you do not feel the same tell me now, and we shall never speak of it again," he said in earnest.

"Why me?"

"I have fallen in love with you. I have also imprinted on you," he admitted.

"Imprinted? What does that mean?"

"It is difficult to explain." He shook his head gently.

"Please try."

He inhaled deep as he looked at her. "I will do whatever I must to protect you, to keep you safe. Even if doing so defies my Regent, and even my Queen. I desire you and your approval above any other. Imprinting occurs beyond our control. We cannot fight it or deny it."

"Imprinting? So, you basically love me because you can't help it?" she said with a smirk.

"Imprinting and passion are not the same. I imprinted on you the moment I first saw you. Before you even opened your eyes on Veda. Imprinting is not about love, and even if it were, who can stop themselves from loving someone? Are you able to control who you care for? My falling in love with you and imprinting on you are separate matters," he said as he raised his chin but maintained eye contact. "Imprinting is one thing, falling in love is another, but having both with the same person is a rare thing indeed."

"Is it even possible?" she asked, shrugging a shoulder.

"It has already happened."

"No, I mean for us to be together in that way?"

"With caution, I do not see why it would not be possible."

"What do you mean?"

"It could be risky. When I see you, I desire nothing more than to please you. To embrace you in my arms and make love to you, but I do not wish to harm you. I cannot harm you. Even with great care, I may still injure you. If we could not be together in that way, knowing we have a mutual affection for one another would be enough," he said as he took another step toward her.

"You'd really have a relationship with someone without sex?" she asked, furrowing her brow.

"There are other ways to have physical intimacy. We desire to please our women. Whether it be earning their favor or pleasing them in other ways. I would receive just as much pleasure by pleasing you as I would through sexual intimacy. We do not require copulation to be satisfied."

"Why could it be risky? You have me curious now, I'm sorry," she stifled a chuckle.

Kel inhaled deeply and raised his chin, searching for a translation. "I have a large physique. I am also more powerful and have greater stamina than any human," he said as he looked at her, hoping his words did not frighten her. "You are smaller and are built differently. Though, you do have full hips," he said as he gazed over her body, "Specter females have wider hips to accommodate their mates."

Katlyn looked at him briefly as he stepped closer to her. "I'm not sure what to say," she said, looking out the window toward the nebula.

"Katlyn," Kel breathed in deep, his breath shuddered as it escaped through his barely parted lips. "Please, do not torment me. I have professed my desire for you. Do not leave me in anguish. You must tell me if you feel the same, or am I a fool?" he demanded sternly but passionately as he stepped closer and reached out for her but stopped himself.

Katlyn lowered her chin, and her voice trembled when she spoke. "You're not a fool."

Kel sharply exhaled the breath he did not know he was holding. "May I touch you?" he asked. The overwhelming desire to embrace her was becoming too much to bear.

With shuddered breath, Katlyn said, "You don't ever have to ask for permission to touch me. You can touch me whenever you wish, for any reason. I know you'll never hurt me in anger. Even the last time, I know you weren't angry."

"I should not have done that, but it was not out of anger. It was out of frustration and my passion for you. When I grabbed you, I wanted to embrace you, I desired you, but you were afraid of me. I was confused and afraid for you, of what might become of us if I acted on my urges. And I did not know whether you felt the same," he confessed.

"I do."

"You do what?" he asked as he gently gripped the small of her back, pulling her close, his cool hand brushing her warm, bare skin. She was still wearing barely any clothing and wrapped in a simple linen cover.

She grasped the lapel of his robe and took a shuddered breath. "I feel the same. I'm in love with you, and I want to be with you, but I'm afraid."

He looked at her with the longing he always felt when he gazed at her. The words she spoke lit a fire within him, but quelled it at the same time.

~Katlyn

She felt his passion as he looked at her. It was the same look he always gave but with more intensity. He was fixated on her. His pupils were black specks in a sea of polished rubies. They were filled with hunger and desire as if he'd been searching for something his entire life and finally found it.

His reaction caught her off guard, and she shuddered against him when he lowered his chin to lean in closer to her. Her breathing was staggered as her pulse quickened. Their lips were a hairsbreadth apart, and his finger caressed her cheek, wiping away the tear that fell from her eye. She pulled her head back, putting some distance between them. She gasped lightly when his hand embraced the side of her face and neck. She closed her eyes and pushed into his touch. His skin was cool on her fevered flesh.

"Do not be afraid," he whispered as his thumb forced her chin up so their lips could finally meet.

Kel gripped the back of her neck with one hand and the small of her back with the other, forcing her into him, but she didn't resist. His lips were cool, but heat filled her mouth and radiated throughout her body. He pressed against her with such force; she felt as if he were going to consume her. But she wanted to be consumed; for him to touch every nerve of her body with his intoxicating sensations. She was so overcome with passion that her legs refused to carry her weight. Her body succumbed to him, and she collapsed into his arms. He pulled her all the way to him. Her tender body pressed securely against his firm physique, their lips still embracing.

When they finally pulled away, she wrapped her arms around his neck, and her legs around his waist when he lifted her body. He pulled her hips into his torso and buried his face into the crook of her neck. She was weeping with her face buried into his shoulder.

"Will you stay with me?" he asked. She nodded, giving a muffled response as she gripped his neck and waist tighter.

He pulled the privacy curtain to his bed aside and dropped to his knees. She still gripped him tightly as he laid her onto his bed.

If that was all their night entailed, it was enough. He loved her, and she loved him. Their mutual affection was enough. Neither of them knew or understood why they ever fought or resisted the desire they had for each other. It felt so natural, as if it should have always been that way.

Their story continues...

BOUND

Katlyn woke to a gentle kiss on the back of her shoulder and a soft caress against her hip. She turned her head to see Kel already dressed and sitting on the edge of the bed. She tugged at the sheet that covered her naked body as she rolled onto her back so she could see him.

"Good morning," he said, then kissed her forehead and rubbed his hand along her stomach. Katlyn gave a broad smile and reached her hand up to his face. He captured it with his own as she caressed his cheek. "I brought you breakfast."

"Oh, really?"

"I am sorry it is only fruit and water. I do not know how to prepare a meal."

"Fruit and water are perfect," she said, sitting up and capturing his lips in a kiss.

Katlyn wrapped her arms around his neck as he pushed her down onto the bed. She pulled at him greedily when he pulled away. His cool hand caressed her cheek as he sat back up.

"There are things I must attend to this morning. We will return to the planet around midday. I still need to hunt. I

263

typically go in the evening, stay overnight, and hunt at sunrise. You are welcome to accompany me if you wish."

"I would love to. I haven't been camping in forever!"

"It may get chilly. I will build a fire, but you will need a blanket and food for yourself," he said when he stood up. "And please gather your things from my room. I trust Nia and Rory to be discreet if the situation calls for it, but I would rather hold off if possible. I hope you understand."

"Yes, I understand. I know we can't run naked through the corridors or anything." They both chuckled.

"I am not concerned about my men. My Regent is a whole other matter."

"I understand."

Katlyn stood up, clutching the sheet together above her breasts. Her hair fell around her body into a tousled mess. She swept her eyes up to Kel, then back down and bit her bottom lip as she attempted to brush her hair with her free hand. Kel's eyes remained locked on her, gazing at her in his usual way, but it was different somehow.

"You are beautiful," he whispered, then clasped his hand around the side of her neck. She moaned and pushed into his touch.

She couldn't help but admire him as he stood in front of her. He was the epitome of masculinity—the alpha male, but tender and gentle. He didn't need to roar or growl to show his dominance. His emphatic aura was enough.

She wrapped her hand around his. "What happens now?"

"This will be difficult. Many people, yours and mine, will be against this," he said. "And at some point, you will be faced with a choice."

"What choice?"

Kel sighed. "Whether to return to Earth or remain with me, but we will discuss this another day. I must go. I will return when it is time to leave."

He turned and activated the door control, but before leaving, he spun around to face her. He captured her hand and kissed the inside of her wrist. "Ardor," he whispered, then turned on his heel and left.

After eating breakfast, Katlyn ran herself a bath. As the water caressed her body, she thought about what Kel said, her having to make a choice. Their relationship was far from typical. Sure, long-distance relationships could work if both people wanted it to, but theirs was a record for long-distance. They literally came from two different worlds, and him going to hers wasn't an option. He was right; she would be faced with a very real, and exceedingly difficult decision—go home or make this her home. If she wanted to be with him, she would have to stay, but what kind of life would that be?

She sat in the water, thinking about the night before, remembering Kel's hands exploring her body, learning about her. He spoke as if there were things he didn't know, but he knew. If he didn't know, he was a quick study. The way Kel touched her was different. She had never experienced anything like it before. It was almost as if his regular touch had a bit of that healing energy. The previous night was incredible. Just thinking about him made her body flush despite the hot water surrounding her.

She sank her head under the water before washing her hair and body and getting out of the tub. After drying off and getting dressed, she packed a bag with a couple of blankets and the scarf Kel gave her. She then made a quick trip to the kitchen for a few things to eat for the next couple of meals. When she got back to Kel's quarters, she didn't have to wait long before he showed up. He caressed the side of her neck before grabbing her bag and escorting her to the hangar bay.

~Kel

"Conscripts?" Katlyn asked when they boarded the small transport ship.

Two warriors piloted the last couple trips to the planet, but Kel wished to speak with Bry'aere.

"Yes, we may speak freely among them," he said just as Bry'aere entered the transport. "I have told her, Bry'aere."

Katlyn sat down as the ramp lifted, and Bry'aere sat across from her.

"I assume it has worked in your favor," Bry'aere said.

Kel sat next to Katlyn and took her hand in his, bringing it up to his mouth and kissing her palm. "Yes, we must discuss how to proceed," he said.

"I am not sure what you mean, Kel'ardent."

"Katlyn is aware that she must choose at some point whether to stay or go."

"I did not realize her staying was an option. That is not a wise decision," Bry'aere said. His jaw clenched, and the blacks of his eyes restricted. Kel sensed his agitation, but knew it was out of concern.

"Why?" Katlyn asked.

Bry'aere tilted his head. "Our Regent would be very angry, for several reasons," he said, looking at Kel.

Kel raised his chin. "I will not force her to leave. It will be her decision."

Bry'aere sat back against the seat, looking at Kel and Katlyn. "I did not expect this, Kel'ardent. I assumed she would go at some point."

"You encouraged this!"

"I encouraged you to enjoy her company while she was here. Not for her to stay and put us all at risk!"

"You know I will do whatever she asks of me. If staying here pleases her, then I cannot forbid it!" Kel embraced Katlyn's hand tighter and placed it on his thigh.

"I'd really appreciate it if you didn't talk about me as if I weren't here," Katlyn interjected, to no avail.

"Will you not follow me?" Kel continued.

Bry'aere leapt to his feet and clenched his fists at his sides. "Never question my loyalty!" Kel released Katlyn's hand and stood with him. "I will follow you anywhere, even if she"—he pointed to Katlyn—"is by your side. As your friend and second in command, it is my duty to inform you of the risk you are taking. I knew you were captivated, but I had no idea it was this serious."

Kel shook his head, placed both hands on his hips, and shifted his weight onto one leg. "I do believe you are now the one who is in denial. You knew how serious my feelings were before even I knew."

"Perhaps," Bry'aere said as he sat back down, resting his elbows on his knees.

"I don't want to put anyone at risk," Katlyn said.

"You already put us all at risk!" Bry'aere's tone was elevated.

Kel gritted his teeth at Bry'aere. "Do not!" Then he sat back down next to Katlyn. "Do not allow Bry'aere to influence your decision."

"But, he's right," she said. "It's not something I thought about until he said it."

"I could rip your throat out, brother, for your interference," Kel hissed through clenched teeth.

"Just stop! We'll see how things play out. You might get sick of me sooner than you think. I am a handful after all," Katlyn chuckled.

"You must be careful," Bry'aere said. "If our Regent suspects anything, this will end as quickly as it began. How do you expect to be with someone you should not be with? Even if she were Specter, you still could not be with her."

"Why?" Katlyn asked.

Bry'aere tilted his head and furrowed his brow. "That is not for me to say, mistress."

"That is why we must discuss this," Kel said.

"There are many things we should discuss, but right now is not the time, Kel'ardent. If you were any other man—"

"If I were any other man, this would never have happened." Kel sighed as he sat back against the seat and took Katlyn's hand. "I have imprinted on and fallen in love with the same woman, Bry'aere. You know better than anyone what that means."

"Yes, I do. I also know there is no precedence for this. Even if she were Specter, considering your station, there is still no precedence."

"What does that mean?" Katlyn asked.

"We will finish this discussion another time," Kel said.

"I know there are things you're not telling me, but I'm going to overlook that for now," Katlyn said. "For now!" She flashed Kel a stern expression. "I don't like secrets, but I understand these are extenuating circumstances, and I'll respect that."

Bry'aere chuckled and shook his head. "If this does work in your favor, you both will be a force to be reckoned with. You are quite the woman to have stood up to a centurion as you did. Or any of us for that matter."

All three sat in silence for the remainder of the trip. Kel pulled Katlyn's hand up to his chest while she rested her chin on his shoulder, looking up at him. Bry'aere sat with his arms crossed in front of his chest, watching them both.

GLOSSARY

Some words in the Specter language have no English translation. In real-world English, a doyen is the most respected or prominent person in a field. In the Specter language, it doesn't have a translation. In Chapter Twenty, Kel tells Katlyn it means 'leader,' which is not inaccurate, but the closest translation would be 'prince,' but prince is not in their vocabulary.

Doyen - no translation – the son of a queen or her sibling—male royalty.

Nevos is what they call the son of a sibling. In English, it would be 'nephew,' but nephew is not in their vocabulary. In Chapter Seventeen, we discover that Kel is the Queen's nevos.

Nevos – no translation – the son of one's sibling.

Nexus – to join or link. Joining of lineages. English translation is marriage.

Specter Names

The first part of a Specter's name is given to them upon their birth. Most have a meaning of some kind or translates into something. The second part of their name is what their mind projects telepathically. It can be an emotion, a feeling, their disposition, any one of their character traits, a color, or even something tangible.

Below are all the Specter names mentioned in this series so far.

Bry'aere – warrior – honorable, devotion, loyalty, strength
Kel'ardent – decisive, resolute – passionate, fervent, fierce
Roe'lys – calm – light, flash

ABOUT THE AUTHOR

MaryAnn has always wanted to write, but life got in the way. She wrote a short story in fifth grade that her teacher encouraged her to publish, but she never did.

In March 2020, just when the COVID-19 pandemic hit the U.S., she sat down with pen and paper and started writing Doyen. The premise for the story came to her months before, however, but when families were self-isolating all over the country is when she decided to put her story to paper.

MaryAnn lives in Oklahoma with her family.

Made in the USA
Columbia, SC
07 October 2020